The Knights of the Limits

Books by Barrington Bayley

Annihilation Factor
Collision with Chronos
Empire of Two Worlds
The Fall of Chronopolis
The Forest of Peldain
The Garments of Caean
The Great Hydration
The Grand Wheel
The Knights of the Limits (short story collection)
The Pillars of Eternity
The Rod of Light
The Seed of Evil (short story collection)
The Sinners of Erspia
The Soul of the Robot
Star Virus
Star Winds
The Zen Gun

The Knights of the Limits

Barrington Bayley

Cosmos Books, an imprint of **Wildside Press**
New Jersey . New York . California . Ohio

The Knights of the Limits

Published by:

Cosmos Books, an imprint of Wildside Press
P.O. Box 45, Gillette, NJ 07933-0045
www.wildsidepress.com

Publishing history: Allison & Busby, hardback, 1978.

Copyright © 2001 by Barrington Bayley. All rights reserved.
Cover design copyright © 2001 by Juha Lindroos.

No portion of this book may be reproduced by any means, mechanical, electronic, or otherwise, without first obtaining the permission of the copyright holder.

For more information, contact Wildside Press.

ISBN: 1-58715-383-1

In an unwritten occult teaching
various ascending orders of spacetime
are defined in terms of "the Knights of the Limits".

Acknowledgements

"Mutation Planet" first appeared in *Tomorrow's Alternatives,* edited by Roger Elwood. "The Problem of Morley's Emission" was written for *An Index of Possibilities* and is included in this collection by permission of Clanose Publishers Ltd. All other stories first appeared in *New Worlds*.

The six-based number spiral and the concept of Hyper-One described in "The Bees of Knowledge" are borrowed, with thanks, from the mathematical efforts of W. G. Davies.

Contents

The Exploration of Space	9
The Bees of Knowledge	28
Exit from City 5	57
Me and My Antronoscope	84
All the King's Men	109
An Overload	129
Mutation Planet	151
The Problem of Morley's Emission	175
The Cabinet of Oliver Naylor	185

The Exploration of Space

The physical space in which we and the worlds move and have our being may easily be presumed to be a necessary and absolute condition of existence, the only form of the universe that is possible or even conceivable. Mathematicians may invent fictitious spaces of higher dimensions than our own but these, our intuition tells us, are no more than idealistic inventions which could nowhere be translated into reality and do not therefore properly deserve the designation "space". The space we know, having the qualities of symmetry and continuity, is intimately and automatically the concomitant of any universe containing things and events, and therefore is inevitable; without space as we know it there could be no existence. The commonplace mind accepts this notion without question; thoughtful philosophers have spoken of the symmetrical, continuous space of three dimensions as an *a priori* world principle whose contradiction would remain a contradiction even in the mind of God. Yet not only has this belief no axiomatic justification but, as I shall attempt to show presently, it is untrue.

I had just smoked my second pipe of opium and was settling into a pleasant reverie. The opium smell, a sweet, cloying and quite unique odour, still hung in the air of my study, mingling with the aroma of the polished mahogany bookcases and the scent of flowers from the garden. Through the open window I could see that garden, with its pretty shrubs and crazy pathways, and beyond, the red ball of the far-off sun sinking through strata of pink and blue clouds.

My attention, however, was on the chessboard before me. Perhaps I should say a few words about myself. I believe that my brief participation in "orthodox" experimental research may permit me to call myself a man of science, although these days my studies are more mathematical and deductive. It will surprise some that my main interest throughout my life has been alchemy. I have myself practised the Hermetic Art with some assiduity, if only to feel for myself the same numinousness experienced by my alchemistic forebears in manipulating the chemical constituents of the world. Hence I have known what it is to search for the *prima materia* (which others call the Philosopher's stone, being the root of transformation); and I have pondered long and deeply on that profoundly basic manual, the Emerald Table of Hermes Trismegistus.

Unlike most contemporary men I am not inclined to the belief that alchemy has been rendered obsolete by modern science, but rather that its inadequate techniques and theories have been temporarily outstripped, while the essence of the Art remains unapproached. In the not too distant future the reverent search for *prima materia* may once again be conducted with the full charisma of symbology, but employing the best of particle accelerators. If the outlook I am displaying seems to run counter to the spirit of inductive science, let me admit that my thoughts do sometimes wander, for good or ill, outside the pale wherein dwell the more active members of the scientific community. There is value, I believe, in looking back over the history of science as well as forward to future expectations. I am not, for instance, hypnotised by the success of atomic theory, as are practically all of my colleagues. If I may be permitted to say so, the objections to the atomic view of nature listed by Aristotle have never been answered. These objections are still valid, and eventually they will have to be answered — or vindicated — on the level of sub-nuclear physics.

Opium has the happy conjunction of both inducing a feeling of relaxation and well-being and of opening the inner doors of the mind to a realm of colourful creativity. By opium, it is conjectured, Coleridge glimpsed the poem *Kubla Khan*, only fragments of which he managed to remember. By opium I met my new, though sadly soon-departed, friend, the Chessboard Knight.

A chessboard, to recapitulate the obvious, consists of 8x8 locations, or "squares" arranged in a rectilinear grid. To us, the chessboard represents a peculiarly restricted world. The entities, or "pieces" of this world are distinguished from one another only by their power of movement: a pawn can only move forward, one square at a time; a castle can move longitudinally for up to eight squares, a bishop likewise diagonally, and a knight can move to the opposite corner of a 2x3 rectangle. For all pieces movement is always directly from square to square, with no locations existing between the squares: none of them possesses the power of continuous, non-discrete movement we enjoy in our own world. On the other hand none of us possesses the power of simultaneous transition from location to location enjoyed by chessmen, particularly by the knight, who is unimpeded by intervening obstacles.

A rapid succession of similar thoughts was passing through my head as I gazed at the chessboard, though ostensibly to study the game laid out thereon, which I was playing by letter with a distant correspondent. As sometimes happens when smoking opium, time suddenly slowed down and thoughts seemed to come with incredible speed and clarity. Normally, I mused, one would unhesitatingly suppose our real physical world to be the superior of the chessboard world, because no limitation is placed upon the number of locations we may occupy. No arbitrary laws restrict me from moving in any way I please about my study, my garden, or the countryside beyond. But is that so important? The significance of chess lies not in its very simplified space-time environment but in the relation the pieces hold to one another. By this latter criterion our own degree of freedom undergoes a drastic reduction: the number of stances I can hold in relation to my wife, to my friends or to my employer (though being retired, I have no employer) is by no means great; insignificant, in fact, when compared to the infinite number of relationships that would obtain by mathematically permutating all possible locations in our continuum of physical space. Is it an unfounded presumption, then, that our own world of continuous consecutive motions is logically any more basic to nature, or any richer in content, than one based on the principle of the chessboard, comprising discrete transitions between non-continuous locations?

I had reached thus far in my speeding express-train of thought when before my dazed eyes the chess pieces, like a machine that had suddenly been switched on, began flicking themselves around the board, switching from square to square with all the abruptness of the winking patterns of lights on a computer console. After this brief, flurried display they arranged themselves in a formation which left the centre of the board empty and were still — except for the White King's Knight, who went flickering among them in his corner-turning manner, executing a dizzying but gracefully arabesque circuit of the board before finishing up in the centre, where he turned to me, bowed slightly, and lifted his head to speak to me in a distant, somewhat braying tone.

In my drugged state this happening did not induce in me the same surfeit of bewilderment and incredulity that would normally, I believe, have been my reaction. Astonished I certainly was. It is not every day that one's chess set shows a life of its own, or that the pieces remain so true to their formal nature as laid down by the rules that they move from one position to another without bothering to traverse the spaces between. Not, let me add for the sake of the record, that the pieces showed any carelessness or laziness, or that they took short cuts. In order to move, say, from Qkt4 to Kr4, a castle was required to manifest himself in all the intervening squares so as to show that he came by a definite route and that the way was unimpeded — only the Knight flashed to his opposite corner unperturbed by whatever might surround him. These manifestations were, however, fleeting in the extreme, and nothing was ever seen of the castle in between adjacent squares — because, naturally, in a game of chess there is no "between adjacent squares".

But I jump ahead of myself. My astonishment was so great that I missed the Knight's first words and he was obliged to repeat himself. What he said was:

"We enter your haven with gratitude."

His voice, as I have said, was distant, with a resinous, braying quality. Yet not cold or unpleasant; on the contrary it was cordial and civilised. I replied:

"I was not aware that you were in need of haven; but that being the case, you are welcome." In retrospect my words might appear to have received weighty consideration, but in fact they were flippant and extempory, the only response my brain could form to an impossible situation. And so began my conversation with the Chessboard Knight, the strangest and most informative conversation I have ever held.

So total was my bemusement that I accepted with an unnatural calmness the Knight's announcement that he was a space explorer. My sense of excitement returned, however, when he went on to explain that he was not a space explorer such as our imagination might conjure by the phrase, but that he was an explorer of alternative types of spatial framework of which, he assured me, there were a good number in the universe. What we are pleased to call the sidereal universe, that is, the whole system of space-time observable by us on Earth, is merely one among a vast range of various systems. Even more astounding, in the circumstances, was the revelation that the Knight hailed from a system of space identical to that which I had a moment before been contemplating! One analogous to a game of chess, where space, instead of being continuous and homogeneous as we know it, was made up of discrete locations, infinite or at any rate indefinite in number, and to which entities can address themselves instantaneously and in any order. There is no extended spatial framework in which these locations are ordered or arrayed and all locations are equally available from any starting point (provided they are not already occupied). An entity may, however, occupy only one location at a time and therein lies the principle of order in this well-nigh incomprehensible world. Structures, systems and events consist of convoluted, arabesque patterns of successive occupations, and of the game-like relationships these manoeuvres hold to one another. The chess-people's analogy of a long distance takes the form of a particularly difficult sequence of locations; alternatively the sequence could correspond to a particularly clever construct or device — the chess-people make little distinction between these two interpretations.

As do the occupants of a chessboard, the entities of this space (which I shall term locational-transitional space) vary in the range and ingenuity of their movements. Primitive organisms can do no more than transfer themselves slowly from one location to another, without pattern or direction, like pawns, while the most evolved intelligent species, like my friend the Knight, had advanced to dizzying achievements as laid down by the possibilities of such a realm. Their most staggering achievement was that of travel to other spaces; this was accomplished by a hazardous, almost infinitely long series of locations executed at colossal speed and comprising a pattern of such subtlety and complexity that my mind could not hope to comprehend it. Indeed, few even in the Knight's spatial realm comprehended it and for their science it constituted a triumph comparable to our release of atomic energy from matter.

The discerning reader who has followed me this far might justly wonder at the coincidence which brought these bizarre travellers to my presence at the very moment when I had been theoretically contemplating something resembling their home space. This question was uppermost in my mind, also, but there was, the Knight told me, no coincidence involved at all. On entering our continuum (which the Knight and the companions under his command did indirectly, via other realms less weird to them) the space explorers had become confused and lost their bearings, seeming to wander in a sea of primeval chaos where no laws they could hypothesise, not even those garnered in their wide experience of spatial systems, seemed to obtain. Then, like a faint beacon of light in the uncognisable limbo, they had sighted a tiny oasis of ordered space, and with great expertise and luck had managed to steer their ship towards it.

That oasis was my chessboard. Not the board alone, of course — tens of thousands of chess games in progress at the same moment failed to catch their attention — but the fact that it had been illumined and made real by the thoughts I had entertained while gazing upon it, imbuing it with conceptions that approached, however haltingly, the conditions of their home world. Hence I owed the visitation to a lesser, more credible coincidence: chess and opium. At any rate, having landed their ship upon the board and thus bringing it under the influence of that vessel's internally maintained alien laws, they had carried out simple manipulations of the pieces in order to signal their presence and establish communication — the real ship and its occupants not being visible or even conceivable to me, since they did not have contiguous spatial extension.

My reader, still suspicious of my truthfulness, will also want to know how it was that the Knight spoke to me in English. The appalling difficulties offered by any other explanation have tempted me to decide that we did not really speak at all, but only telepathically from mind to mind. And yet my grosser, more stubborn recollection belies this evasion: we *did* speak, the air vibrated and brought to me the thin, resinous tones of the Knight's voice. His own remarks on the matter were off-hand

and baffling. There was scarcely a language in the universe that could not be mastered in less than a minute, he said, provided it was of the relational type, which they nearly all were. He seemed to find my own mystification slightly disconcerting. The only comment I can contribute, after much reflection, is that for a locational-transitional being what he says may well be the case. Language, as he pointed out, largely concerns relations between things and concepts. To the Knight relations are the stuff of life, and he would find our own comprehension of them far below the level of imbecility. In our world to have but one fraction of his appreciation of relations, which to us are so important but so difficult to manage, would make us past masters of strategy and I believe no power would be able to withstand such knowledge.

But here lies the antinomy: the Knight and his crew were coming to *me* for help. They found the conditions of our three-dimensional continuum as incomprehensible and chaotic as we would find their realm. They had not even been able to ascertain what manner of space it was, and begged me to explain its laws to them in order that they might be able to find their way out of it.

There was a certain irony in being asked to describe the world I knew when I yearned to question the Knight as to *his* world. (Indeed my imagination was exploding—were there galaxies, stars and planets in the locational-transitional space? No, of course there could not be: such things were products of continuous space. What, then, was there? Some parallel to our phenomena there must be, but try as I might I could not picture what.) However, a cry of distress cannot go unanswered and I launched into an exposition.

It was quite a test of the intellect to have to describe the utterly familiar to a being whose conceptions are absolutely different from one's own. At first I had great difficulty in explaining the rules and limitations by which we stereo beings (that is the phrase I have decided upon to describe our spatial characteristics) are obliged to order our lives. In particular it was hard to convey to the Knight that to get from point A to point B the basic strategy is to proceed in a straight line. To give them credit, the chessman crew had already experimented with the idea that continuous motion of some kind might be needed, but they had conceived the natural form of motion to be in a circle. When sighting my chessboard they had proceeded in the opposite direction and approached it by executing a perfect circle of a diameter several times that of the galaxy. I could not help but admire the mathematical expertise that had put both their starting point and their destination on the circumference of this circle.

After a number of false starts the Knight successfully mastered the necessary concepts and was able to identify the class of spaces to which ours belongs, a class some other members of which had been explored previously. They were regarded as dangerous but none, he informed me, had so far proved as hazardous and weird as our own, nor so difficult to move in. He still could not visualise our space, but I had apparently given him enough information for the ship's computer to chart a course homeward (computers, theirs as well as ours, are notoriously untroubled by the limitations of imagination).

During the conversation I had naturally enough sought his opinion on various contemporary theories of the space we inhabit: on Riemannian space, Poincaré space, special and general relativity. Is our space positively or negatively curved? Spherical, parabolic or saddle-shaped—or is it curved at all? Is it finite or infinite? I acquainted him with the equation for the general theory of gravitation and invited his comments:

$$R_{ik} - \tfrac{1}{2} g_{ik} R = T_{ik}$$

His reply to all this was discouraging. The only definitive datum he would give me was that our space is infinite. As for Einstein's equation, he said that it merely gave an approximate, superficial description of behaviour and did not uncover any law. He told me that in our continuum motion depends on a set of expansion*

Our whole idea of analysing space by means of dimensions is inadequate and artificial, the Knight advised. The notion is an internally generated side-effect, and to anyone from outside, e.g.

---

* A break in the manuscript occurs here—Ed.

from another kind of space, it is neither meaningful nor descriptive. The essence of a spatial structure is more often expressed by a plain maxim that might appear to be ad hoc and rule-of-thumb, but that actually contains the nub of its specific law. At this I could not refrain from interrupting with the boast that privately I had once reached the same conclusion; and that if I had to state the basic physical law of our space (which I then thought of as the universe) it would be that in moving towards any one thing one is necessarily moving away from some other thing. The Knight complimented me on my insight; his ship's computer was at that very moment grinding out the implications of a formulation quite close to the one I had come up with.

Following this, the Knight expressed his gratitude and announced his intention to leave. I begged him to stay a while; but he replied that to continue meshing the spatial laws of the ship (i.e. locational-transitional laws) with the pieces on the chessboard was proving to be a drain on the power unit. Guiltily, I confess that I allowed selfishness to come to the fore here. Did he not owe me something for the help I had given him, I argued? Could he and his crew not spend a little more energy, and would it truly endanger their lives? My unethical blackmail was prompted solely by my burning desire to learn as much as I could while the opportunity remained. I think he understood my feelings for, after a brief hesitation, he agreed to remain and discourse with me for a short time, or at least until the power drain approached a critical level.

Eagerly I besought him to tell me as much as he could of this vast universe of divers space-times to which he had access but I had not. To begin with, where did the Knight's own spatial realm lie? Was it beyond the boundaries of our own space (beyond infinity!) or was it at right angles to it in another dimension? (I babbled carelessly, forgetting his former objection to the term.) Or was it, perhaps, co-extensive with our continuum, passing unnoticed because its own mode of existence is so unutterably different from it? To all these hasty suggestions the Knight replied by chiding me gently for my naivety. I would never know the answer while I persisted in thinking in a such a way, he said, for the simple reason that there was no answer *and no question*. While I was still capable of asking this nonexistent question the non-answer would never be apparent to me.

Somewhat abashed, I asked a more pertinent question: was each space-time unique, or was each type duplicated over and over? As far as was known, the Knight said, each was unique, but they were classified by similarities and some differed only in details or in the quantitative value of some physical constant. It was to be expected, for instance, that there would be a range of stereo space-times resembling our own but with different values on the velocity of light. To my next request, that he describe some alien space-times to me, he explained that many would be totally inconceivable to me and that there was no way to express them in my language, mathematical or spoken. The majority of the spaces that were known to the chess-people were variations on the locational-transitional theme. There was a theory in his home world that locational-transitional (or chessboard) space was the basic kind of space in the universe and that all others were permutations and variants of it; but he agreed with me that this theory could be suspected of special pleading and that deeper penetration into the universe by the chess-people's spaceships might well bring home a different story. He would not bore me, he added, by describing meaningless variations on locational-transitional space, but felt that I would be more entertained by those spaces whose qualities made striking comparisons with the qualities of my own realm.

There was, for instance, a space that, though continuous, was not symmetrical in all directions but was hung between two great poles like a magnetic field. Motion along the direction of the axis between the poles was as easy as it is for us, but transverse movement was an altogether different phenomenon that required a different type of energy and a different name. This polarisation continued down into every event and structure, which was invariably positioned between two opposing poles of one kind or another. There was stereo space with great cracks of nullity running all through it, chasms of zero-existence which were impossible to cross and had to be gone round. There was space where an entity could travel in a straight line without incident, but where on changing direction he shed similar, though not identical, duplicates of himself which continued to accompany him thereafter. Prior to their rescue by me the Knight and his crew had believed themselves to be in such a space, for they had chanced to catch a glimpse of a woman accompanied by several daughters of various ages who closely resembled her. Also along these lines, there was a space where the image of an object or entity had the same powers and qualities as the original. This space abounded in mirrors and reflecting surfaces, and an entity was liable to project himself in all directions like a volley of arrows.

When you think about it, the necessity to be in only one place at a time is a pretty severe restriction. Many are the spaces where this law has never been heard of, and where an entity may multiply himself simultaneously into disparate situations without prejudice to his psychic integrity, roaming over the world in a number of bodies yet remaining a single individual. Chameleons have caused some puzzlement among biologists because their eyes operate independently of one another; the right eye knoweth not what the left eye is doing but each scans separately for prey or enemies. Does the consciousness of the chameleon give its full attention to both eyes simultaneously? If so, the chameleon is a mental giant which no human being can equal. This feat is a natural function, however, in the space of "multiple individuality" I have described.

The Knight warned me against a restrictive concept of motion. It was not, he said, an idea of universal validity, but what we understood by motion could be subsumed under a more generalised concept he called "transformation", a much larger class of phenomena. Thus there were spaces where to go was to come, where to approach was to recede, where to say goodbye was to say hello. In short, my maxim which says that to approach one point is to recede from another is not a universal law but a local case. Inversely, there were types of transformation that no mangling of the English language could succeed in hinting at. Once again the Knight suggested that I waste none of our precious time in trying to understand these inconceivable variations.

He spent some words in describing spaces that were not totally homogeneous. The space with cracks was one of these; another was "sheaving space" with a quite odd quirk: the space split itself up into branches not all of which had any possible communication or influence with one another, even though they might all communicate with some common branch. Thus both A and B might communicate with C, but it would still be impossible for any message or particle to pass from A to B even via C. The separate branches usually contained innumerable worlds, with bizarre results.

Space can also vary in the quality of time it contains. (The Knight was quite firm in asserting that time is a subsidiary feature of space.) Time is not always irreversible, but in some spaces can be revisited by retracing one's steps. The Knight fascinated me by telling of one space which he called "a space of forking time" where every incident had not one but several possible outcomes, all equally real. Thus space branches continually in this continuum to develop alternate histories; where this space differs from the stock science-fiction notion, however, is that *every past event is recoverable,* and hence *all possible histories communicate.* By retracing his steps in a certain manner a man (or entity) can go back to the crucial moment that determined the shape of events and take a different path. When I reflected on how the fate and happiness of men is tyrannised over in our space by the singleness of time and the cruel dice-throwing of fleeting happenstance, this realm appeared to me to be a perfect abode of happiness.

It will be obvious that causality is governed by the type of space in which it takes place. The Knight mentioned that our space contains the principle of "single-instance causality", which is also the principle obtaining in most space-times, and means that prolonged and complex processes can come to completion only with difficulty. The reason is thus: if A causes B, and B causes C, it still does not follow that A will lead to C because in the interim B might be modified by interceding influences and fail to cause C. There are, claimed the Knight, space-times of extended causality where every process or project reaches completion and no tendency is ever interrupted. As the realising of ambitions is automatic any "effort to succeed" is quite redundant in this space-time. The struggle and drama of life consists not of trying to actualise intentions but of the struggle to form intentions in the first place.

In this respect the Knight included his only description of a species of locational-transitional space: a space where there was no sequential causality at all, but in which everything happened on a purely statistical basis. Wondering what it could be like on the inside of such a stochastic wonderland, I asked whether there could ever be the slightest possibility of intelligent, conscious entities arising there. To my surprise the Knight averred that it was well stocked with such entities: statistically intelligent, statistically conscious entities.

I have touched but lightly on the role of matter in the space-times I have discussed; it would be needless to tell my intelligent reader that matter and space are inextricably entwined. He will already have guessed that besides the innumerable spaces that form a receptacle for matter, there are also those that are Aristotelian in the sense of complying with that philosopher's erroneous theories: where matter, instead of being atomic, is continuous and identical with the space it occupies, motion being accomplished by a process of compression and attenuation. There is no empty space in these continua, exactly as Aristotle reasons. In at least one such continuum all the matter is dense and solid, so that it consists of a blocked infinity of solid rock or metal (I am not sure which). In this continuum, the Knight admitted, the possibility of conscious intelligences could be discounted. In contrast to such immobility I particularly liked what the Knight called "folding space" but which I have since named "origami space" (origami is the Japanese art of paper-folding). Origami space has an inner richness that makes our own space look bland. Objects can be folded so as to develop entirely new qualities. A man (or entity), by folding a piece of paper in the right way, may make of it a chair, a table, an aeroplane, a house, a fruit, a flower, a live animal, another man, a woman, or practically anything. The art of such folding, it need hardly be added, far surpasses anything to be found in our Earthly origami. Mass and size are not constants in this continuum but can be increased (or decreased) by folding, hence a square of paper a foot on the side may end up as an airliner able to carry a hundred people.

After recounting these wonders the Knight paused to allow me to gather my mental breath. As if by way of relaxation he briefly outlined some primitive-sounding space-times that lacked our centreless relativity but were organised around a fixed centre. Remembering that earlier he had referred to our version of stereo space as a particularly rigid and restricted variety, I seized on this latest exposition to remark that at least the world I inhabited had the dignity of being infinite, symmetrical and unconstricted by having a centre. The Knight's amusement was genuine, if gentle. With a dry laugh he instructed me that my mistake was a classic of unsophisticated presumption, and he regretted to have to inform me that my world did not have relativistic symmetry but that *it had a centre*.

Where was this centre? I asked. Once more came the Knight's mocking chuckle. He had neglected to mention so far, he said, that also intimately related to the question of space is the question of *numbers*. Our space might have no identifiable centre in terms of motion and direction, but in its regard to number it was very strongly centred.

At first his meaning escaped me. Number was another way of classifying the innumerable kinds of space in the universe, he explained. There was at least one space for every possible number (a theorem stated that there were more spaces than one for every possible number), and they were arranged in an ascending series, each space having its "centre of gravity" about a particular number. We are near to the bottom of the scale as our "centre of gravity" is the number One (there are spaces preferring fractions and at least one preferring Zero). The consequences are immediate and self-evident: singleness is what signifies a complete object in our world; integral unity is all, and the state of there being two of a thing is incidental—a thing comes into its own when it is *one*. We all accept this innately. Every entity and thing is itself by assigning the number One to itself. Higher numbers introduce additional qualities, but do not carry the same weight as *one*.*

In the space next above us in the scale completeness attaches to the number *two*. "Two-ness" is ideal, and singleness is incomplete in the same way that a fraction or a part is incomplete in our world. I reflected on what a mass migration there would be if communication could be established with that world — for we also have the yearning after *two* in our shadowy, tantalised way. Our lives are full of complementary pairs. The tragedy of

---

* By way of example, we conceive of Two as "Two Ones".

THE EXPLORATION OF SPACE 23

lovers is that they are thwarted by the One-ness of the spatial system: each remains alone and solitary, however much they strive and strain to be completely merged as *two* — for the vain yearning of lovers is not to be made One, which would negate the whole proceeding, but to be, as it were, indistinguishably blended as Two. Should a pair of Eros-struck lovers by some magic or science transpose themselves to this other realm where Two is All, then their bliss would be beyond describing.

More remotely, other worlds model themselves on Three, Four, Five, and so on up the scale of integers to infinity. In addition there is a corresponding scale of negative integers, as also of worlds modelled on every possible fraction, on irrational numbers, on imaginary numbers, and on groups, sets and series of numbers, such as on all the primes, all the odd integers, all the even integers, and on arithmetic and geometric progressions. Beyond even these abstruse factualities are the ranges of worlds centred on numbers and number systems not possible or conceivable to us. The only truly symmetrical, non-centred, relativistic space-time, said the Knight, is one giving equal weight to all numbers.

Georg Cantor, wrestling with the enigma of the infinite, discovered a branch of mathematics called transfinite arithmetic, in which he developed a progression of numbers analogous to the positive integers but whose first term was infinity and whose succeeding terms were as qualitatively different from and beyond infinity as are Two, Three, Four, etc., beyond One. In short, he found that there are numbers larger than infinity. As might be expected, the Knight confirmed the reality of this number system and of the transfinite space that goes with it. There is a whole range of transfinite spaces, probably even larger than the range of finite and infinite spaces (since the number of total spaces is both finite, infinite and transfinite). At this point the Knight seemed to think that we were wandering from the type of description from which I might be expected to profit, and proposed to resume expatiating on those nearer to familiarity. I objected; it was diverting, but less challenging, to be presented with nothing but modifications of an existence I already knew. In a sense I could almost have invented these modifications myself. Would not the Knight consent to offer me, or at least attempt to make me

understand, worlds having no common ground with my own —
for even the Knight's own locational-transitional space-time, I
reminded him, was not hard to describe. I longed to hear something so original as to blow my mind free of all its preconceptions. After some hesitation and muttering as to the perplexities
engendered by my request, the Knight agreed to make the effort
and favoured me with the following amazing descriptions: *

Suddenly the Knight broke off to warn me that the power drain
was now significantly close to tolerable limits and that he would
not be able to linger much longer. A brief feeling of panic assailed
me. There must be one question that above all others needed to
be asked — yes! The choice was obvious, and I did not delay in
putting it. Did the chess-people have any single, particular
purpose in undertaking their admirable explorations of space?

The instinct of exploration, said the Knight, is a natural one.
There was a central quest, however: to try to determine whether,
in the multiplicity of space-times, there is a common universal
law or principle, and thereby to discover how existence originates
and is maintained.

I cursed myself for not having broached this subject sooner,
instead of leaving it until it was almost too late. I had given much
thought to this Basic Question myself, I tendered. And, if it was
of any interest, I had once come to a tentative conclusion, that
there *was* a basic law of existence. It is simply: "A thing is
identical to itself." This principle explained the operation of cause
and effect, I claimed. The universe being a unity, it is also
identical to itself, and an effect only *appears* to follow a cause. In
actuality they are part of the same thing, opposite sides of the
same coin.

Once again the Knight had cause to chide me for my lack of
imagination. This axiom certainly held in my own space, he conceded, but I shouldn't suppose because of that that it was a
universal law. There were numerous space-times where *things*

---

* A second break occurs in the manuscript here. The Narrator pleads
that this section was too ephemeral to remember or too abstruse to
be outlined in words; The Editor surmises that his invention had run
dry—Ed.

were not equal to themselves. In fact even in my own space the principle adhered only approximately, because things were in motion and motion involved a marginal blurring of self-identity. My axiom held as an absolute law only in those spaces where motion was impossible.

Unabashed, I offered my second contribution, this one concerning the maintenance of existence. There was a theory, I told him, that used an electronic analogy and likened existence to a television screen and a camera. The camera scanned the image on the screen, and fed it back to the screen's input, so maintaining the image perpetually. Thuswise existence was maintained: if the feedback from the camera to the screen should be interrupted, even for a split second, existence would vanish and could never be reconstituted.

A pre-electronic version of the theory replaces the screen and camera by two mirrors, each reflecting the image of existence into the other. It is my belief that this is the meaning of the ancient alchemical aphorism "As above, so below" found on the Emerald Table of Hermes Trismegistus, it being imagined that the mirrors are placed one above the other. Other authorities unanimously assert that it refers to the supposed similarity between the macrocosm and the microcosm; but I consider that this, besides being of doubtful veridity, is a crude, pedestrian interpretation unworthy of the thought of the Geat Master. The full text of the saying runs:

> That which is above is like to that which is below, and that which is below is like to that which is above, to accomplish the miracles of one thing.

It has to be understood that the mirrors themselves are part of the image, of course, just as the screen and camera are part of the scanning pattern — if it is asked how this could possibly be, I would refer the enquirer to that other Alchemical symbol, the Worm Ouroboros, who is shown with his tail in his mouth, eating himself.

The Knight appeared to look on this exposition with some approval. Hermes Trismegistus, he said, was certainly a king among men of science. I asked what theories or discoveries the chess-people had on the subject; but, the Knight announced, time had run out and he could delay departure no longer. The few seconds remaining would not suffice to tell what he otherwise might have to say; but, he added, he had not so far revealed that the question of space was also intimately bound up with that of *consciousness*, and that it was towards consciousness that the chess-people were now directing their researches. He mentioned a space where an entity, as it might be a man, was forced to enjoy a double consciousness — not only was he conscious in himself, but he was also conscious at every moment of his appearance to the physical world around him, which was also conscious. The Knight invited me to ponder on what existence would be like in such a state — but his words now came in haste and he bade me goodbye.

Again I begged him to stay, just for a little while. But he turned and looked commandingly around him over the chessboard. The pieces began to move and to execute their flickering dance pattern around the board. The Knight joined them, gyrating around the board like a dance master directing the others. As the invisible ship lifted away the pieces surged round the board in a circular movement as if caught in a vortex; then they were still. The Knight could no longer speak to me in his resinous, friendly voice: he was only a chiselled piece of dead wood.

I came out of my shocked reverie with a start. On the disappearance of the alien influence the pieces had reverted to their original positions, ready to resume the game. There would be no need, I thought blankly, for me to write to my partner for the details.

I pushed myself away from the table. The sweet opium smell still hung on the air. The breeze from the garden was only marginally cooler. The far-off sun was still in the act of descending to the horizon through an elegant Technicolor sky.

It was hard for me to admit that only a minute or two could have passed, when I was sure that I had been talking and listening for hours. I will never be able to know absolutely, and certainly never be able to prove, that what I say took place really did take place. I can only speak of the compelling veridity of my recollection. But whatever the truth, it has at least brought to my notice that for all our knowledge of the universe, even when we project our giant rockets into space and imagine that at last we are penetrating the basic void that holds all things, we still have not touched or even suspected the immensities and the mysteries that existence contains.

The Bees of Knowledge

It scarcely seems necessary to relate how I first came to be cast on to Handrea, like a man thrown up on a strange shore. To the Bees of Handrea these details, though possibly known to them, are of negligible interest since in their regard I rate as no more than an unremarkable piece of flotsam that chanced to drift into their domain. Let it suffice, then, that I had paused to say a prayer at the shrine of Saint Hysastum, the patron saint of interstellar travellers, when an explosion in the region of the engine room wrecked the entire liner. The cause of the catastrophe remains a mystery to me. Such accidents are far from common aboard passenger ships, though when they do occur subsequent rescue is an uncertain hope, owing to the great choice of routes open to interstellar navigators and to their habit of changing course in mid-flight to provide additional sightseeing.

My timely devotions saved my life, though reserving me for a weirder fate. Within seconds I was able to gain a lifeboat, which was stationed thoughtfully adjacent to the shrine, and, amid flame and buckling metal, I was ejected into space. After the explosion, picking my way through the scattered debris, I learned that no one but myself had escaped.

The crushing sense of desolation that comes over one at such a moment cannot adequately be described. Nothing brings one so thoroughly face to face with blind, uncaring Nature as this sudden, utter remoteness from one's fellow human beings. Here I was, surrounded by vast light years of space, with probably not another human soul within hundreds of parsecs, totally alone and very nearly helpless.

My feeling of isolation mounted to a state of terror when I discovered that the rescue beacon was not operating. Once again I had recourse to prayer, which calmed me a little and brought me to a more hopeful appraisal of my situation. The lifeboat, I reminded myself, could keep me alive for up to a year if all went well. There would have been little point in activating the beacon immediately in any case. The star liner would not be reported missing for several weeks, and taking into account the delay before a search was organised, and the dozens of possible routes to be surveyed, a sweep within range of the beacon might not occur for months, if at all. During that time its repair seemed a feasible project, or at any rate not a hopeless one.

But it could not be done conveniently in space, and I peered again through the lifeboat's portholes. On one side glimmered a reddish-yellow sun. Close by on the other side hung a big murky globe resembling an overripe fruit — the planet Handrea, to provide a view of which the star liner had been slowing down at the time of the explosion. It had received its name but an hour previously from one of the passengers (the privilege of naming newly sighted worlds being another of the minor perquisites of interstellar travel) and had already been ascertained as being tolerable as regards chemistry and geology. So, heartened by having at least some course of action to pursue, I turned my small lifeboat towards it.

As I passed through them I made a careful recording of the bands of magnetism and radiation that planets of this type usually possess, noting as I did so that they were uncommonly strong and complicated. I was perturbed to find that the atmosphere was a deep one, descending nearly seven hundred miles. Upon my entering its outer fringes the sky turned from jet black to dark brown and the stars quickly vanished from sight. A hundred miles further down I entered a sphere of electrical storms and was buffeted about by powerful gusts. It had been my intention, had Handrea looked unduly inhospitable, to fly straight out again, but before long it was all I could do to keep on an even keel, not being an expert pilot. Eventually, much relieved after a harrowing passage, I entered the layer of calm air that lies close to the surface and accomplished a landing amid large tufts of a plant which, though maroon in colour, could fairly be described as grasslike.

I peered at the landscape. Vision was limited to about a hundred yards, and within this span I saw only the mild undulations of the ground, the drab colouration of the vegetation, the dull grey air. Instruments told me that the air was dense, but not of the intolerable pressure suggested by the depth of the atmosphere, consisting of light inert gases and about five per cent oxygen. The temperature, at twenty degrees, was comfortable enough to require no special protective clothing.

After a while I put on an oxygen mask — not trusting myself to the outside's natural mix — and equalised pressures before opening the hatch. Taking with me the lifeboat's tool-kit, I stepped outside to remove the beacon's service plate.

Underfoot the maroon grass had a thick-piled springy texture. As I moved the air felt thick, almost like water, and perfect silence prevailed. I tried to close my mind to the fact that I stood on an alien and unknown planet, and concentrated on the task in hand.

I worked thus for perhaps twenty minutes before becoming aware of a low-pitched droning or burring sound, which, almost before I could react to it, swelled in volume until it made the air vibrate all about me. Like the parting of a curtain the opaque atmosphere suddenly disgorged two huge flying shapes. And so I saw them for the first time: the Bees of Handrea.

Describing them offers no particular difficulties, since unlike many alien forms of life they can be compared with a terrestrial species. They are, of course, vast if measured alongside our earthly bees, and the resemblance is in some respects a superficial one. The body, in two segments, is three or four times the size of a man, the abdomen being very large and round so as to make the creature closest in appearance, perhaps, to our bumble bee. As in the terrestrial bee the fur is striped but only slightly so — a relic, I would guess, from some previous evolutionary period the Bees have passed through — the stripes being fuzzy fawn and soft gold, so that the Bees seemed almost to shine in their monotonous environment.

On Earth this great mass could never take to the air at all, but the density of Handrea's atmosphere enables such a creature to be supported by two pairs of surprisingly small wings which vibrate rapidly, giving off the pronounced drone I had first noticed. The Bees move, moreover, with all the speed and agility of their earthly counterparts. Their arrival occasioned me some alarm, naturally, and I attempted to make a hasty retreat into the lifeboat, but I had time to take only a couple of steps before one of the huge creatures had darted to me and lifted me up with its frontward limbs which ended in tangles of hooks and pincers.

The desperation of my initial struggles may be imagined. From acquaintance with earthly insects I had expected instantly to receive some dreadful sting which would paralyse me or kill me outright, and I fought with all my might to free myself from the monster. In the struggle my oxygen mask was torn loose and fell to the ground, so that for the first time, with a cold shock, I drew Handrea's air into my lungs. All my efforts were to no avail; no sting was forthcoming, and the Bee merely modified its powerful grip so as to leave me completely helpless, and I was borne off into the mists, leaving the lifeboat far behind.

The two Bees flew, as near as I could tell, in a straight line, keeping abreast of one another. The narrow patch of landscape in my view at any one time presented no change of aspect, but we travelled through the foggy, impenetrable air at what seemed to me a prodigious speed. Unhindered now by my oxygen mask, the world of Handrea met my senses with a new immediacy. The breath that coursed through my nostrils smelled damp, bearing hints of dank vegetable fragrance. Quite separate from this, I was aware of the much stronger smell of the Bee that carried me — a sharp, oddly sweet smell that could not be ignored.

Reminding myself of insect habits, I was fearful now of a much worse fate than being stung to death. My imagination worked apace: these Bees would hardly have seized me for nothing, I told myself, and in all probability their intention was to use me as a body in which to lay eggs, so that the larvae could feed off my live flesh. In my despair I even contemplated the sin of suicide, wondering how I might kill myself before the worst happened. When I remember these fears now, my present circumstances seem relatively good.

On and on we droned, the increasing distance between myself and the lifeboat, and the virtual impossibility of my ever returning to it, causing me no small agony of mind. At least an hour, and possibly several, passed in this fashion before the Bees' destination came looming out of the fog.

At first I took the shape ahead to be an oddly-formed mountain until its artificial nature became apparent. Then it emerged as an uneven, elongated dome whose limits passed entirely out of sight in the dimness: a stupendous beehive. I now know its height to attain several thousand feet, with nearly the same proportions at the base. As we came closer a generalised humming could be heard emanating from the huge edifice. At the same time I saw giant bees flitting hither and thither, coming and going from the great hive.

We approached an entrance set about a hundred feet from ground level and without pause passed through to the interior. I observed a number of Bees stationed just within the opening, some apparently standing guard, others vibrating their wings rapidly, presumably to ventilate the hive as bees do on Earth. Indeed, their work set up such a wind that the clothes were nearly torn from my back as my captors alighted on the floor of the vestibule. From this chamber several passages radiated —that, at least, was my first impression. As my captors set off down one of these I realised that in fact the openings all connected up with one another; the internal structure of the hive was largely an open one, the space of any level being divided by the pillars which supported the next.

I will not dwell on how fully I appreciated the horror of my apparent situation as I was dragged into this den. Bees swarmed everywhere and their pungent-sweet smell was overpowering. To think that I, a human being bearing a spark of the divinity, was reduced to the role of some smaller insect for these beasts, as if I were a caterpillar or a grub, affected me almost as strongly as the thought of the physical horror which I had no doubt was to come. Deeper and deeper I was carried into the hive, descending and ascending I did not know how many levels. It was like a vast city, filled with the rustling, buzzing and chittering of its inhabitants. Once my captors (they remained together) were accosted by a group of their fellows and performed a kind of waggling dance, at the same time emitting loud noises which sounded like the wailing of a whole team of buzz-saws. Finally our journey came to an end: the two Bees halted in a bowl-shaped depression some tens of feet across, and the hold on my aching body was at last released.

I tumbled, rolled over, and steeled myself to take my first good look at the Bee's head: the faceted eyes glinting with myriad colours, the rolled proboscis, the tufted cheeks and the swollen cranium, all of which are now so familiar to me. Unable to bear the suspense any longer I squeezed my eyes shut and tried not to exist. Now it would come — the deep-thrusting sting, mortal as any sword, or the cruel insertion of the ovipositor.

The muscular limbs turned me over and over, bristly fur scratching my skin. When, after some time, nothing else transpired I opened my eyes a little. The two Bees were huddled over me, holding me almost in a double embrace, and fondling me with their forelegs. Their wings trembled; their droning buzz-saw voices, with no articulation that I could discern, rose and fell in harmony. The movements of the forelegs became light and caressing, so that I wondered what kind of insect ritual I was being subjected to. Then, to my surprise, the manipulatory claws began clumsily to strip me of my clothing. Shortly I lay naked, while my garments were lifted one by one, inspected and tossed aside.

The Bees' attention returned to my naked body, probing it with a feather-like touch, examining orifices, holding me upside down or in whatever fashion was convenient, as though I were an inanimate object. I experienced a moment of supreme terror when a stiff digit entered my anus and slid up my rectum. The organ withdrew in a second or two, but I was left in little uncertainty of mind as to what had taken place.

At length the Bees seemed to have finished. One wandered off, while the other lifted me up and took to the air again. I observed that we were in a spacious vault, allowing the Bees ample room for flight but somewhat dimly lit (unlike much of the hive I had passed through). We swooped low to pass under a barrier, swam up a sort of gully, and emerged in yet another vault even larger, whose far side was not clearly visible but which contained great indistinct piles. On one of these the Bee unceremoniously dropped me, and I sprawled and slithered down a slope composed of loose objects, like a rubbish heap.

After the Bee had flown away, my great concern was with the eggs I felt sure it had deposited in my rectum. I felt up with my finger as far as I could, but encountered nothing. I decided it was imperative to sweep out the passage straight away. After a great deal of frantic straining I managed to pass an amount of faecal matter and examined it anxiously for sign of the eggs. There was none, and eventually I concluded with immense relief that the Bee's intrusion had been exploratory, nothing more.

Finding myself unexpectedly alive and unharmed, I was able to take a more leisurely interest in my surroundings. The first question to pique my curiosity was how the interior of the hive came to be lighted, when it should have been in complete darkness. Some parts of it, in fact, were bathed in a fairly bright haze. Peering at the near-by wall of the vault, I saw that the material out of which the hive was constructed was itself fluorescent, thus explaining the mystery. I pondered a little further on the nature of this material. Being phosphorescent it was very likely organic in origin, I reflected. Possibly the Bees used their own excrement as a building material, as termites do on Earth.

Perhaps this luminosity was an accidental by-product and extraneous to the Bees' needs. But if it formed part of their economy then it was a wonderful example of the ingenuity of Nature, which had evolved phosphorescent excrement for such a purpose.

I pulled myself upright on the unsteady pile where I was precariously perched and took a closer survey of my immediate environs. I stood on a jumble of objects of various shapes and sizes, all indistinct in the gloom. Bending, I picked one up.

The thing was made of a substance indistinguishable from wood. And it was a carving of some kind of animal, perhaps another giant insect, with a peculiar flowering snout. I was not sure whether the representation was meant to be a naturalistic one or whether it was fanciful; what was in no doubt was that it was the product of art.

I dropped it and selected another object. This turned out to be something whose purpose I could not decipher: a black rod about three feet in length with a hemispherical bowl attached to one end. But again, I judged it to be artificial.

In a state of fresh excitement I extended my explorations. The heap proved to be varied in its composition; most of it consisted of decayed vegetable matter. But buried in it, strewn on top of it, piled here and there, was a treasure house of alien artifacts too diverse to describe. Many of them were rotted, broken and crushed, but others seemed intact and even new.

What was the reason for this rubbish heap? Who had manufactured the artifacts? Not the Bees — somehow that did not strike me as a likely proposition, and the impression was confirmed when I found what I could only call, from its shape and size, a drinking cup.

Bees would not use drinking cups.

Somewhere on this planet, then, was an intelligent race. While I was mulling this over there came a loud droning noise and another Bee entered the vault, dropped an article on the heap and departed. I scrambled towards the discarded object and discovered it to be a mysterious instrument consisting of hinged and interlocking boxes.

I recalled the manner in which I had been snatched from the ground while attempting to repair my rescue beacon, and all seemed to become clear to me. The Bees had a magpie instinct: they were collectors of any object they came across that attracted their attention. I, just like anything else, had been added to their mindless hoard.

For some time that remained the total of my understanding of the Bees of Handrea.

At length I clambered down from the pile and began to explore beyond the vault. By now hunger was beginning to affect me, and while I still could not speculate as to what my future might be, I wondered as to the possibility of obtaining food.

My needs were answered much sooner than I had expected. Half an hour of probing (trying always to keep track of my movements) brought me to a wall which exuded a heavy, sweet aroma. This wall was made of a golden bread-like substance which crumbled and broke easily in the hand to yield chunks from which seeped a light yellow syrup. It had every appearance of being edible, and though afraid of poisoning myself I sampled a morsel, recalling that though the protein structure of alien life may differ from our own, that protein is everywhere constructed out of the same small group of amino acids, into which the digestive system decomposes it. I was soon reassured: the bread was delicious, sweet without being nauseous, and of a texture like honey-cake. As a food it proved completely satisfying. I ate a quantity of it, reasoning as I did so that in all probability this was a corner of the Bees' food store, or at any rate of one of a number of such stores.

My meal was interrupted by a rustling sound. I was alarmed to see the approach of an insect-like creature, smaller than the Bees and indeed somewhat smaller than myself, but nevertheless of horrifying appearance. I was put in mind of a fly — not the common housefly, but something closer to a mosquito, with small folded wings and a spike-like proboscis. I ran for my life, but on rounding a corner of the passageway, and hearing no sound of pursuit, I stopped and cautiously peeped back. The Fly had inserted its proboscis into the honey-bread and was presumably sucking out the liqueur.

I decided to risk no further confrontation but made my way back to the vault where lay the junkheaps. There I discovered some pools of brackish water and further refreshed myself. Then I set about finding a weapon in case I should need to defend myself against monsters such as I had just witnessed — or, for that matter, against the Bees, though I fervently hoped I should not be called upon to fight such prodigious creatures. After some searching I found a long metal pole with a pointed end which would serve tolerably well as a spear.

The vault seemed empty, lonely, silent and echoing. From afar came the continual murmur of the business of the hive, like the ceaseless activity of a city, but it barely broke the silence. Already I had begun to think of the place as a refuge, and eventually I found a spot for myself where, wearied and strained by my experiences, I settled down to sleep.

On waking I drank more water and made the short trip to obtain more honey-bread. Then, naked though I was, and armed with my spear, I set out to explore the hive in earnest.

Thus began a fairly long period in which I acquainted myself with the life of the great bee-city, though in what I now know to be a superficial way. Slowly and tentatively I explored the passages and galleries, making sure all the time that I could find my way back to the familiar territory of the junkheaps where I was at least assured of water and food, and to which I periodically returned to rest. Always I made my way upwards, searching for the entrance by which I had been brought into the hive.

The Bees, who busied themselves everywhere, consistently ignored me. I discovered that the hive was host to numerous other parasites like myself, species of insects and giant worms who had made their home here and were apparently tolerated, if they were noticed at all. Usually (but not invariably) they were smaller than the Bees, and either stole honey-bread or stalked one another for food. Thus for any but the Bees themselves (who of course were never attacked) the hive was a jungle in which every ecological niche was filled.

The dangers to myself were considerable, and I soon found that I had been lucky in my choice of weapons, for the spear enabled me to keep most predators at bay. Nevertheless my early experiences were horrifying. On my first reconnoitre I was attacked three times: twice by grub-like beasts with hideous scissor-type jaws, and once by something resembling a giant mite whose habit it is to drop a net on passers-by from above. I could not free myself from this trap for some time, during which I was obliged to fight for my life while still enmeshed, wielding the spear through the holes and finally killing my adversary.

I quickly learned which species were harmless and which to beware of. I learned to recognise the kind of corners and approaches the predators were apt to lurk in, and so these bouts of deadly combat became much less frequent.

My third sortie brought me at last to the entrance. I hesitated on the approach to the vestibule, seeing ahead of me the humped shapes of the guards, and bracing myself against the wind set up by the whirring wings of the ventilator Bees. So powerful was this dense current that when I finally went forward I was obliged to edge myself across the floor with the help of my spear. I stopped close to the broad slot-like opening and looked out into the free air of Handrea.

A fog-like cold smote my skin, in contrast to the warmth of the hive. I could see only thick misty air which eddied and swirled as more Bees came to alight inside the entrance. The ground was quite out of sight.

I believe the guards would not have prevented me from leaving the hive. I could have scrambled down its rough surface to the ground. But where to then? I had no means of achieving the goal which had been uppermost in my mind: that of returning to the lifeboat and completing the repair of the beacon. Not only had I no idea of which direction to take, but I had no way of holding to that direction if I found it. Once away from the hive I would be unlikely to locate it again, and would die of hunger or thirst or else fall victim to larger predators that I had not yet seen.

But could I accept the corollary: that I must live out my remaining years in the hive with the status of a parasitic worm? A curiously forlorn, deserted feeling came over me: I felt that I had been treated badly during the explosion on the passenger liner; my companions had all died and been spared any further problems, but I had been excluded from the common fate and left alone, abandoned by death.

This odd and sinful feeling lasted but a minute or two. With heavy heart I made my way back down below, wondering if I could pluck up the courage for the near-suicidal attempt to retrace the course of the Bees who had brought me here. When I arrived at the junkheaps an extraordinary sight met my eyes. There, flung at a lurching angle atop the nearest pile, was the lifeboat!

I scrambled up the heap towards it with a cry of joy. On reaching the small spacecraft, however, I was in for a crushing disappointment. It had been gutted. Everything had been stripped from it, inside and out, leaving only an empty shell.

Strewn over a fairly wide area round about was all the equipment with which the lifeboat had been stocked. To my astonishment every item had been torn to pieces: the Bees seemed to exhibit a destructive animal curiosity over everything they touched. I found the beacon after searching for some minutes. Like everything else it was completely wrecked, practically disintegrated component by component. Any kind of repair was absolutely out of the question, and after staring at the remains for some while in a state of shock, I sat down and buried my face in my hands, sobbing to think what life was to mean to me from now on.

For some time afterwards wild schemes were apt to enter my head. It occurred to me that perhaps I was not necessarily doomed to remain indefinitely in the hive. Judging by the contents of the junkheaps intelligence existed somewhere on the planet, and the Bees visited the scene of that intelligence. I entertained the notion of clinging to a Bee's back, possibly attaching myself there by means of a harness, and flying with it to where life might be more agreeable, even though I still would not be among my own kind.

It was even possible, I conjectured (remembering that some of the artifacts I had seen denoted a fairly advanced technology) that once learning of my plight the creatures I met would be kind enough to set up a beacon of their own to signal the rescue ship, if I could explain its mode of operation clearly enough.

These plans served chiefly to ward off my despair, for common sense told me how unlikely they were to succeed. My faith also came under great strain at this time, but I am glad to say I retained it, though with some difficulty at first, and prayer was, as ever, my solace.

But as the days succeeded one another my mood turned to one of apathy, although I tried to rouse myself to action and to remind myself that the time remaining before a search expedition arrived within signalling distance was not unlimited. Thinking that I should fashion a harness with which to carry out my project of riding on a Bee, I began to sort through the junkheaps. The detritus of alien industry was fascinating to browse through. I presumed at first that the artifacts were all the product of the same civilisation, but later I realised that I had no verification of this. Indeed I could construe no picture of a single culture out of the objects I perused; rather they suggested a number of different, quite unconnected civilisations, or even species.

I was also struck by the number of artifacts which were clearly not tools or ornaments and whose use could not easily be discerned. At length I discovered some of the more curiously shaped of them to bear close-packed markings, and I surmised that these and others, including some I believed to be electronic in operation, were books or records of some kind, though I could not explain why they made up such a large percentage of the junkheaps.

My desultory efforts to escape the hive were all brought to an end when an extraordinary event occurred. I had gone on another exploratory foray with the intention of making some rough assessment of Bee anatomy when the usual bumbling activity of the hive turned to a state of agitation. I heard sounds of rending and general destruction, and on investigating perceived that numbers of the Bees were engaged in tearing down parts of the hive. The reason for this soon became apparent: they were clearing a passage for a huge object, too large to enter the hive by any of its entrances or to negotiate its interior spaces.

The object proved to be a ship, clearly built to ride on water. Of a wood-like material, it had a sweeping profile at least a hundred and fifty feet long, with an elegant pattern of raised decks at intervals, stepped slightly higher forward and aft. In its general lines the closest resemblance would be, I suppose, to a Greek galley, a resemblance heightened by the carving which adorned the fore and aft railings and the protruding wales which swept from stem to stern. The brute force by which the Bees moved this ship was a sight to behold. They must have flown it here an unknown distance by the concerted power of their wings alone — a feat which even in Handrea's thickened atmosphere was astonishing — and now they nudged, heaved and strained at it in their hundreds, wings buzzing in a deafening clamour (for it appeared to be their wings they mostly used to gain traction). The ship lurched forward foot by foot, grinding and crushing everything in its path, shouldering aside masses of building material where the cleared pathway was not wide enough, and causing yet more to come crashing down behind it. Where it had passed Bees set to work immediately to repair the damage, a task which I knew they could accomplish with unbelievable rapidity.

Steadily the ship was being edged into the heart of the hive. I crept forward, dodged past Bee bodies, and found myself able to clamber up the side of the vessel. Briefly I managed to stand on the deck, which, I was interested to see, was inlaid with silvery designs. I could see no sign of any crew. A moment later I heard an impatient buzz behind me and a bristly limb knocked me over the side. I fell to the ground, winded and badly bruised.

Slowly the ship jerked from view amid clouds of dust and a rain of rubble, swaying cumbersomely. Limping, I followed, still curious and wondering how the Bees were regarded by the intelligent race or races from whom they filched so many valuable artifacts.

It occurred to me that for all my wanderings I had remained in the peripheral region of the hive, my mind obsessed by the idea of escape. Vaguely I had imagined the hive to present the same aspect wherever one stood in it, but venturing deeper into the interior in pursuit of the ship I saw my mistake. The light strengthened to become a golden ambience in which the golden fur of the Bees shone. The architecture of the hive also changed. The monotonous tiered floors gave way to a more complex structure in which there were spiral ramps, great halls, and linked chambers of various shapes, sometimes comprising whole banks of huge polyhedra of perfect geometrical regularity, so that the hive came to resemble more and more the "golden palace" beloved of the more sentimental naturalists when writing of earthly bees. And the sharp-sweet odour of these Bees, to which I thought I had become accustomed, became so strong that I was almost stifled.

All these wonders, like everything else about the Bees, I understood up to this moment to be the product of instinct. I had almost caught up with the lurching ship when I saw something which gave me pause for thought.

A number of artifacts had apparently fallen from the ship in the course of its progress and lay about in the rubble. One Bee lingered and was playing with a device made of a shiny brown material, in shape somewhere between a sphere and a cube and numbering among its features several protuberances and a circular plate of dull silver. The Bee touched a protuberance with a foreleg, and the plate came abruptly to life.

I edged closer to spy on what was taking place. The plate showed a full-colour motion picture that at first was of no recognisable object or scene. After some moments I realised that it was displaying a series of geometrical figures arranged in a logical series. A mathematics lesson!

To my bemusement the huge insect's gaze seemed intent on the picture plate. Shortly it again touched the protuberance, which was a control of the sliding sort, and the picture changed to a text in some kind of writing or ideograms, illustrated by enigmatic symbols. Again the Bee followed the lesson with every appearance of understanding it, but even when this was succeeded by the Bee's manipulating various knobs in seemingly skilful fashion, eliciting information at will, I still could not grasp what the evidence of my eyes suggested.

The Bee turned to another pastime. It turned the device over and in a few moments had removed the outer casing. A mass of close-packed parts was revealed, which the Bee took to pieces with surprisingly delicate pincers. I thought I was seeing the usual destructiveness I already had cause to complain of on the part of these insects, but was astonished by what followed. With the machine in fragments, the Bee suddenly set to work to put it all together again. In a minute or two it was again functioning perfectly.

Along came a second Bee. A buzz-saw exchange took place between them. Wings trembled. The first Bee again stripped down the machine. Together they played with the components, assembling and disassembling them several times over, their droning voices rising and falling, until finally they tired of the game and the pieces were flung carelessly to the ground.

There could be no doubt of it. The Bees were intelligent! And they understood technology!

Saint Hysastum, I thought, you have answered my prayers!

How foolish I had been to give practically no thought to this possibility! How ridiculous to plan journeys across Handrea when the answer lay right here under my nose!

But why had the Bees behaved towards me like brute beasts? I recalled that I had been outside the lifeboat when they arrived. Possibly I had been taken for a denizen of their own planet. They had mistaken my nature, just as I had mistaken theirs.

But it was imperative that I enlighten them without delay. I dashed forward, right under the gaze of those huge mosaic eyes, and began scratching diagrams in the dust with my spear. A circle, a triangle, a square, a pentagon — surely a sentient creature familiar with mathematics (as my recent observations showed the Bee to be) would recognise these as signs of intelligence on my part? The Bee did not seem to notice and made to move off, but I skipped forward again, placing myself impetuously in its path, and again began my eager scribbling. I made three dots, then another three, followed by six dots — a clear demonstration that I could count! For good measure I scribbled out the diagram that accompanies Pythagoras' theorem, even though it is perhaps too elaborate for a first contact between species. The Bee seemed nonplussed for a moment. But then it brushed me aside and passed on, followed by its companion.

My frantic efforts as I sought to make contact with the Bees during the next hour or two approached the level of hysteria. All was to no avail. I remained a nonentity as far as they were concerned: I spoke to them, gesticulated, drew, showed them my spear and play-acted its use, but was simply ignored. From their conduct, which to all appearances exemplified insect mindlessness, it was hard to believe that they really possessed intelligence.

At last, disheartened and perplexed, I returned to my quiet refuge in the vault of the junkheaps. I was not completely alone there: the Fly, the mosquito-like creature I had first encountered at the honey-bread bank, was pottering about among the rubbish. I often met this creature on my trips to the honey-bread, and occasionally it ventured into the vault and roamed aimlessly among the heaps of artifacts. Never having received any threat from it, I had come to accept its presence.

Sighing and despairing, I fell at length into a light sleep. And as I slept I dreamed.

We came between a defile in the hills and ahead of us, with mist rising and falling about it like steam, lay the hive. Bees came hither and thither in ceaseless streams. Otwun, my Handreatic companion, a member of one of the mammalian species of the planet, laid a hand on my shoulder.

"There it is," he said. "The hive of the Bees of Knowledge, where is made the Honey of Experience."

I glanced into his opal eyes. From the cast of his face I knew he was feeling a certain kind of emotion. "You seem afraid of these creatures," I remarked. "Are they dangerous?"

"They are voracious and implacable," he answered. "They know everything old and discover everything new. They range over the whole world in search of knowledge, which is their food, taking it wherever they find it. Yet no man can communicate with them."

"An aloof intelligence then? No pacts or alliances are made with the Bees? No wars or quarrels?"

"Such is out of the question. The Bees are not beings such as the warm-blooded races. They belong in the class of creeping, crawling and flying things. Come, we must pass by the hive if we are to be about our business."

We went forward, the fine rain laying a mantle about our shoulders and casting the hive in a lush setting. We skirted the hive to the east, but suddenly a huge Bee loomed out of the mist and hovered before us, giving off a loud buzzing sound that wavered up and down the scale. Although Otwun had told me it was impossible to communicate with the Bees the buzzing penetrated my brain like bright light through glass and seemed somehow to bypass the speech centre to impart information directly to my consciousness. A terrifying flood of knowledge of the most dazzling and intellectual kind overwhelmed me and caused me almost to faint. . . .

I awoke with the dream vivid in my mind. It was the kind of dream that leaves behind it a mingling of hopeful emotions, seeming to convey a message more real than waking reality itself. I strove to recover the tacit details of the dream — what, for instance, was the important business on which I and Otwun were engaged? But these were gone, as they often are in dreams, and I was left with only the central theme: the nature of the Bees of Handrea. Of this I had received a direct and compelling impression, much more comprehensive than was implied by Otwun's few remarks.

Every sentient creature's intelligence is modified by its ancestral nature. Bees are honey gatherers. Hence when intellectual curiosity developed in the Bees of Handrea it took just this form. The Bees liked to forage into their world seeking to satisfy their avid thirst for knowledge and to bring back their findings into the hive. The physical objects they brought back were of cursory interest only: their main diet was of intellectual ideas and observations, which they were adept at stealing from surrounding civilisations.

This interpretation of the Bees made such an impression on me that, irrationally perhaps, I accepted it as literally true. I believed I had been vouchsafed a minor vision by Saint Hysastum to help me. Then I recalled a passage by the philosopher Nietzsche who lived some centuries ago. Although a heathen in his outlook Nietzsche had many insights. Here he depicted man's mind as a beehive. We are honey gatherers, bringing in little loads of knowledge and ideas — exactly like the Bees of Handrea.

Nietzsche was also the inventor of the doctrine of eternal recurrence, which posits that since the universe is infinite and eternal everything in it, including the Earth and all its inhabitants, must somewhere, sometime, be repeated. If one follows this argument further then it means that every product of man's imagination must somewhere be a reality — and here was Nietzsche's mental beehive, not as the analogy he had conceived, but as a literal reality! What a strange confirmation of Nietzsche's beliefs!

There was a slurping sound. The Fly was sucking up water from one of the tepid pools.

Elsewhere on Handrea, the dream had reminded me, were other races, less alien than the Bees and more amenable to contact. Should I perhaps stock up with honey-bread and strike out on foot in the hope of finding them? But no — the message of the dream clearly indicated that it was with the Bees that my salvation lay. It would be wrong to reject Saint Hysastum's advice.

Accordingly I turned my mind again to the problem of making my nature and my requirements known. To advertise myself as a calculating, tool-making creature seemed to be the best approach. I conceived a plan, and rummaging through the junk and scrap I gathered together the material I needed and set to work.

In an hour or two I had made my Arithmetical Demonstrator. It consisted of a circular board around whose circumference I had marked, with a soft chalk-like substance I found, the numbers One to Twenty-Five in dot notation, so that any sighted intelligent creature anywhere in creation could have recognised them. Pinned to the centre of the board were two pointers each of a different shape, so that the whole affair looked much like a clock.

The Demonstrator was simple to operate. With the first hand I would point to two numbers successively, and then point to their sum with the second hand. Once I had caught the attention of the Bees in this way I would write the addition sign on the board, then write the multiplication sign and perform a few simple multiplications. In the same manner I would also be able to demonstrate subtraction and division and leave the Bees in no doubt as to my rationality.

Sitting halfway up the junkheap, I practised with the completed board for a short while. Suddenly the sound of dislodged rubbish close behind me made me jump. Turning, I saw that the Fly had descended furtively on me from the top of the heap and its head was craned forward in what I took to be a menacing manner.

In my alarm I half-rolled, half-scrambled down the heap,

forgetting all about the demonstration board and trying to think where I had left my spear. The Fly made no attempt to follow me, however. When I next saw it, about ten minutes later, it had climbed down the far side of the heap and was squatting on the ground as if preoccupied. To my exasperation I saw that it was in possession of my Arithmetical Demonstrator.

Having found my spear I decided to use the Fly's own tactic against it to recover the board. Carefully, making as little noise as possible, I skirted round the heap and climbed up it on all fours so as to bring myself above and behind the Fly. Then I began a stealthy descent, reasoning that a noisy attack at close quarters would be enough to scare the insect into abandoning the board just as I had done.

Less deftly than the Fly I climbed to within a few feet of it. Its hearing did not seem particularly acute: it took no notice of my less than silent approach. But before I launched an onslaught I noticed something purposeful about the movement of its foreleg and stayed my hand.

The Fly was playing with the Demonstrator, displaying computations on it exactly as I had intended.

On each occasion it moved the first pointer twice and the second pointer once.

Five and Eight equals Thirteen. Addition.

Four and Six equals Twenty-Four. Multiplication.

The fourth or fifth manipulation I observed made me think at first that these results were coincidental. Two and Three equals Eight. Incorrect.

Then it struck me. Two to the *power* Three equals Eight!

My amazement, not to say bewilderment, was so great that the spear dropped from my hand. I could not doubt but that the Fly, too, possessed intellectual power.

Here was my introduction to the Bees!

But why was the Fly, if it belonged to an intelligent species, living the life of a scavenger? Was it perhaps trapped in the hive, as I was? Or was *every* insect species on Handrea intelligent, as a matter of course?

I slithered to the ground and stood near the Fly, forcing myself to disregard its powerful stench. It moved back but a few feet when I reached out my hand to pick up the demonstration board and regarded me intently as I spelled out the initial steps of our dialogue.

So began an incredible period of learning and interchange between my friend the Fly and myself. To be honest, the learning was mostly on his part, for I could never have absorbed information as he did.

The Fly's memory was as rapid and unfaltering as a computer's. Everything I showed him he knew instantly. First I introduced him to the Arabic decimal notation and then, though he seemed content to rush into an orgy of abstruse calculation, I induced him to learn alphabetical writing. He mastered words and concepts with machine-like ease, and in the space of a few weeks we were able to converse on almost any subject, using an alphabetical version I made of the demonstration board.

My new friend's curiosity was prodigious. He asked me where I came from, and what was the size and distance of my home planet. He then asked how the spaceship that had brought me here had been propelled, and I explained it to him as best as I was able. I also managed to elicit from him one or two scraps of information about Handrea, though his answers were vague.

The Fly's chief obsession, however, lay in the mathematics of numbers. In this he was a wizard, possessing the type of brain that the human race produces perhaps once in a couple of centuries. I was never able to understand a fraction of what the Fly knew about numbers. It would have taken a Fermat or a Poincaré to keep up with him.

There was much wonderment in the thought of what strange vessels God chooses to imbue with his divine spark. I had little enthusiasm, however, for exploring the more recondite properties of Fibonacci numbers, prime numbers and the like, and as soon as was practicable I broached the subject that was the aim of the entire operation as far as I was concerned: would the Fly help me to establish relations with the Bees, so that I might persuade them to construct a rescue beacon for me?

While I posed this question on the alphabet board the Fly was hunched over the much improved number board. Although I was sure he read my request as I presented it to him he gave no sign of understanding it and continued playing with his own board.

Annoyed, I snatched the number board away from him and repeated my demand. The Fly squatted there, unmoving. As I was coming near the end of my letter-pointing he casually shuffled to the number-board again and continued his rapid calculations, which I believed concerned number curios of a high order but which I was in no position to follow without textual explanations.

I asked:

"Why will you not answer me?"

And was ignored.

I made increasingly desperate attempts at a closer accord and similarly was rebuffed, while the Fly continued his mathematical orgy in what looked increasingly like a frantic ecstasy. It suddenly occurred to me that up until my request for help none of our exchanges had been in the nature of true conversation but had consisted purely of an exchange of dry knowledge. Otherwise the Fly was behaving like someone who had not quite realised I existed — indeed, except for his obvious intelligence, he behaved like an idiot. Or a witless animal.

My failure to create a true relationship with the Fly was extremely disappointing. It taught me yet again how different was the intelligence of the Handreatic insects from my own. I concluded, after taking to the board for further attempts at a more personal contact, that I had been mistaken in thinking that the Fly was speaking to me when using the boards. Except for his initial enquiries into my origins he had been talking to himself, using the boards as a new toy or tool of thought.

So depressing was this reversal of my hopes that I felt unutterably weary. I reflected that I had wasted several weeks on what had proved to be a blind alley, and that if the Fly had rejected me as a fellow sentient being then so, probably, would the Bees. I dragged myself away from the busy insect, and flung myself down to sleep.

Otwun caught my arm and dragged me past the hovering Bee, whereupon normal perception returned to me. The Bee flew away and left us standing in the rain-sodden grass.

"What — what happened?" I asked dully.

"By accident you touched the mind of the Bee with your mind.

It happens sometimes. Come, we must make haste if we are to arrive in time to take part in the assault against Totcune. Our Kessene allies will not wait indefinitely."

I looked down at the arm he held. Unlike his arm, which was pale green, mine was a dark brown. Understanding for the first time that I also was a Handreatic I looked down at the whole of myself. My race was different from Otwun's. I was smaller, squat, like a goblin beside his lankness.

"Come."

He noticed me gazing at the hive. "Men have sometimes entered the hive to taste the Bees' honey," he said. "None have come out again, to my knowledge."

"It would be a great adventure."

"Only for a fool who no longer wishes to live."

"Perhaps. Give my greetings to the Kessene."

I moved away from him, walking slowly towards the hive.

I had slept but a few minutes, and on waking found my mind buzzing with new energy.

The dream. I was sure the dream was telling me what to do. I had taken the Bees too much for granted, not pondering enough as to their true nature. And yet all I had to do was to think about terrestrial bees.

The gathering of nectar was not the end of the bees' food-making process. That nectar was taken into the hive and made into honey. The same must be true, I reasoned, of the Bees of Handrea and their gathering of knowledge. That knowledge was further refined in the depths of the hive. But what was the honey that resulted from this refining?

Men have sometimes entered the hive to taste the Bees' honey.

The Bees of knowledge; the honey of experience. The phrase came into my mind, I did not know from where.

Of course! The answer came to me in a flash. It explained everything — why the Bees ignored me, why they pulled artifacts to pieces and abandoned them, apparently fashioning nothing similar themselves.

Social insects, as individuals, are not complete. They live only to serve the hive, or colony. Usually they are biologically specialised to perform specific functions and are oblivious of any other. Workers do not know sex. Drones do not know anything else.

The individual Bees I had encountered were not, by themselves, intelligent. What *was* intelligent was the *Hive Mind*, the collectivity of all the Bees, existing as some sort of separate entity. This Mind sent out its golden insects to bring back items of interest from the surrounding world. The Bees collected ideas and observations which were then mulled over by the Mind to provide itself with experience. Because the Hive Mind itself had no direct perception; everything had to come through the Bees.

Experience was the honey that was made from this dry, arid knowledge. It was the Hive Mind's food.

And it was the Hive Mind, not the individual Bees, that would understand my needs!

Could it have been the Hive Mind and not Saint Hysastum, I wondered, that had been calling to me through my dreams? At any rate my course of action seemed clear. I must descend deep into the hive in search of the Mind, hoping that I could contact it somehow.

The Fly was still fiddling with the number board when, for the last time, I left the dim vault of the junkheaps. How close I was to the truth — and yet how far! Armed as usual with my spear I set off, heading for the very centre of the hive where I imagined the Mind to manifest itself.

The damage caused by dragging the alien ship into the interior had all been repaired. The ceaselessly busy and largely inconsequential-looking activity of the giant insects went on all around me. The Bees rushed to and fro, buzz-saw voices rising and falling and wings trembling on meeting, or performed their odd waggling dance before one another. Except for their size and some physical differences it could have been any beehive on Earth.

I journeyed through the golden chambers I have already described. Beyond these lay a labyrinth of worm-like tunnels in which were interspersed empty egg-shaped chambers or nests. I discovered this to appertain to the hive's reproductive arrangements, for eventually I entered a part of the labyrinth that was not empty. Here larvae crawled about the chambers, tended by worker Bees. Then I suddenly broke through the labyrinth and was confronted by an enormous honeycombed wall extending far overhead. Each cell of this honeycomb evidently contained an egg, for newly-hatched larvae were emerging here and there and crawling down the surface.

Somewhere, conceivably, was a huge bloated queen, mother to the whole hive. Could this queen constitute the intelligence I sought? I rejected the idea. As among earthly insects, she would be totally overburdened with her egg-laying role and unfit for anything else.

A longitudinal slit, about eight foot in height, separated the honeycomb from the ground. Since my destination lay in this direction I passed through it and walked, in semi-darkness for a time, with the bulk of the honeycomb pressing down above me.

Then the space seemed to open up abruptly and at the same time I was in the midst of a golden haze which intensified with each step I took, so that the limits of the place I was in were indistinct. Vague shapes loomed at me as if in a dream. Among them was the alien ship I had seen carried into the hive, sliding past me as if into a mist.

My foot caught against something. The floor was littered with objects of all kinds so as to resemble the floor of the vault of the junkheaps, except that here they were bathed in the golden ambience covering everything. I went on, picking my way among them. Presently I heard a familiar buzzing sound. Ahead of me were a number of Bees that appeared to be in an ecstatic trance. Their legs were rigid, their wings were open and vibrating tremulously, their antennae quivered, while the droning they gave off had an almost hypnotic effect.

During the course of my journey I had gradually become aware of an oppressive feeling in my head and an aching sensation at the bridge of my nose. These feelings became unbearably strong in the golden haze. I looked at the gathered Bees and understood that this was the place where their honey was processed, or perhaps where it was stored. With that thought the aching in my head became like a migraine and then suddenly vanished. Something pushed its way into my brain.

I tasted the Bees' honey. I experienced as the Bees experience.

The dream had been a precursor. But it could not have prepared me for such total immersion. What is experience? It comes through the senses, is processed by the mind and presented to the consciousness. The Bees' honey bypasses all these, except perhaps the last. It is raw experience, pre-digested, intensified, blotting out everything else.

This honey has an actual physical basis: magnetism. Handrea's magnetic field, as I have mentioned earlier, is unusually strong and intricate. The Bees have incorporated this magnetic intricacy into their evolution. By means of it they are able to perform a kind of telepathy on the creatures they borrow their knowledge from, using magnetic currents of great delicacy to read the memory banks of living minds. By tuning in to Handrea's magnetic field they know a great deal about what is taking place across the planet, and by the same means they can extend their knowledge into space within the limits of the field. Thus they knew of the accident aboard the passenger liner, and perhaps had learned much of mankind, before I ever set foot on Handrea.

Sometimes magnetic strains from this golden store sweep through the hive in wayward currents. Twice these currents had impinged on my mind to create dreams, giving me the information that had led me into this trap.

I do not know how long my first trance lasted. When it ended I found myself lying on the floor and understood that I must have been overwhelmed by the rush of impressions and passed out. Clarity of the senses lasted only a few minutes, however. The magnetic furore swept through my brain again, and once more I was subjected to amazing experiences.

One does not lose consciousness during these trances. It is rather that one's normal perceptions are blotted out by a stronger force, as the light of a candle is annihilated by the light of the sun.

And what are these stronger experiences?

How am I to describe the contents of alien minds?

At first my experiences were almost wholly abstract, but possessing a baroque quality quite different from what one normally thinks of as abstract. When I try to recall them I am left with a sense of something golden and ornate, of sweetish-musk aromas and of depth within depth.

Like my friend the Fly, the Bees are much interested in mathematics, but theirs is of a type that not even he would be able to understand (any more than I could, except intuitively when I was in the grip of the trance). What would he have made, with his obsession with numbers, of the Bees' theorem that there is a highest positive integer! To human mathematicians this would make no sense. The Bees accomplish it by arranging all numbers radially on six spokes, centred about the number One. They then place on the spokes of this great wheel certain number series which are claimed to contain the essence of numbers and which go spiralling through it, diverging and converging in a winding dance. All these series meet at last in a single immense number. This, according to the theorem, is the opposite pole of the system of positive integers, of which One is the other pole, and is referred to as Hyper-One. This is the end of numbers as we know them. Hyper-One then serves as One for a number system of a higher order. But, to show the hypothetical nature of the Bees' deliberations there is a quite contrary doctrine which portrays all numbers as emanating from a number Plenum, so that every number is potentially zero.

These are items, scraps, crumbs from the feast of the Bees' honey. The raw material of this honey is the knowledge and ideas that the individual Bees forage from all over Handrea. In the safety of their hive the Bees get busy with this knowledge, converting it into direct experience. With the tirelessness of all insects they use it to create innumerable hypothetical worlds, testing them, as it were, with their prodigious intellects to see how they serve as vehicles for experience. I have lived in these worlds. When I am in them they are as real as my own. I have tasted intellectual abstractions of such a rarefied nature that it is useless for me to try to think about them.

But as my brain began to accommodate itself to the honey my experiences became more concrete. Instead of finding myself in a realm of vast theoretical calculation I would find myself sailing the seas of Handrea in a big ship, walking cities that lay somewhere on the other side of the globe, or participating in historical events, many of which had taken place thousands of years previously. Yet even here the Bees' intellectual preoccupations asserted themselves. Nearly always the adventures I met ended in the studies of philosophers and mathematicians, where lengthy debate took place, sometimes followed by translation into a world of pure ideas.

There was a third stage. My experiences began to include material that could only have come from within my own brain. I was back in my home city on my home planet. I was with my friends and loved ones. I relived events from the past. None of this was actually as it has happened, but restructured and mixed together, as happens in dreams, and always with mingled emotions of joy, regret and nostalgia. Among it all, I also lived fantastic scenes from fiction; even comic-strip caricatures came to life, as if the Bees did not know the difference between them and reality.

My home world came, perhaps, to be my own private corner of the honey-store, though it is certainly only a minor item in the Bees' vast hoard. Yet what a sense of desolation I always feel on coming out of it, in the periods when for some reason the magnetic currents no longer inflame my brain, and I realise it is only hallucination! I then find myself in this arid, lonely place, with Bees buzzing and trembling all around me, and as I crawl from the chamber for nearby food and water I know that I shall never, in reality, see home again.

For the time is long, long past when a rescue beacon could do anything to help me. Not that there was ever, in fact, any chance of constructing one. Because the Bees are not intelligent.

Incredibly, but truly, they are not intelligent. They have intellect merely, pure intellect, but not true intelligence, for this requires the exertion of both intellect and the feelings — and, most important, of the soul. The Bees have no feelings, any more than any other insect has, and — of this I am convinced — God has not endowed them with souls.

They are merely insects. Their intellectual powers, their avid thirst for knowledge, are but instincts with them, no different from the instinct that prompts the ants, bees and termites of Earth to feats of engineering, and which has also misled men into thinking those to be intelligent. No rational mind, able to respond to and communicate with other rational minds, lies behind their voracious appetite.

It seems fitting that if by some quirk or accident of nature intellectual brains should evolve in that class of creature roughly corresponding to our terrestrial arthropods (and Handrea offers the only case of this as far as I know, even though insect-like fauna are abundant throughout the universe), they should do so in this bizarre fashion. One does not expect insects to be intelligent, and indeed they are not, even when endowed with analytical powers greater than our own.

But how long it took me to grasp this fact when I strove so desperately to convey messages to the Hive Mind! For there *is* a Hive Mind; but it has no qualities or intelligence that an individual Bee does not have. It is simply an insect collectivised, a single Bee writ large, and would not be worth mentioning were it not for one curious power it has, or that I think it has.

It seems able, by some means I cannot explain, to congeal objects out of thought. Perhaps these objects are forms imprinted on matter by magnetism. At any rate several times I have found in the chamber small artifacts which earlier I had encountered in visions, and which I do not think could have been obtained on Handrea. Once, for instance, I found a copy of a newspaper including in its pages the adventures of the Amazing Human Spider.

And recently I discovered a small bound book in which was written all the events I have outlined in this account.

I no longer know whether I have copied my story from this book, or whether the book was copied by the Bees from my mind.

What does it matter? I do not know for certain if the book, or indeed any of the other objects I have found in the chamber, really existed. The fact is that for all the abstract knowledge available to me, my grip on concrete reality has steadily deteriorated. I can no longer say with certainty which of the experiences given me by the honey really happened in my former life and which are alterations, interpolations or fantasies. For instance, was I really a companion of the Amazing Human Spider, a crime-fighter who leaps from skyscraper to skyscraper by means of his gravity-defying web?

I have been here for many years. My hair and beard are long and shaggy now that I no longer trim them. Often at the beginning I tried to break away from this addiction to the Bees' honey, but without it the reality of my position is simply too unbearable. Once I even dragged myself halfway back to the vault of the junkheaps, but I knew all the time that I would be forced to return, so great is the pull of those waking dreams.

And so here I remain and must remain, more a parasite upon

these monsters than I ever had imagined I could be. For monsters they are — monsters in the Satanic sense. How else can one describe creatures of such prodigious knowledge and such negligible understanding? And for my enjoyment I have this honey — this all-spanning knowledge. Mad knowledge, too great for human encompassing and fit only for these manic Bees and the work of their ceaseless insect intellects. Knowledge that has no meaning, nothing to check or illuminate it, and which produces no practical end. And yet I know that even here, amid the unseeing Bees of Handrea, far from the temples and comforts of my religion, God is present.

Exit from City 5

Kayin often wondered why the autumnal phase of the City's weather-cycle brought with it such an atmosphere of untidiness and decay. He sat holding Polla's hand in the park, watching as the light over the City dimmed with the approach of night. Here, the gentle breeze that blew continuously through City 5 collected by fitful gusts into a modest wind, skirling up a detritus of torn paper, scraps of fabric and dust.

Rearing above the park's fringe of trees, the ranks of windows in the serried arrays of office buildings began to flick into life. The park was situated on a high level and well out towards the perimeter of the City, so that from this vantage point City 5, with its broken lines, blocks and levels, presented the appearance of a metal bowl finely machined into numerous rectilinear surfaces like an abstract sculpture. From the broken perimeter to the central pinnacle the City rose in a wide countercurve to the curve of the crystal dome overhead, creating a deliberate but false impression of spaciousness. And indeed for a brief period in the late morning, when the light was brightest and the air filled with the sounds of industry, City 5 did manage to generate an atmosphere of liveliness, almost of excitement. But by mid-afternoon the illusion was gone. The crystal dome, glinting in the falling light, became oppressive, and when night arrived it grew overreachingly, invisibly black, filling Kayin's imagination with vacant images of *outside*.

"Why don't they leave the light on?" he said irritably. "I don't need any night-time."

Polla did not answer. The reason was known to them both. Of all the carefully-arranged principles by which the City lived, routine was the most vital. Instead she disengaged her hand and put her arm round his neck in a fond, artless gesture. "You *are* getting moody lately," she told him.

He grunted. "I know. Can you blame me? This trouble with the Society. I'm out, you know. They don't dare let me back after this. And the City Board will come down on my neck like a ton of steel."

"Oh, they'll go easy on you. What you did wasn't really shocking by today's standards. Anyway, something like that doesn't usually bother *you*, Kayin."

Kayin sighed. "You're right, it's not the Society. They won't achieve anything anyway. Poll, have you ever taken a walk through the City from end to end?"

"Sure," she laughed, "lots of times."

So had he. Its diameter was a little short of five miles. Streets, offices, factories, houses, parks, level piled on level. Some parts of the City were laid out neatly, efficiently, others were warrens of twisting, turning passages. There was a fair amount of variety. But for some reason, on these walks of his, Kayin always seemed to find himself out at the perimeter, where the City proper met the crystal dome, piling up against it in irregular steps like a wave. It was not possible actually to touch the dome: the way was barred by a solid girdle of steel. For interest's sake, Kayin would usually return through the basement of the City, where acre upon acre of apparatus managed the precise transformations of matter and energy that kept City 5 biologically viable, skirting round the vast sealed chambers that contained the old propulsion units that had brought them here centuries ago.

"I feel I know every foot of this place," Kayin said. "I feel I know everybody in it. That's ridiculous, of course — you can't know two million people. But you understand. . . . I'll admit I've had some good times here. It's all right if you like living in what is essentially an extended, highly technical village. But there's something a bit dead about City 5. Nothing ever comes in from outside. Anything that happens has to be generated right here."

Polla's expression was both worried and uncomprehending. "What are you talking about? What could come in from outside?"

He ignored her question. "I'll tell you something, Poll," he said, "the City Board ought to have tighter control. I don't like the kind of symbolisations and plays they've been putting on lately. They really shouldn't allow these independent art groups and independent scientific groups like the Society. Ambition is a curse, it's frustration."

"I never expected to hear you say that! You were always going to be the teenage rebel."

Kayin shook his head. "I still can't feel happy at having to spend the rest of my life in City 5. I know that's a queer thing to say. I have my job in the Inertial Stocktaking Department, I spend my time in the same way everybody else spends theirs, and I wish I could be content with that. But instead I feel restless, dissatisfied. I just wish I could *go* somewhere."

With an impatient shake of her head Polla stood up. "All right then. Let's go home and have a session. I feel randy."

"Okay." Automatically he rose and followed. But before leaving the park he headed for its most obtrusive feature, the now defunct observatory. The building, a tall, ribbed dome, bulked large against the background of trees and shrubbery. Beside it a squat tower loomed, housing the exploratory nucleon rocket that had once been part of the observatory's ancillary equipment. He beckoned Polla and, crossing a stretch of sward, led her through a small door in the base of the building.

Although abandoned, the observatory was still kept in good order and any citizen had the right to visit and use it. Few people ever bothered, but Kayin, along with his ex-colleagues in the Astronomical Society, had spent a fair amount of time there lately.

Not that there was anything to see. The experience was a purely negative one, and subsequent visits could do nothing but repeat it. A soft light, faintly tinged with green, filled the vaulted chamber. Kayin switched on the observatory and saw the glow of life come into the control panels, heard the waiting hum from the machinery that moved the main telescope.

The instrument was the best of its type ever designed, fitted with the complete range of auxiliary apparatus — radio, X-ray, laser and maser detectors, image amplification and the rest. When built, its makers had boasted that it could detect emitting matter anywhere in the sidereal universe. Kayin set the big cylinder in motion and brought it to rest pointing directly to zenith. The wall display screens remained dark and opaque. As if performing a ritual Kayin moved the telescope again, directing it towards City-perimeter-west. On the screens, again nothing. North: nothing. East: nothing. South: nothing. Kayin and Polla stood stock-still in the capacious, echoing dome, staring at the black screens like children recalling an often-repeated lesson.

City 5 was an oasis of light in an immense darkness. A few minutes ago Kayin had said he wished he could go somewhere. He realised now that that wasn't quite right. What he meant was: *he wished there was somewhere to go.*

He thought of the nearby nucleon rocket. Recently he actually had gone somewhere — almost.

Near the centre of the City, in the upper echelons of the Administrative Ramification, Kord awoke after his customary year of suspended animation.

Strange . . . the freeze process stopped everything, body and brain. Logically he should come out of it with the feeling that only a second or two had passed since he lost consciousness. Inexplicably, it was not like that. Each time he felt as if he had been gone a long, long time, and privately he suspected that he aged a year mentally despite the biological stop.

He thrust the thought from his mind. If his task was ever completed, perhaps then he could give his attention to philosophical diversions. Until then there was only one thing to occupy his whole being.

Having lifted him out of the casket and given him a thorough check, the doctors helped him down from the inspection slab, one of them assisting Kord to fit on his prosthetic leg, the legacy of a brief period of civil strife early in the history of the City. At length he stood up, feeling fit and alive, and paced the room experimentally, limping slightly on the artificial limb. Other men entered with clothes and attentively helped him to dress.

Not until they had finished did he speak. "Are the others awake?"

"Yes, Chairman. Will you proceed to briefing?"

He nodded, and left the room by a side door to find himself in a small, discreetly lighted chamber containing only a table and a chair. A man wearing the uniform of the Social Dynamic Movements Department entered briefly to hand him a file.

Kord sat down, opened the file and began to read. It was written in the special language of sociodynamic symbology, legible only to specially trained persons. From it Kord could gain a complete picture of social tendencies over the past year, every nuance, every incipient crystallisation and fragmentation, every vibration between the poles of conservation and change. If the symbolic analysis was not enough, Kord had implanted under the skin of his neck a set of filaments connected directly to the memory area of his brain. A lead from the City Archives Monitor Desk, taped to his neck, would induce in them currents carrying audio-visual recordings of conversations, happenings, a million cameos of life easily gathered and recorded by the watchful electronics of a closed system like City 5. By drawing on the memories he would suddenly find in his mind, Kord's knowledge of the past year would be experiential, not merely symbolic.

In adjoining cells the other four members of the Permanent Board were reading similar files. As he progressed through his, Kord knew that he would be calling on the Monitor Desk. He had been aware of dangerous tendencies present in the society of City 5, but he had not anticipated this sudden alarming acceleration of events. Grimly he realised that when the twenty-four-hour period was up he would not, as was the custom, be returning to deep freeze.

That night Kayin did not, as he would normally have done, attend the meeting of the Astronomical Society, but spent it instead alone with Polla. Ham-Ra, President of the Society, had already put his decision to him and in fairness Kayin had agreed with his judgment. He was out.

The Society gathered in a comfortable, otherwise unused room in one of the rambling parts of the City. A video recorder in one corner contained the edited minutes of their previous meetings and what little information or few resolutions they had been able to formulate.

The object of the Society was to re-establish the sciences of astronomy and space exploration. It numbered fifteen members, without Kayin, between the ages of about seventeen and twenty-three. In most societies like this one youth was the order of the day.

"We have a lot to present this session," Ham-Ra said by way of introduction. "For the first time we're really getting somewhere. However, you'll all have noticed that Kayin isn't here. A few of you know why. For the rest, it will become plain later just why he can't attend.

"Now then, friends, when we last convened over a month ago we were getting depressed and ready to give up. But what Tamm has to show us today is really going to knock you out. Take over, Tamm."

The freckled red-head rose, grinning shyly, and stood by the table, on which stood a video unit. "As you know, public knowledge concerning the origin of City 5, the whereabouts of Earth and so on, has fluctuated considerably over the years by reason of the Mandatory Cut-Off of information, as the Administrative Ramification vacillated between the theory that total ignorance is best and the theory that full knowledge is best. Over the past ten years Mandatory Cut-Off has been relaxed considerably — otherwise our Society couldn't exist — and along with the upsurge of interest in scientific matters we have been able to gain access to some information that wasn't available before.

"Nevertheless our astronomical knowledge has been slight, particularly where it affects our relations with Earth. We know that the City came from Earth some hundreds of years ago, that we can never go back, and that essentially we must remain here for all time. I think we can take it that the pendulum of policy is swinging towards freedom because, by sedulously bending the ears of a few sympathetic parties in the Administrative Ramification, Ham-Ra and myself gained official permission to make use of the City's last remaining nucleon rocket in order to undertake an expedition to the sidereal universe, or as close to it as we could safely get."

"That's fantastic!" said a voice into the ensuing silence.

Tamm nodded. "The condition we had to agree to is that the results of the expedition, and the information we gained from it, remain the property of the Ramification and should not be divulged outside the Society. Furthermore only two members were permitted to go on the trip. For various reasons Ham-Ra stood down in favour of Kayin, who together with myself made up the crew. It would have been nice if you could all have seen what we saw, but we made complete video recordings throughout, so to that extent you can share the experience with us.

"You will see that the expedition was not only one of exploration; it was also a concession on the Ramification's part on divulging historical knowledge in the form of an instruction tape on the rocket itself. What you learn will probably not surprise any of us much, but it will still give us a great deal to think about."

He pressed a stud on the video unit. A large wall screen lit up. Tamm and Kayin were in the nucleon rocket's main cabin in bucket seats before a curved control panel. Kayin's keen, intelligent face turned towards the pick-up.

"We are going out through the egress sphincter now. In a few moments we should be the first people of our generation to see the City from outside."

With a flicker, because of rather hasty editing, the picture changed to show a view through one of the ports. Everyone in the room held his breath. At first they only saw what appeared to be a vast curving wall, just visible as a dull metallic sheen due to an unseen source of illumination. Then, as the rocket drifted away, they got a full view of the City seen side-on: a huge disc-shaped slab surmounted by a graceful glittering dome in which could be discerned a low profile of shadowy shapes.

The rocket mounted above the City and hovered over it, somewhat to one side. They were looking down on the dome now and the City was suspended in space at an odd angle, blazing with light in an otherwise unbroken, impenetrable blackness.

They could have stared at it forever; but suddenly they were back in the cabin again and this time Tamm was speaking to them while Kayin piloted the rocket. "Although we can see nothing out here even with the ship's telescope — apart from the City, that is — we have been given a guidance tape that should take us to the sidereal universe, or the material universe as it is alternatively called. The distance is about three light-years, so we should be there very quickly."

The picture flickered wildly again; Tamm had cut out half an hour of uneventful tape. When they came back it was in the middle of a word. Tamm was shouting wildly.

"— look at that! Just look at that!"

The pick-up was once more pointing outside. The sight that met their eyes was more spectacular even than the panorama of the City. The first impression was of a blaze, of scattered light, of fire. Nearby, a few huge misty spirals hung in the void; further away, on either side, above and below, and far off into the depths, masses of similar spirals and glowing clouds and streamers receded into the distance, while a sort of diamond dust seemed to be infused among them all.

The scene was hypnotic, and the pick-up camera lingered on it for a considerable time. After the first impact, the impression was gained that the phenomenon, though big, was limited in size: the larger-looking spirals, though majestic, were some distance away and on the straggling edge of the cloud, whose limits seemed to define a slight but perceptible curve.

At that moment they became aware that the rocket's instruction tape had clicked into action, delivering a neat lecture in the quiet, calm voice of an electronic vodor. So unobtrusive was the voice at first that they failed to hear it in the general excitement:

". . . we have now passed the first threshold beyond which the material universe becomes visible, and are approaching the second threshold. You are warned severely against attempting to cross the second threshold; such a manoeuvre is generally agreed to be almost impossible or at any rate prohibitively difficult, and if by chance you should succeed and actually enter the material universe, you will not be able to leave again and will suffer the fate of all the matter it contains. Proceed with care: your visual instincts will probably tell you that the edge of the material universe, the metagalaxy as it is sometimes called, is light years away or at least many millions of miles away. It is, in fact, very close. The galaxies you are now seeing are only a few miles in diameter, many of them less than a mile in diameter, and the entire conglomeration of galactic and stellar systems is still shrinking steadily.

"The cause of the shrinkage of matter has not been ascertained with any certainty. It was first detected in A.D. 5085, Old Reckoning, when specific anomalies relating to the velocity and wave-length of light revealed that all phenomena having the properties of mass-energy were shrinking relative to the unit of space. Extrapolation of the equations led to the conclusion that a point would be reached, and that fairly soon, when the fundamental particles would be too small to maintain their identity in the space-time frame and that therefore all matter everywhere would vanish from existence.

"Since the shrinkage related to the metagalaxy as a whole, it was theorised that if an entity or system could escape beyond the by then known boundaries of the sidereal universe then it might also escape the field of the shrinking process and survive. Luckily the centuries-old Problem of Velocity had recently been solved, and already ships had been built capable of traversing the whole diameter of the metagalaxy in a fairly short period of time. The first attempts to pass into the space beyond the metagalaxy, however, met difficulty. Either the shrinkage field or the metagalaxy itself set up an interface with the rest of space that constituted a barrier to the passage of matter. Penetration of the barrier was, however, theoretically possible, and was attempted over a considerable period of time by ships equipped with specially powerful drive units. Eventually one such ship succeeded, to return with the report that the void beyond the metagalaxy, though it appeared to contain no matter itself, would accept the existence of matter placed in it and maintain it in a stable, non-shrinking state.

"As the universe shrank, the barrier grew more impenetrable. If anything was to be preserved, it was essential to act quickly. Twenty self-contained cities were constructed and equipped with the most powerful drive units. As they headed at top speed for the perimeter of the material realm they were able to observe a large number of ships, cities and similar constructs doing the same from various points in the universe. None of these alien launchings met with success and mankind's effort did only marginally better. As they encountered the barrier and strove to make their exit, all but one of the Earth cities either blew up or otherwise failed to break through. It can now be said with certainty that City 5 is the sole fragment of matter to have escaped the shrinking metagalaxy, where the current state of materiality is such that biological life is believed to be no longer possible.

"In recent years an acceleration in the rate of shrinking has been observed, leading to the belief that the moment is now very close for the extinction of this island of materiality unique in the spatial frame. For a long time it has been effectively invisible from City 5, or indeed from anywhere outside the interface region, for the reason that the enveloping barrier has an outer and an inner surface known as the first and second thresholds. The inner threshold is permeable to radiant energy but offers a strong resistance to the passage of solid masses. The outer threshold may be crossed quite easily by slow-moving masses, but is opaque to light and other radiation passing to it from the inner threshold. In order to view the sidereal universe it is therefore necessary to position oneself between the two.

"City 5 was designed to be self-subsisting in perpetuity. Physicists on Earth nevertheless entertained the expectation, or rather the hope, that other areas of materiality where humanity could again proliferate would be located in the void, even though they might be immensely remote from the home universe. For a long time long-range spaceships were built and despatched from City 5 in efforts to discover even one atom or electron of matter. Any one of these missions covered a distance equal to many billion times the diameter of the old metagalaxy at its original full size, a feat that has added poignancy when we reflect that by pre-shrinkage standards of measurement City 5 itself is slightly over half an inch in diameter. All such projects have long since been abandoned as useless and the exploratory rockets dismantled. It is now accepted that materiality is not a normal feature of the space frame and that it does not exist anywhere apart from the sidereal universe already known to us. All future endeavours on the part of humanity must perforce make do with such material as was transported in City 5 at the time of the migration, and the City has therefore had to face the problems of perpetuating the life of mankind in complete isolation. The technical aspects, though prodigious, do not present any insoluble difficulties; the chief problems lie in the social and psychological fields."

The screen went suddenly blank. "I think we might as well end the tape there," Tamm said matter-of-factly. "That's the valid part of the mission."

His audience was silent, thoughtful, perhaps a little stunned. Finally Ham-Ra said: "Well, that fills in some gaps in our knowledge. Any comments?"

"It shouldn't come as any great shock," someone said after a moment, "but somehow it does. We have always known we were isolated and alone, that we can't return to Earth. But I always presumed that Earth and the rest of the universe still existed somewhere and would always continue to exist. It makes a difference."

"That's a fact," said another. "It means we have to rethink our aims and objectives. Which brings me to the point that it still hasn't been explained why Kayin is absent."

Tamm cleared his throat and glanced at Ham-Ra, who nodded for him to go ahead. "When Kayin and myself returned to City 5 we still had very little technical data of a useful kind. While beyond the first threshold we did of course take a whole library of image and spectral recordings which we can all study at our leisure. But a great deal of the other instrumentation we took along proved useless. More specifically, the nucleon rocket's instruction tape had whetted our appetite to know more about the early efforts to explore the empty void, as this seemed to be the direction in which the Society's interest would lie. Unfortunately the requisite documents lie well behind the Mandatory Cut-Off, and no one we could reach in the Administrative Ramification had authorisation to give us access. So we devised a scheme to tap the archives illegally."

The audience was torn between fright at this manoeuvre and admiration for its audacity. The brighter of them had already anticipated the outcome of the story. A skinny, scowling youngster with a sharp face snorted. "The tap was detected, of course?"

"Yes, but only Kayin's part in the matter is known to the Ramification. It was his training that made the attempt possible. Now, although both Ham-Ra and myself, and to that extent the whole Society, were involved, the only chance to save the Society from dissolution is to disavow responsibility. We all agreed that Kayin should be expelled and his actions condemned."

"Isn't that a little unfair?"

"Kayin doesn't seem to think so."

"What will happen to him?"

"Nothing much, not the way the wind's blowing at present. You could say our loss is just as great as his — we've lost one of our only two members to have seen the sidereal universe with their own eyes."

The news seemed to have agitated, energised the Society. They began speaking all at once, shouting each other down.

"What do we do now?"

"We ought to force the Ramification to act!"

"We ought to steal the nucleon rocket —"

Ham-Ra held up his hands for silence. The hatchet-faced, damp-haired young man who had spoken before rose to his feet. Ham-Ra nodded.

"Obviously the Ramification expected us to accept what we've learned and to give up quietly, maybe even to dissolve ourselves voluntarily," said the youth, whose name was Barsh. "Their message to us is: *there is no science of astronomy, there is no exploration of space*. I don't think we should take it lying down. Instead, I think we should revive the whole question of whether there is matter in the empty void and of launching new missions going even further than they did before."

"That's right! Last time they gave up too easily."

Curtly Ham-Ra once again stopped the rising hubbub. Tamm was smiling wryly. "I don't imagine they gave up easily. I think they tried as hard as it's possible to try. These days the Ramification has trouble of a different kind."

He flicked a switch, reeling back a few inches of tape. The screen glowed with its incredible picture, accompanied by the instruction tape's closing remark:

". . . the chief problems lie in the social and psychological fields."

The others heard the words, but the blank looks in their eyes betrayed their lack of interest. "What are we going to do about outfitting an expedition into deep space?" Barsh said.

To Kiang, Chairman of the Temporary Board, the meeting with Kord was slightly frightening, slightly thrilling. The man was large — tall, broad, and bulky; his face, which gave one the impression that it had never smiled, was also large, and lined with the impress of years of wilfully directed thought. Its colour was grey, not the grey of illness but the grey of granite, of obdurate strength. When Kord spoke, everybody listened. He was that rare man, the great leader who in times past would have directed the affairs of continents, of planets. There was something heartbreaking in seeing that powerful personality applied with full force to the promotion of stasis and conservation on this pathetic scrap of a vanished universe.

The boardroom was divided down the centre by a long, polished table. On one side sat the Temporary Board, headed by Kiang and backed by Haren, Kuro, Chippilare and Freen. Facing them sat the Permanent Board: Kord flanked by Bnec, specialist in physics, the science of materiality; Engrach, specialist in technology; Ferad and Elbern, specialists in sociodynamics. Elbern was one of Kord's strokes of strategy, for he was a converted member of the old opposition of centuries ago. Kord knew that the errors promulgated by the vanquished party would occur again and again in the history of City 5, though he hoped with steadily diminishing force, and he realised the advantage of having a man who understood the kind of mentality that fostered them.

Kord permitted himself a direct glance into Kiang's mobile face. They're afraid of us, he thought. They feel young in our presence; they're aware that we were old and wise, sitting on this board, before they were babies. But they'll fight us if they have to.

The members of the Permanent Board lived for only one day a year. Thus one year of ageing for them spanned three hundred and sixty-five years of City 5 history. Without this device of a permanent guiding hand, Kord believed, the City would never have maintained its historical stability thus far — and in this small, unique, precious island of life stability was all-important. If social tendencies slowed down enough to require less readjustment, the dormant period could be extended to ten years, perhaps even to a hundred years.

At the moment those long, restful sleeps seemed a long way off. Inwardly Kord sighed. He was the last of a line of leaders, including men like Chairman Mao and Gebr Hermesis, who had tried to reform the mind of humanity and fix it with an eternal pattern. Always the problem was one of training the new generation to think in every way like the old. Humanity had survived their failures, but Kord was convinced that it would not survive his.

Angrily he flung the file he had studied at Kiang. "A hundred years ago you would have been executed for the contents of that file. I spare you now only on the assumption that rectification of the situation will immediately be taken in hand."

". . . We do not necessarily agree, Chairman, that rectification is necessary."

"How many times do I have to spell it out to you, gentlemen?" Kord said, his voice becoming gravelly with displeasure. "We are concerned with preserving the City, not for a thousand years, not for a million, but *forever*, for *eternity*. Due to the nature of the human psyche this is only possible if life is regularised in every detail. There must be no new directions, no individuality, no innovations or originality of thought. The City is small. It must be protected from itself." Kord felt himself sweating. Only a few years ago the consciousness of what was required for survival was infused in the Ramification, in the mind of the City itself. Yet over and over again, through the centuries, he had gone through exactly such arguments as this. It seemed that the tendency to deviate, to forget, was ever-present and in time entered even the Temporary Board itself. Even so, Kord was shocked to find that the position had deteriorated so quickly in the past year; his perpetual nightmare was that one day he would awake to find that his authority was no longer valid.

"You have made the severest mistake," he continued, "committed the greatest crime, in giving youth its head. The absolute pre-condition for a permanent social pattern is the complete subordination and conditioning of the younger generation. But what do I find? Led on by your own foolish ambitions, you have permitted youth to set in train what threatens to be a virtual renaissance in the arts and sciences."

"We have been giving the matter considerable thought for some time, Chairman," Chippilare put in. "As we see it, you fear initiative because it will upset the balance; but we fear stasis because it produces a movement in the other direction, towards decay. The City can die through a progressive depletion of psychic energy, as well as through an explosion of it."

"There has been a noticeable air of apathy and drabness about the City of recent years," Kuro said. "Perhaps you, in suspended animation, have missed it. It was to counteract this decline in tone that we decided to liven things up a bit."

"In fact," added Freen, "we now question whether a society can be kept in good health without innovation and change."

"It can," answered Kord firmly, aware by now that he had a full-scale rebellion on his hands. "There were many such societies on Earth, usually of a primitive nature, which were eventually destroyed *only* by change and innovation introduced from outside. In particular, the aborigines of the prehistoric period on the continent of Australia maintained a fully developed culture for thousands of years, believing their origins to be in an immensely distant 'dream time'. We have to create a 'dream time' for our people."

"That's right," said Elbern, looking at Freen with a certain amount of hostility. "The reason for the long-term stability of the aborigines was that, living in a sparse, poorly-endowed land, all their energies were taken up in the considerable skills needed to survive. We are perhaps unfortunate in that with our level of technology we can take care of our basic needs fairly easily — that is why we have tried to replace preoccupation with short-term needs with preoccupation with long-term needs, in the maintenance of the basic machinery, in the continual drawing up of new plans for the re-design of the City, and above all in the inertial stocktaking, which takes up an enormous amount of the population's labour-time and is concerned with accounting for every atom of the City's mass. I do not need to remind you how important that activity is if we are to conserve all our mass and energy over billions and billions of years."

The Temporary Board looked embarrassed and cast covert glances at one another. At length Kiang ventured: "Our recent philosophical studies have cast doubt on the very basis of the City's plan for existence. We have been studying the very fact of matter itself. It has been known ever since the early formulation of dialectical materialism that motion and tendency, opposing forces and so on, are the very basis of matter whether it takes physical, mental or social forms. If the principle of opposition, as for instance in a class strugle of some sort, is fundamental then how can you be sure that a static or self-perpetuating state *is even possible?* You cannot name any Earth society that remained stable for all time."

Kiang was voicing Kord's private fears, but he said nothing, only stared stonily.

"Furthermore," Kiang continued, "we have to take note of the fact that materiality is an extraordinary and temporary occurrence in the space-time frame. More and more we have become convinced that the materiality of the sidereal universe consisted of an accidental polar opposition with no inherent tendency towards stability. It had to move some way, and in so doing the transient balance was lost; hence the shrinkage of matter and its final disappearance. But where does that leave us? The materiality of City 5 is even more isolated and vulnerable. At any moment in time it may suddenly collapse and disappear. So there is not much point in our planning for eternity."

Throughout this argument the Permanent Board had listened in silence. When Kiang had finished Bnec, Kord's specialist in physics, let out an expression of disgust.

"A very pretty speech! You palpitating fool, is your brain so addled that you have forgotten your special access beyond the Mandatory Cut-Off? Or do you believe yourself to be too progressive to learn anything from the superhuman efforts of your ancestors? Can you seriously imagine that these questions were not thrashed out, researched and resolved millennia ago?"

Kord held up his hand to quell the brewing quarrel. "Have no fear, the material of the City is sound as far as science can tell. Also, we shall not run out of energy provided we lose no appreciable mass: it has been found that we are in a privileged position here, in that there is a conservation of mass-energy. The material polarity, as you correctly call it, is self-conserving. When atomic energy, say, is released from matter to perform useful work, it is not dissipated but we absorb it elsewhere in the City. Thus as long as the total mass remains constant the same energy can be released again and again in a cyclic action. Apart from that we have proved that we can keep the genetic material of the population stable. So our problem concerns only the conscious, active life of the City, without which none of these principles can be maintained."

He clenched his fist. "Get this! Everything that happens, happens beneath the crystal dome. *There is no external world.* There is no longer any universe, any creation . . . so any uncontrolled process beneath the dome is a danger to the City. The element in the human psyche that reaches out, explores and discovers must be eradicated. It means destruction to us. The outward, aspirational life must be replaced by an inward life of symbolism and extremely close personal relationships.

"None of this can happen at once, of course. In a sense we are still in our first stages of arrival in the empty void. We have still to make the adjustment, which we are doing by degrees, progressing two steps forward and one step back. Thus at the moment the dome is transparent and lets out a blaze of light. This means a loss of energy but for us it is a symbol, an announcement of our presence. At some date in the future the dome will be made totally impervious and no quantum of mass-energy will ever be allowed to leave the City. Then again, we still call the City by its original name, City 5, bringing with it the awareness that there were other cities and other places. Eventually it will be known simply as the City."

"And is ignorance also part of the prescription for survival?" Haren's tone was mildly contemptuous.

"A careful balance is needed." The long arguing was making Kord tired, but he refused to let his energy flag. "Full consciousness of our situation would be too much for the collective mind; it would cause mental disorders and ultimately destroy us. Likewise, complete ignorance would destroy us for different reasons. We must steer a middle course until the day when the non-deviating republic has been established and we can safely permit the whole city to live with the full knowledge and consciousness of where we are."

Kord stood up, his bulk looming over them. "I trust I have made things clear. We will recess for a short while and meet in the Executive Complex in three hours' time. It will be necessary to make some arrangements."

With opaque faces the Temporary Board rose and left the room. The others remained behind, looking pensively at the table top.

"A fairly bad business," Elbern said.

"We can handle it. But I think the Board we leave behind when we freeze again will have some different names in it." Kord picked up the file he had thrown at Kiang and leafed through it moodily. The section on the Archetypal Dramas had been the first giveaway. Kord had always known that the symbols and archetypes that would emerge from the collective unconscious would decide the fate of City 5 in the long run. That was why he had encouraged the development of art forms for which practically the whole City was an audience, films, plays and archetypal dramas delivered in a semi-hypnagogic state, in which these entities could find expression, symbols, characters and stories merging into a dream-like, hypnotic blend. The section on the dramas was always the first thing he turned to when given the briefing. If the symbols were rounded, square, on the Jungian mandala or quaternity patterns, then he was pleased. The image he looked for was the cave, the female, the square table, the square room, the circle. Today there was an altogether unacceptable number of thrusting, probing images, the tower on the plain, the pointed lance, the long journey, the magician, the supreme effort. These images were all culled from the generalised social unconscious of the time. Aware of the part played by the sexual polarity in the structure of the social psyche, Kord had long since realised that it was necessary to create a womb-centred, vulva-centred civilisation, instead of a phallus-centred one.

Brooding, he closed the file. He had faced many difficulties in the past. It was disappointing to find that they might not, after all, be diminishing.

When they again met the Temporary Board three hours later, they found that the spirit of disagreement was still present. Further, the rebels had used the time to reconsolidate their position among some complexes of the Ramification. Kord was obliged to resort to strong measures. Within twenty-four hours he had set in motion an efficient and informed state police. Two days later, the general purge began. Within a week public executions were being held daily in the main park.

Kayin was in hiding, having taken Polla with him, in a part of the City that had not been rebuilt for a few hundred years and where he had friends. To his surprise he remained hidden, whereas others failed to evade the combination of delation and electronic scanning by which the Ramification discovered everyone's whereabouts. The reason, as he at last surmised, was simple: his expulsion from the Society had saved him. He was no longer associated with a subversive movement, and his other crime was not, in the context of present events, viewed with the same gravity.

Accordingly he began to venture out. In the main park he watched as the unrepentant Ham-Ra, Tamm and Barsh received the customary lethal injections in the neck. As he wandered away, feeling bitter and sick, he heard someone call his name.

It was Herren, an acquaintance he had not seen for a couple of years. About the same age as himself, Herren appraised him speculatively.

"How are you, old chap? Everything all right?"

The bright, breezy manner simply left Kayin scowling. He turned away, but Herren followed him, speaking sympathetically. "Yes, I know, it's an awful shame. But the game's not lost, you know. Things really are moving. I thought you might be interested."

Kayin shrugged.

"Well, all right, it is a bit open here. Listen. I happen to know where you're staying. Surprised?" He laughed. "News travels these days. Friends, you know. I'll call on you tonight. Pity if you were left out of everything."

Kayin looked at him thoughtfully. "It's up to you." He felt oddly detached. Herren might be a Ramification agent, for all he knew, but he didn't much care.

In the event, Herren was playing it straight. He called just as Kayin and Polla were finishing their evening meal. The wall screen was showing an old drama from several years ago — the new-style dramas had been taken out of circulation — but they were paying it too little heed to be drawn into the semi-hypnagogic state in which it could have been fully appreciated.

Herren entered the room and rudely switched the screen off. "Not interested in that old rubbish, are you?" He looked around, then produced a small metal cylinder from his pocket and carefully placed it on the table. "This will fool any hidden scanners," he explained. "They'll pick up nothing but an empty room."

Kayin stared at the gadget blankly. "Where did you get it?"

The other winked. "There's a certain amount of underground stuff being manufactured these days."

Despite his own misdemeanour, Kayin found the idea hard to grasp. "Do you mean insurrection? The City is fragmenting?"

"They are talking of civil war."

"But that's . . . crazy. . . ." Kayin wondered if Herren knew what he knew of City 5's situation, of the facts concerning the sidereal universe.

"I haven't been getting much news lately," he ended weakly.

"Let me fill you in. Kord has already killed three members of the Temporary Board. Chippilare and Kuro escaped, thanks to the loyalty of sympathetic elements both in the Ramification and outside. They have organised an opposition and are holding out in the Western Segment, down near the Basement. It's more or less an enclave. The State Police aren't strong enough to go in and get them out."

"Has Kord given the police arms?"

"They're getting arms now. But the opposition is manufacturing arms, too. It's a revolution! Because the opposition isn't just in the enclave, it's all over, gradually being organised. Youth is waking up!"

Polla stared from one to the other of the young men in disbelief. "Kayin, can this be true? What's happening?"

"Kord is finding out that he can't enslave the mind of humanity forever," Herren said. "We are discovering freedom."

"It's all over a difference of opinion," Kayin told her wearily. "Kord and his people think that the City can best be preserved by rigid control and a low level of aspiration. Our technology is sufficient, so there's no need for further development in the arts or sciences. The others, like Herren here, believe that that approach leads to a slow but sure disaster, and that the City must be kept bubbling to stay healthy, that life isn't worth living any other way anyhow. They both feel strongly enough about it to go to war. They're all in the minority, of course. The great majority of the population have the good sense to interest themselves in nothing much except the inertial stocktaking."

"But which side is right?"

"Right?" Kayin said with a grimace. "Neither! Both roads will lead to disaster. . . . There isn't any solution. . . . The City exists in a place where it isn't supposed to be. . . ."

Herren leaned forward and gripped his slumped shoulder comfortingly "Steady, old chap. I know how it must have been for you this afternoon, seeing your friends executed. Believe me, we've all been through it. But you'll pull through. I know we'll be able to depend on you when the time comes."

Kayin remembered the wry smile on red-headed Tamm's face, just before they injected the poison.

When Kuro finally answered Kord's invitation, he found the centuries-old Master of City 5 looking drawn and strained. For his part, it had been a mortal blow to Kord's confidence when he had failed to contain the situation. He suspected that for some years the briefings he had been given had been tampered with to play down the actual motion of events. Now, though he held the central premises of the Ramification, he effectively controlled only two thirds of the City.

"Very well," he said curtly, "you are strong enough to fight us."

"And we will."

Kord spoke in an exasperated tone. "Already there have been gun battles in the City! Yesterday fire broke out in the Northern Segment." Angrily he rapped his artificial leg. "Do you know how I got this? In a civil war pretty much like this one is becoming. Sheer lunacy! It's suicide to fight inside the City; we can't allow it again."

"So?"

"If we have to fight, it will have to be done *outside the dome.*"

"My conclusion exactly," Kuro said sombrely, "as far as heavier weapons go, anyway. We can both construct space vessels of some sort. For the arrangement to be effective each side must be allowed to transfer sufficient forces outside, without interference."

"Agreed, then. We shall set up an independent commission to control the egress port."

He paused reflectively. "By the way, I got some news today. You know that there is an instrument in the Ramification set to record the moment when the material universe finally vanishes altogether. Just after eight last night, the event registered."

Kuro made no comment. After they had completed the formal arrangements he left, feeling only slight discomfort about what was going on.

"It's like a nightmare," Polla said.

The City appeared to be huddling, expectant. In the north could be seen the fire-blackened region, and a faint smell of smoke still hung in the air, not quite eradicated by the circulatory system. The crystal dome sparkled; but beyond it vague shadowy forms were moving as the contending forces arrayed themselves.

"Well, at least the City will be safe," Kayin replied. Herren had come to him and expected him to take part in the street fighting. When he had declined, he had again come to him and invited him to help man the weapons carried by the new spacecraft. Kayin could imagine what kind of a battle that would be: hastily built ships manoeuvring in an utterly empty void, carefully avoiding proximity with the City and offering perfect sitting ducks to one another. With luck, none of them would return and the City could live in peace.

Kayin was fingering a key in his pocket. It was a special key, working by electronic impulses, and it gave its owner possession of the observatory's nucleon rocket. Kayin had never handed it back after his mission with Tamm.

"Poll," he said, "let's go somewhere."

"Where?"

"Out," he answered sardonically, "outward bound. The early expeditions failed because they always turned back when they reached the point of no return, when their engines wouldn't have got them back if they'd gone further. *We'll keep on going.* What does it matter?"

She didn't understand what he was talking about, but she followed him to the park where they used to meet. He headed for the observatory, but this time bypassed the dome and pressed the key into a small slot in the base of the tower.

A door slid open. He stepped inside, taking Polla by the hand and tugging her through. There was a gap of about twelve feet between the hull of the rocket and the shell of the tower. The spacecraft loomed above them like a huge shaft.

He pressed the same key into a slot in a large box inside the door. It clicked and hummed; automatically the rocket was being readied for use.

"*Kayin,*" Polla protested in sudden alarm. "What's going on? I'm not going anywhere —"

Without waiting for her fright to become hysteria, he closed in on her. For a few moments she was gasping as they grappled, then he had her held securely over his shoulder. Still she struggled, bewildered, but there wasn't far to go. He carried her to the embarkation platform; swiftly it took them up the side of the rocket to the port. Inside the rocket he stepped down a short passage and threw her down in the luxurious living apartment.

"What are you *doing?*" She sat up on the floor, her legs asplay.

He switched on the wall screen, tuning it to the external scanners. "Enjoy the show," he said, then left for the control cabin, locking the door behind him.

The controllers of the egress port were used to a constant stream of craft applying for exit; they asked no questions in his case. For the second time in his life he floated up above the dome, seeing the City spread out below him. But this time there were big, clumsy cylindrical objects floating in the vicinity of the City, some of them sporting wicked-looking equipment welded on in various places. The war was due to begin soon.

Kayin chose a direction at random and started up the nucleon engines at full power. In a second City 5 was gone. He and Polla were alone in the void, the eternal, infinite, vacant void.

On and on and on and on and on. The engines never stopped. Although they ran silently, Kayin checked their action constantly on the instruments in the control cabin.

Polla had wept and screamed, then sulked for weeks, and then gradually became friendly again. By now Kayin himself felt defensively sullen about what he had done. It was boorish and uncharacteristic of him. But he stubbornly refused to apologise, even to his own conscience.

At this distance it was impossible even with the most powerful magnification available on the rocket to gain as much as a photon's worth of image from the City. Shortly after departure he had picked up brief flashes that came not from the City itself but from the spaceships that were fighting one another with nuclear weapons. Even if they had not been travelling at billions of times the speed of light, such minute flickers would not have been detectable by any means now.

So there was only the emptiness on all sides. Looking out into it, one could not even discern distance; there was only absolute lightlessness.

After they had been travelling for nearly two months Kayin took to spending long periods in the direct observation blister that, projecting from the hull of the rocket in a perfectly transparent bulge, formed a cavity or extrusion into space. Here was the only place in the rocket where the artificial gravity (derived from the same principle as the nucleon engine) did not operate.

With the cavity light switched off, one might as well have been floating in free fall in the void itself. Kayin spent what seemed like hours staring out of the blister, into what to his eyes was simply blackness but which his mind knew to be infinity. His mind began working in new directions. Matter, he reasoned, had structure, but space was simply emptiness. Yet space, too, had structure of a kind. It had extension and direction. Was there, he wondered, a substratum to the void, a richer reality lying beneath it? After a while, for some dim sense of pleasure only vaguely known to himself, he took to coming into the cavity naked.

SENSORY DEPRIVATION

The human mind is not made to be without incoming sensory data for any but the briefest periods. The first consequence of sensory deprivation is that the subject loses, first the sense of his bodily outline, and then his sense of identity. Then, since the consciousness will not tolerate lack of perceptions, and being denied them fom the external direction, it draws upon them from the inner direction, projecting on to the senses first hallucinations of a random, dream-like character, and then, if the process is continued, unlocking the archetypal symbols from the unconscious.

Kayin went through all these stages fairly quickly. Out in the void he saw vast wheeling mandalas, glimmering forms whose size was beyond the mind to compute. He saw the mystic triad, the mystic quaternity, exemplified in a thousand dazzling forms. He did not think or remark on what he saw, *for he was not there.* His personal identity was gone; his being consisted merely of an impersonalised consciousness of the symbols he saw.

Once he must have moved accidentally and bumped into the wall of the cavity. The bodily sensation brought him momentarily to himself. Flashing waves of excitement, of joy, swept through him. *I'm seeing it,* he thought. *This is the reality underlying space, the structure of the world transcending it. Stay here long enough and it shows itself.*

Then he was merged once again with the contents of the unconscious, a kind of paradisical, compelling, luring world. His next bodily sensation was a feeling of hotness. Vaguely he returned to himself, realising that genuine light was in his eyes. He turned slowly. The door of the cavity was open and Polla was drifting in, having turned on the illumination to a dim, soft glow.

She smiled at him distantly. They both rotated and twisted slowly round one another, hanging in the air. The hem of the short frock she wore was riding up, warping and twirling. To Kayin it was the most vivid thing he had ever seen, a vision thousands of miles across. Her face flashed with angelic light. The texture and colour of her skin radiated a soft, irresistible power.

He undid the clasp at her neck and pulled off the loose frock. They continued to turn and bend soundlessly in the cavity, the frock drifting away from them. Her body was angled slightly away from him, slightly above him. Reaching up, he first fondled then drew off her soft undergarment. Hot waves of unconsciousness swept through him.

The symbols and signs were still all around them, the very substance of their world. Kayin heard choking gasps, squeals and screams. He was submerged, spinning in endless glyphs of power and enjoying a withering, burning fire that ran in wide searing rivers and consumed the world.

Briefly he came again to consciousness of himself. They were suspended in the centre of the cavity. He was gripping Polla by her upper arms, and she his. Their bodies, held away from each other while he thrust between her legs, and joined at the genitals, were arched violently and bucking like wild animals, savagely butting, fucking. Dizzily vision again faded from his consciousness. He and the world were one identity, consisting of a huge, powerful and stiff phallus moving forward with steady purpose. Then he was at the same time a large opened vulva against which the phallus mashed and poked, making them both throb.

A murmur caught his ear. He was pressed up against Polla, his lips against hers and their bodies straining and heaving. Would they merge, blend, generating between them an androgyne with supernatural sexual powers?

Then, with a groan, they fell slightly apart and began grappling with the whole length of their bodies, limbs twisting and tangling, biting, gripping and kicking. Finally, after a last lunge at her,

Kayin, fully restored to himself now, pushed her away and they hung staring at one another avidly.

END OF THE LINE

Kayin and Polla lay weakly in the living apartment. For weeks they had been exhausting themselves in the outside cavity, pushing to the utmost every kind of sex that a male and a female can engineer between them.

It was a discovery that Kayin would have liked to take back to City 5. There was nothing like it. Twenty minutes alone in the cavity, and sex became like it had never been before. It seemed that all unconscious power was released and flooded into action.

"Would you like to go home, Poll?"

"I don't care," she sighed quietly.

In between their frequent bouts Kayin had also given himself time to think. At first he had thought the visions he saw in the void, even in the blister cavity itself, were real, a hopeful revelation of a positive reality beneath the nothingness through which they moved. More soberly, he had now recognised them for what they were: projections from his own mind, the exteriorisation of basic psychic patterns, which spilled into the open when the constraining effect of sensory impressions was removed. One interesting thing about them was that both he and Polla frequently experienced the same images at the same time during their lovemaking, further evidence that the unconscious was a collective one.

"Then we're going home," he said firmly.

"You don't want to find the other universe?" she spoke timidly, like a child. Such powerful and abundant sex as they had been getting seemed to have made her regress to something like a childish state.

"There *isn't* any other universe. What's more, I'm pretty certain by now that *there isn't any space. No empty void.*"

She didn't understand what he meant, so he didn't try to explain. The idea had formed itself slowly in his mind, and he felt sure that it was right. Space was a consequence of matter, not matter of space. Outside the sidereal universe, where there was no matter, there was no space either. *When City 5 had escaped the metagalaxy, it had simply escaped into non-being.*

It would not appear that way to observers, of course. Since space was always associated with matter, City 5 extended its own island of space. Projectiles sent out from it always did the same, generating as they went a fictitious measuring system of distances and velocities by which they orientated themselves.

The nucleon rocket was not going anywhere. It merely created its own "appearance" of space as it "moved" through an incomprehensible nullity. It was, in fact, hard to argue that it moved at all; such a statement was quite meaningless, as was its obverse that the rocket didn't move.

None of which made any difference as regards piloting it. The rocket acted according to the laws of its materiality, for in nullity there were no laws. Kayin turned the ship round and gave the computer the problem of finding City 5. The moment of their return being mathematically certain, he and Polla then waited patiently for the rocket to deliver them there, indulging often in the pastime of which they never grew tired.

When the rocket signalled completion of the journey, they went to the now familiar outside cavity, eager for their first glimpse of their life-long home to be by line of sight.

Polla fainted dead away. Kayin grabbed a stanchion to steady himself, and avoided the same only by a determined effort of will. The crude cylindrical ships, the litter from the war between the followers of Kord and the followers of Kuro, were scattered all over the space surrounding the City, gutted, gashed and broken, trailing bodies and equipment.

Evidently the fight had been pressed too hard, and the contendants had grown desperate over relinquishing control of the City. City 5 blazed into the darkness, as it would automatically continue to do for millennia. But the crystal dome was shattered, gaping like a broken tooth. As the rocket came closer he saw the masses of dead bodies in the airless plazas and streets. About one third of the buildings seemed to have been wrecked by an explosion, and Kayin noticed, as his glazed eyes roamed over the dead City spinning slowly like a great mandala in the void, that the big housing tower for the nucleon rocket had been broken off at the base, and lay like a fallen giant across the sward.

Me and My Antronoscope

My dear Asmravaar: Many thanks for your last burst, and apologies for the long delay in answering. Not that it has been wholly my fault, because my burst sender broke down — for the third time this trip! When I get back home I shall have something to say to the Transfinite Communicator Co., and you can tell them that from me.

However, to be honest, I repaired my sender some time ago and so my silence cannot all be laid at the door of our unspeakably muddling technicians. The rest of the time I have been kept busy keeping track of a gripping little "adventure" that I chanced to catch in my sights, almost in passing as it were. At the moment I am feeling tired, but also very excited, and I just cannot resist staying awake a little longer so that I can get it all down and burst it to you. It's a fascinating story and I'm hoping it will even change your mind about a few things, you grumpy old stay-at-home!

At this point I am going to allow a note of triumph to creep into my account. Why not? — I have won a philosophic victory! For too long, Asmravaar, you and others of your ilk have laughed at the explorer-wanderers such as myself. You say that there is no point to our wanderings, that we are on a fool's errand — that the universe, though endless, is everywhere of a dreary sameness and that one might as well stay at home where there is at least a little variety. Well of course I have to admit that there is *some* substance to your allegations, and none knows that better than myself. I, more intimately than any of you pessimists, have seen what the universe consists of: an infinite series of spatialities, every one more or less the same, each containing innumerable worlds conforming to only a small number of basic types, and — as you complain — rarely any life to be found anywhere. I grant that if we were to believe in the existence of a Creator of this immensity of ours, then we could justifiably charge Him with lacking imagination. Once one gets over the awesomeness of sheer physical grandeur then there is precious little else!

Yet I am reluctant to accuse nature of being niggardly. No, it is *you* I accuse, Asmravaar! You are guilty of "philosophical defeatism"! In my belief the universe still has a few surprises in store for us, if we keep looking. It can still ring a few changes!

And I have proved it!

Well, I'll get on with it. I was transiting through the 10^{5298}th range of spatialities, not expecting to find anything unusual, when I came across a world which turned out to contain life. Not very much life, it is true, but life. Physically the species is not of our reticulated tendricular type but of the much rarer oxygenated, bipedal type. Moreover I do not believe they can be native to their present habitat but must have migrated there a considerable period ago. At any rate, I was suddenly thankful that I had recently invested in a fine new high-powered Mark XXXVI sound-and-vision antronoscope,* as well as in a new instant semanticiser — for this is what I saw. . . .

Against the yielding rock wall the big vibro-drill was working well, despite its age. Tremoring invisibly, the rotating blades sliced through the basalt at a steady rate, shoving the finely divided rubble to the rear to be dealt with by a follow-up machine — which, since this was only a demonstration run, was in this case absent.

Erfax, Keeper of the Machine Museum, flicked a switch and the drill died with a protesting whine. His friend Erled nodded. He was impressed. In a few minutes the drill had already buried half its length in the rock wall, carving out the commencement of a six-foot diameter tunnel.

"So this is how they tunnelled in the old days," he said.

"That's right. The ancients may have been primitive in some ways, but technologically they weren't bad, not bad at all. This type of machine made possible the great epic explorations — the migratory ones. If one is to believe history — and personally I do — with such drills they tunnelled hundreds of thousands of miles. These days we could do better, of course. They must have spent

---

* An instrument for peering into caves and hollows through the surrounding rock.

an awful long time travelling those distances with a vibro-drill, apart from wearing out God knows how many machines in the process."

Erled smiled wistfully. "A few centuries was nothing to those people. They had *will-power.*" He watched as the drill was withdrawn from the dent-like cavity it had made and was turned round for the short journey to its resting place in the Museum. Behind it a packing machine moved into place, scooping up the rock that had been thrown out and ramming it expertly back into the hole. He tried to imagine the drill spinning out a tunnel thousands of miles into the infinite rock, pushing relentlessly forward on a vain search for other worlds. He imagined thousands of people passing along that tunnel as their home cavity gradually filled up with the rock from the excavation — until, eventually, they gave up the search, filled up the tunnel itself and settled in the new cavity they were thus able to hollow out — *this* cavity in which Erled had been born. Yes, he thought, those ancestors of ours had a quality we have lost.

"I should congratulate you," he told Erfax. "It looks as good as new."

Erfax laughed shyly. "Part of my duties is to keep the machines entrusted to me in working condition," he said. "Ostensibly that drill is five hundred years old, the last of its type — but between you and me it's had so many parts replaced it might just as well have been made yesterday."

Erled nodded again, smiling. "Yes, I suppose so. Well, thanks for showing it to me, Erfax. It's helped — seeing how they did it in the old days, I mean. I feel encouraged, now. If they had the nerve to explore the universe with relatively primitive equipment like this, then we can certainly do it with what we have available. Maybe we will succeed where they failed."

Erfax's assistants were guiding the vibro-drill under its own power down a broad, even-ceilinged corridor. He and Erled followed, turning away from the rock perimeter and walking Inwards. Erled was a tall, sharp-eyed man, a few years beyond the freshness of youth but still fairly young. Erfax, rather older, was a shorter, rounder man who walked with short, quick strides and he had to hurry to keep up with the other.

A short while later, at the gates of the Machine Museum, Erfax turned to Erled.

"You are very confident, friend. But whatever the hazards of the voyage might be, the greatest hurdle you will have to overcome is still here, in the Cavity. You still have to gain the assent of the Proctors. However, I wish you luck."

"The Proctors?" Erled answered lightly. "They will be no trouble at all, you can depend on it. Why, Ergrad, the Proctor Enforcer, is the father of Fanaleen, my betrothed. This is practically a family affair!"

Erfax merely smiled uncertainly, waved farewell and disappeared through the gates of his Museum in the wake of the whining, elephantine vibro-drill. Erled went on down the low passage whose ceiling, as everywhere in the Cavity, was barely six or eight inches over head. He was not discomforted by this pressing closeness; it was the condition of life he had always known, that everyone had always known.

Centuries ago, had Erled raised his eyes and looked about him, he would have seen a vast cavern several miles in extent with a roof that curved perhaps a mile overhead: such was the Cavity as it had first been hollowed out, the total emptiness capacity of the known solid universe all in one piece. In the intervening centuries humanity had increased in numbers and had learned to use the space available to it with greater efficiency, compartmentalising all of it into closely calculated living and working spaces. In its present honeycombed form the Cavity petered out indeterminately into the surrounding rock like an amoeba trapped in a solid matrix. Its diameter was roughly fifteen miles and its population was three quarters of a million. Incessantly computations were carried out to see whether, by an appropriate readjustment of existing arrangements, more living space could be gained from the inert plenum.

One thing was certain: no new emptiness could be created. That was a scientifically established law of conservation. Emptiness could be rearranged in any number of ways, or it could be moved from place to place by the substitution of solid matter, but its total volume could not be increased. Like solidity itself, that remained unchanging throughout time.

Which meant that humanity could never expand beyond the space that was already available to it; that its numbers could never increase beyond a certain tolerable density.

Unless.

Unless, as Erled had told himself a thousand times, new worlds, new Cavities, could be discovered in the infinite solidity.

After walking half a mile Inwards Erled took the public conveyor system which carried him speedily towards his destination: the workshop on the other side of the Cavity where he and his colleagues were preparing for the most exciting enterprise for many, many generations.

Erled's confrontation with the Proctors came only a few workcycles later.

It was not what he had expected.

He was summoned abruptly from his home during the relaxation period. On ariving at the Chamber of Proctors he was ushered directly in, and almost before he had time to compose himself he found himself faced with the interrogating stares of the men and women who ruled his life.

There was Erfloured, Ergurur and Erkarn, all representing different vital departments of life — Sustenance, Machine Technology, and Emptiness Utilisation. To their left, wearing ceremonial robe and sash, sat Erpiort, Proctor of Worship, and beside him the man who made Erled feel most nervous because he already knew him slightly: Ergrad, Proctor Enforcer, wearing the wide shoulder-sleeves and dark cowl of Law Enforcement.

Sitting to the left of Ergrad were the only two women on the Council: Fasusun, Proctress of Domestic Harmony, and Fatelka, Proctress of Child Care. Both were in the full bloom of an officious middle-age, and were looking at Erled with particular suspicion.

"Be seated, Erled," said Erkarn, the man from whom, as Proctor of Emptiness Utilisation, Erled was expecting the most enthusiastic support. However, he was surprised to observe that the Proctor was apparently extremely annoyed with him.

"Over the past few days we have discussed your quite interesting proposal very seriously," the Proctor announced, "but before we deal with that, it has come to our notice that recently you and Keeper of the Machine Museum Erfax, without permission and entirely in defiance of the law, operated a tunnelling machine Outward of the perimeter."

"But no excavations were carried out, Proctor!" protested Erled, bewildered. "It was a demonstration run only. The run Outwards was only a few feet and it was made good immediately. I cannot see that we transgressed the law in doing that."

"You will allow *us* to decide when the law is transgressed," put in Ergrad darkly. He leaned towards Erled and suddenly looked menacing and sinister. "The law against uncontrolled excavations is a very strict one — as it must be, if emptiness is not to be eroded. Only state-commissioned vessels are allowed to operate in the solidity, as well you know, and the degree of the transgression is not the point in question."

Erled looked crestfallen.

"However," resumed Erkarn, "we shall leave that aside for the time being. While ignorance is no excuse it is possible that we may, in this instance, exercise our own discretion. Let us move to the main burden of the meeting: the proposal that long-range expeditions should be sent into solidity. While we have your full argument in the written tender, it would be better, for the sake of procedure, that you give us a brief account of it now so that it may appear on the transcript of this meeting."

"Very well, Proctor." Erled licked his lips. There was a sinking feeling in the pit of his stomach. The Proctors had done everything they could to put him at a disadvantage and that could only mean that they were opposed to the project.

"Essentially our effort is designed to be a continuation of the exploratory sagas of ancient times," he began. "As you are aware the difficulty with the ancients' method, apart from its slowness, is that it requires a permanent tunnel. Eventually all available emptiness is drawn into this tunnel, necessitating that the entire population should migrate along it and take part in the exploratory drive.

"An alternative, much preferable method is for the drilling vessel to fill up the tunnel behind it as it proceeds, thus becoming a genuine vehicle isolated in solidity — thus leaving the Cavity intact. In the old days this was impracticable since there was no way of solving the supply problem. No vessel could possibly carry enough sustenance to support its crew during time periods which might extend to years or generations. But today the situation is different!" Erled's voice rose as his obsession gripped him once again. "We are no longer limited to the vibro-drill. The modern tunneller works by disassociating solid matter into a perfectly fluid dust which, as the solidity-ship moves forward, it passes to its rear through special vents and simultaneously reconstitutes into the original rock. With this type of system almost incredible speeds can be achieved — close on forty miles per hour. Furthermore, by now it has proved its reliability, having been employed for over a generation in the vessels that are used to survey the close rock environs of the Cavity. The time is long overdue when we should rediscover the passion of the ancients for the discovery of new worlds!"

The vibrant voice of the Proctor of Worship answered his declamation. "The ancients were endowed with intense religious zeal and embarked on their migrations in search of God, not of new worlds," Erpiort said critically. "Dauntless and resourceful though they were, it is also true that the ancients were at the primitivist stage of religious knowledge. To our more sophisticated intellects it is obvious that God is not to be found by travelling through the horizontal universe, no matter to what distance. Why should we repeat their follies?"

Erled knew exactly what Erpiort was driving at. It had been recognised for a long time that the universe was stratified. In any transverse direction the rock remained, as far as was known, unchanged to infinity. Downwards, one entered a Region of Intense Heat, while if one attempted to travel Upwards one encountered a Region of Impassibility. Above this region, which could be entered only by the souls of the righteous after death, God was acknowledged to dwell. Conversely the profound Region of Heat was a place of torment reserved for the souls of the wicked. Both regions were held to be infinite in themselves, but to Erled, or indeed to anyone else in the room, the very idea of travel either Up or Down for more than a few hundred miles was virtually a metaphysical notion. These transcendental directions were literally beyond possible human experience. Only horizontal directions had any practical meaning, and it was these that one normally meant by infinity.

Erled's interest was not religious, though he agreed that to hope to find God by travelling through the rock was naïve. "But what of the urge to discover new worlds, to determine once and for all whether there really are other cavities in the solidity?" he countered in a dismayed tone. "We should not stifle such aspirations, surely?"

His dismay was caused by the fact that this aspiration was, to him, a burning ideal that had become second nature, and he simply could not understand why some other minds did not appear to share it. "Besides, the discovery of unknown cavities would make new emptiness available for mankind," he added placatingly.

Erpiort's mouth twisted cynically. "The ancients also exercised their minds with this hypothesis of other worlds," he remarked. "As we all know, they found nothing. Your proposition has come at a very unfortunate time, my fellow. A deposition is currently before the Holy Synod to declare the Doctrine of One Cavity, long preached by all devout priests, an article of faith! This deposition, if accepted, will make it a heresy to believe anything other than that God made but one cavity in the whole of solidity!"

"But that may not be true!" Erled blurted. "Why, Ereton, who is working with me on the project, has produced a calculation — hypothetical, I admit — to show that there may be a definite ratio of emptiness to solidity in the universe. If the ratio is one part emptiness to one quadrillion parts solidity, as he thinks, then there must be innumerable cavities—" He broke off, suddenly aware that he might be causing trouble for Ereton. "Well, at any rate shouldn't the matter be decided scientifically?" he ended lamely.

"Silence!" thundered Erpiort. "The age of cold intellectualism is over, along with the age of religious disputation. We have entered the age of faith!"

Erled fell silent.

The silence was broken by Ergurur, Proctor of Machine Technology. He was a mild-faced man with an easy manner, and he addressed an apologetic smile at Erled.

"Er . . . you gave few details of the design of your proposed exploratory vessel when you submitted the tender," he said. "Perhaps you could say a little more about it now?"

Erled nodded. "We gave little information before because we wanted to make an early application to the Council so as to lose no time," he said. "At that stage our solidity ship was still undergoing development and the final designs were not complete."

"And now?"

"Both the designs and the ship itself are complete," Erled replied woodenly. "Completed and ready to embark on its first voyage. The engine is basically a sturdier model of the engines used in the Cavity environs surveyor vessels. The ship has its own sustenance recycling plant and can supply itself with food and air for at least a year, perhaps a year and a half. It carries a crew of two."

"And its speed?"

"Nearly forty miles per hour!" announced Erled triumphantly. "At least, that is what we gained on the test rig," he added hastily. "The ship has not yet been tested in a true rock environment, naturally."

Ergurur listened to these details in fascination. Erkarn, alert in his Proctorship of Emptiness Utilisation, broke in with a voice like ice.

"You boast that the despatch of your solidity ship will not deprive the Cavity of emptiness," he said. "Nevertheless it must carry *some* emptiness with it, and if for any reason you failed to return then that emptiness would be lost forever. Just what *is* the vacuity volume of your solidity ship?"

"Much thought has been given to this question," Erled answered. "We even thought of cutting down the vacuity volume to near-zero by immersing the crew members in a liquid and allowing them to breathe through flexible tubes directly from the recycling plant. However, we decided that such an existence would prove intolerable during a long voyage, and so we have merely economised as much as possible. The vacuity volume of the ship is only a hundred cubic feet."

"Pah! And if you had your way you would despatch a hundred such ships into the rock, which if they failed to return would deprive mankind of ten thousand cubic feet!" Erkarn leaned back, smugly satisfied with this damning calculation.

"Quite so," murmured Ergrad. "Erled, I fear your solidity ship must be confiscated and destroyed."

"Could it not be placed in the Machine Museum?" suggested Ergurur regretfully.

At this moment Fasusun spoke, giving Erled a look of sorrowful annoyance. "What compelled you to think up this wicked scheme, Erled?" the Proctress said. "I fear your soul is bound for Hell, but I shall pray for you."

"Not wicked, Proctress," Erled replied evenly. "It is merely the natural scientific desire to explore and discover."

"But of course it is wicked! You are defying nature, defying God, trying to upset society! Were you not taught as a child that God intended us to remain where He put us? That He created the Cavity specially for us, and therefore could not possibly have created another? Think again, Erled! Try to lead a better life! Spend more time in the temple and study the scriptures!"

Erled kept silence, unable to devise a suitable reply. My God, he thought, why do they have to allow women on the Council? For bigotry and narrowness these two, Fasusun and Fatelka, had even old Erpiort beat. They spent their time attempting to produce a population trained in doctrinaire placidity, being particularly active in the nurseries.

In addition they were almost certainly fundamentalists, taking literally every word of the scriptures. Believing, for instance, that God created the Cavity in the twinkling of an eye, complete with sustenance, machines and atomic energy, and a small tribe from which mankind grew — that was before the Cavity had by artificial means been moved several hundred thousand miles, of course. Even Erpiort had too much intelligence to swallow that one, Erled thought. Doubtless the Proctor of Worship held, with some reservations, to the scientific, evolutionary theory that Erled himself accepted — that first the Cavity had appeared, possibly by act of God or in some unknown manner, and that life had then developed by an evolutionary process. First, by spontaneous generation, there had appeared sustenance, the edible yeast-like growth that could recycle body wastes and air. Then there had appeared tiny animalcules to feed on the sustenance. Rapidly these had evolved through various stages into present mankind. It was also necessary to suppose that far before present mankind had appeared, the primeval pre-human ancestors had been endowed with an instinctive knowledge of machines and of how to release atomic energy.

Finally the silence was broken by Erkarn. "Well, you can see how it is, Erled. The decision of the Council was unanimous except for one abstaining vote." He glanced disapprovingly at Ergurur. "You are to forget these mad dreams and that's a command."

"You're stifling something that can't be stifled forever," Erled muttered peevishly.

"You will mend your ways and forget the whole matter," Erkarn said sternly. "There is still the business of the illegal drilling hanging over you. We are willing to suspend the charges *if* it is seen that you show contrition — do you understand?"

"Yes," said Erled sullenly.

"Very well, then. The disposal of the solidity ship will be considered later. Much emptiness to you."

"Much emptiness," muttered Erled, and turned away.

Erled's resentment did not abate during the next few hours, but he had no thought of defying the Council. He was powerless against the Proctors, and he did not relish the thought of the criminal charges, with which he was being frankly blackmailed, being laid against him.

It would have to be left to some future generation, he told himself, to carry out the great task of exploring the universe.

He did not immediately convey the news to his colleagues in the project. Instead he felt in need of some different kind of comfort, and when the relaxation period arrived he made his way to the dwelling of Ergrad's family, to call on his betrothed, Fanaleen.

The thought of facing his future father-in-law so soon after his humiliation partly at his hands caused Erled a slight degree of trepidation, but he reassured himself that on such visits Ergrad usually put in only a brief appearance or none at all. However, as he approached Ergrad's well-appointed dwelling through a low-ceilinged passage, the tall, hooded figure of the Proctor Enforcer suddenly appeared from nowhere and barred his way.

This section of the passage-way was dimly lit. Erled felt menaced by the looming form. Dark black eyes flashed at him from beneath the cowl.

"Proctor Ergrad," he stuttered. "I have come to see Fanaleen—"

"Turn round, Erled, and go home. You're not welcome here."

Erled was astounded. "But — Proctor —"

Ergrad clenched his fist in exasperation. "Can you be so thickheaded?" he growled. "Didn't you see what went on in the Chamber today? You're *finished*, Erled, you'll be a nobody for the rest of your life. Not the sort of man I'll allow to marry into my family. You'll never see Fanaleen again."

Abruptly the Proctor turned and strode towards his dwelling. For nearly a minute Erled stared after his retreating back, the finality of what had happened slowly seeping into him.

Never see Fanaleen again.

There could be no revision of that sentence. It was a strict law that the union between a couple must be agreeable to the parents. And the word of a Proctor was inviolate.

Dazed, Erled allowed his feet to carry him to the only place where he was likely to find understanding: the Inn of Vacuous Happiness, the haunt of his friends and colleagues in the solidity ship project. As he anticipated, they were all busy drinking there, and Ereton, with whom he shared co-leadership of the project, greeted him eagerly. So, in their favourite room where the ceiling beams touched one's head if one stood erect, he explained the double disaster.

Ereton squeezed his shoulder consolingly. "It appears that we chose the wrong time," he said sombrely.

"There'll *never* be a right time in this generation," Erled exclaimed heatedly. "And we'll never get a chance to search for other worlds. What right have the Proctors to dictate to our consciences like this? It's tyranny!"

The others agreed fervidly, after which Erled retired to a corner and brooded. His resentment was building up like a burning fire, and as with so many men before him, the tragedy of thwarted love turned his mind to lofty sentiments, so that he began to think again about his lifelong dream: the existence of other cavities. As if hypnotised, he returned to the cosmological questions that at various times had haunted him. Was the rock really infinite? It had to be — for if at some extreme it ended, what lay beyond that end? An infinity of emptiness, as Ereton, in a fit of brilliant extravagance, had once suggested? Erled soon pushed the idea aside. Baffling though the concept of infinity itself was, an empty infinity was something the mind simply could not grasp, and besides the notion was needlessly artificial.

He had expected to get drunk, but two hours later he found that he was still completely sober, having drunk but little. Ereton, too, did not seem to be in a mood for drinking. All seven others, however, drank heavily, and as their intoxication increased so did their indignation at the Proctor's decision. Erled found himself aggravated by the noise and he was about to suggest to Ereton that they leave when there was the sound of a disturbance and the flimsy screen door burst open.

Ergrad, at the head of four or five other enforcers, entered the inn and stood surveying the room, his head slightly bent beneath the big black beams.

"Looks like the whole pack is here, eh?" he barked. "All right, Erled, the Council has just now ordered that your solidity ship be destroyed, so lead us to it so that we may get on with the good work."

"Do you need us for that?" Erled retorted. "Do the job yourselves."

Ergrad looked at him thoughtfully. "Don't try to be obstructive, Erled, or it will go all the worse for you. It seems that you've managed to keep the site of your workshop to yourselves, at any rate Erkarn found himself unable to locate it for some reason or other, which looks damned peculiar to me. Well, anyway, we knew you people came here for relaxation and I'll thank you for the information."

A chain of thoughts flashed through Erled's mind. For a workshop, or any other site for that matter, to be unlocatable by the Proctor of Emptiness Utilisation was not only peculiar, it was downright incredible. Only one explanation came to Erled. Since the machines and workspace had originally been allocated by Ergurur, who was sympathetic to them, then somehow he must have concealed this legally obligatory information from Erkarn! An ecstatic hope accelerated Erled's heart. Even in the Council there was dissension! Ergurur was trying to help them!

Around him the others were crying "Shame!" and protesting to the law enforcers. Ergrad rounded on them, his face livid.

"To your homes, all of you, or you'll learn what it means to cross the law!"

Threateningly, he brandished his truncheon and his followers produced theirs. There was a moment's pause.

Then a heavy glass came sailing through the air and struck Ergrad on the temple. He staggered, while the glass fell to the floor and shattered. With a howl of rage Ergrad ordered his men to attack and in seconds the inn was the scene of an unsightly brawl.

Erled and Ereton, already made nervous by the tense situation, had backed to the far end of the room. They looked on the brawl appalled. Then a cry floated through to them, from Ervane, Erled believed.

"Save the solidity ship! Save the solidity ship!"

That cry prompted Erled into action. Surreptitiously he eased open the rear exit and beckoned to Ereton. Together they slipped away. Minutes later they were headed for the perimeter, having changed direction several times on the public conveyor system to elude pursuit.

"This is terrible!" Ereton said, although he had obeyed Erled as if he had no will of his own. "Do you think we should go back, Erled, and apologise to Proctor Ergrad? Otherwise everyone will be punished severely."

"Our friends would never have dared to attack the enforcers if they hadn't been both drunk and angry," Erled admitted. "Perhaps that will count in their favour when they come to trial. As for us, a wild intention has entered my mind of which I think the others would approve, Ereton."

They spoke no more during the rest of the journey, aware that anyone sitting near them on the transporter chairs might be eavesdropping on their conversation. Before long they came to the workshop on the edge of the Cavity where the solidity ship was housed.

The area was deserted, no residences being nearby and this being the rest period. Erled opened the gate and they crept inside. Before them the solidity ship stood on a short ramp, its snout facing the bare rock of infinity but a few yards away.

The ship had the form of a fluted cylinder, either end being squarely blunt and intricated with drive machinery. "To destroy this ship would be a crime," Erled said. His mouth curled in disgust. "They talk of faith. But isn't *our* effort a matter of faith?

— faith that the universe contains more than just our one cavity? That there *are* other worlds if only we will look?"

"You want us to take the ship and go illegally into solidity," Ereton said tonelessly.

"Yes, why not? What else is left to us? It's either that or abandon all our dreams and live useless, frustrated lives. We've got this one chance, so let's take it!"

In his heart Ereton had known that this was why they had come here, but the thought of such a step made him go deathly pale. "Do you realise what it means? It will be the death sentence when we return!"

"Not if we return with news of other emptiness in the rock!" Erled replied triumphantly. "We have friends even in the Council, you know!" One friend, anyway, he told himself privately.

Ereton opened his hands in a hopeless gesture. "And suppose we find no new emptiness? How long did the ancients search?" He shook his head. "We're both mad."

"*Both* of us, eh?" Erled grinned. "I *knew* you were with me! Don't prevaricate, we may only have minutes in which to make our get-away!"

Smilingly wryly, Ereton patted him on the shoulder. "Of course I'm with you, old friend. As you say, what else is there to do at a juncture like this?"

Hastily they scrambled aboard the solidity ship and made a rapid check of all the equipment. The newly completed craft slid along its ramp until reaching the further wall, when the rock touched by its snout seemed to collapse and to flow like fine oil. The ship lurched suddenly forward, and seconds later it had merged and disappeared into the bare, blank rock.

"Incredible," murmured Erled.

Ereton joined him from aft and peered over his shoulder at the flickering bank of instruments. "What is it?"

"I think we're being followed."

They had been *en voyage* for just over two weeks. In the cramped space, Ereton leaned closer. Pretty soon there was no doubt of it: the image plates of both sonicscope and tremorscope sharpened to reveal that a second solidity ship was following them. And it was close.

While they stared in amazement they heard a *ping* and a light came on over the rockvid receiver. Erled flicked a switch. Across the plate streamed recurrent ripples that slowly built up a crude, low-definition picture carried by sonicwaves from the following ship.

The hooded face of Ergrad stared at them from the plate, distorted somewhat by the incessant ripples.

"I never dreamed they'd go this far!" Erled breathed.

The Proctors, presumably, were so furious at their escape that they had sent Ergrad in hot pursuit! The second ship must have been put together in a hurry by modifying a surveyor vessel. At that, Erled thought, the enforcer had done very well indeed to catch up with them so quickly. He must have strained the engines to the utmost, at considerable danger to himself.

Ergrad spoke, the words coming blurred through the speaker.

"Erled, Ereton! Halt and turn your ship round at once! I am here to escort you back to the Cavity, where you will stand trial for your crimes!"

Erled and Ereton looked at one another quizzically.

"No return!" Erled said fiercely. "We keep going!"

Nodding, Ereton spoke into the transmitter microphone. "Sorry, Proctor, we can't turn back now."

"Be warned that we are armed with quake beams and will not hesitate to use them! Obey or be destroyed!" Ergrad glowered, and his voice was like iron.

"What shall we do?" Ereton hissed, switching off the microphone. "Those beams can shake us to pieces!"

"Perhaps we can dodge them."

Ereton crouched down behind Erled as the latter took over the controls. The solidity ship surged forward at top speed and began to weave about through the rock. Shortly afterwards there was a screeching, rumbling sound and the ship shook as though it were a bell struck by a giant hammer. Erled gasped as the vibrations caught hold of him and made him feel that he was being turned inside out.

Although they had been struck only a glancing blow, Erled had been counting on the fact that quake beams travelled fairly slowly through their rock medium and therefore were difficult to aim at a fast-moving object. Unfortunately, Ergrad — or whoever was operating the weapon — seemed to be skilled in its use.

Finding the controls unaffected by the strike, Erled put the ship through a dizzying series of turns. He knew that he had to avoid another hit and at the same time to put distance between himself and the pursuer, because their only hope lay in the probability that Ergrad's vessel was limited in its range and therefore he would soon have to turn back.

He peered at the sonicscope and tremorscope plates, trying to judge precisely where the pursuing ship lay and where it might strike next. But suddenly both plates erupted into an unreadable, screaming flurry as the quake beam went into action again. All around them the tortured rock quaked and imploded and the metal of the ship shrieked as if demented. Erled and Ereton immediately lost consciousness, but the injured solidity ship, its engines still working at full blast, plunged blindly on at top speed through the eternal rock.

Erled did not know how much later it was that he came to himself again. His first impression was of a grating noise jarring on his ears, telling him that all was not well. He saw that Ereton too was stirring, and then he climbed back to his bucket seat and scaled down the accelerator.

"Are you hurt?" he asked Ereton.

"I don't think so," groaned the other, and he hauled himself to his knees in the confined space, "What in God's name is that noise?"

"We've sustained some damage, I think. Something amiss in the traction motor by the sound of it."

He glanced at the 'scope plates. They were both working normally but showed no hint of anything unusual in the vicinity. "No sign of Ergrad," he announced.

"Eh?" Ereton stared at the plates in delight. "What can have happened to him? He should be able to track us down easily enough."

"It's possible he believes us destroyed," Erled said with a shrug. "Or he might already have been at the point of no return when he caught up with us and is unable to follow us any further. It could even be that the quake beam backfired on him — that happens sometimes, you know. Anyway the first thing we've got to do is check the ship."

When they had done so the news was not good. The steering gear was severely damaged. Worse, the relatively delicate sustenance recycling plant had also suffered damage. Erled and Ereton debated what to do.

Erled said gloomily: "We may well die here in the rock. But even if we manage to turn round now and head back home, what future have we? Our rank rebellion earns the death sentence, apart from the possibility that Ergrad may have died, for which we will be held responsible. Let's continue as best we can, Ereton."

Dourly Ereton agreed.

In the ensuing months they spent much of their time trying to repair the damage. The recycling plant required enormous attention to keep it functioning properly. Sometimes the air became foul and the food uneatable, and neither could help but notice that even its best output was deteriorating over a period of time.

The traction motor never quite lost its ominous grating noise, but they did manage to jury-rig a steering system.

But despite all their successes the confined conditions of their existence, combined with persistent hard work, anxiety, poor food and air, were sapping their strength. As time advanced something like a stupor overcame them. Eventually each privately despaired of reaching their goal, though neither would speak of his despair to the other. During that time only one thing happened to break the monotony. Ereton was taking his turn on watch, staring with heavy-lidded eyes at the image plates. Suddenly he gave a hoarse cry which brought Erled hurrying forward.

"Look!"

Furious ripples were appearing on the tremorscope, threatening to break out at any moment into a maelstrom of violence. "Definitely not a cavity," Erled mused. "To me it suggests only one thing: a natural quake— and a big one! Furthermore it's directly ahead!"

"A natural quake?" said Ereton wonderingly. Theoretically they were possible but none had ever been observed. It was calculated that the violence of such phenomena, if they did actually occur, would be simply colossal — enough to wipe out in an instant any cavity luckless enough to be caught in them.

Erled knew that they would not survive even for seconds in the giant rock storm that lay ahead.

"If we're to get out of its way we're going to have to turn ninety degrees or more," Erled said. "Preferably to the right."

"Do you think we can?"

"We'd better have a damned good try."

Both were having a hard time to stay alert in the foul air. Cautiously they put their temporary steering system into operation. Reluctantly the ship turned a little. Then a little more. There was the sound of something snapping and an alarm sounded. Gritting his teeth, Ereton forced a little more pressure from the collapsing valves that were supposed to bring the head of the ship round in the rock. The ship turned a few degrees more, then the whole system gave way under the strain.

"Ninety degrees," said Ereton, breathing deeply. "Just about!"

But they were without steering of any kind, and both knew that they did not have the strength to try to jury-rig the system again. Leaving the ship on automatic, they returned to their bunks.

Their morale was now falling rapidly. Whenever they could either Erled or Ereton attended to the recycling plant, but the rest of the time, completely debilitated, they simply lay on their narrow bunks and waited for whatever fate would bring.

Four months after their departure from the Cavity Erled was awakened from a deep slumber by the ringing of an alarm. He was perplexed to find that the engines were silent and that the ship was apparently motionless. Dragging himself from his bunk, he saw that the emptiness indicator was flashing — and, he guessed, had been flashing for some time.

Feverishly he shook Ereton to awareness and coaxed him to the control panel. The instruments told their own story: with no one at the controls to heed the "emptiness ahead" warning, the solidity ship had plunged straight on until encountering that emptiness, upon which the automatic cut-out had brought the vessel to a stop.

The two friends did not even speak to one another. Wordlessly they broke open a locker containing oxygen masks which were included in the ship's kit in case the air of alien cavities proved unbreathable. Thus equipped, Erled summoned up his last remaining strength to force open the hull door.

The solidity ship had emerged halfway from a sheer rock wall. As luck would have it, it had struck emptiness only a couple of feet above one of the many rock ledges jutting from the cliff face. After testing the ledge for firmness, Erled and Ereton stumbled down and looked about them.

The new emptiness was faintly illumined by streaks of luminescent stone in the otherwise inert rock. These streaks occurred in the home cavity, also, and were held to be one of the prerequisites for the primeval development of life. The two men, having spent long periods inside the solidity ship in total darkness, adapted to this faint light with little difficulty. At first a terrible cosmic fear gripped Erled; for although he saw the great rock wall stretching unevenly away in all directions nearby, and below he could dimly discern floors, boulders and plateaux, ahead of him there seemed to be nothing but unending void. Was Ereton's wild notion true? Had they come to the edge of solidity, to look out on an infinity of *emptiness*? But as he peered harder Erled saw that the impossible dream was not to be. He saw a dim film of *something* hanging, like a curtain, far away in the distance, and he knew that this was a cavity such as the one in which he had been born. Except that *this* cavity apparently contained no life.

"So it's true!" he declaimed in a cracked voice, the words coming muffled through his mask. "There *are* other cavities in the rock! Some of them *must* be inhabited! Our faith is justified — we are not alone in the universe!"

At that moment his strength failed him. He felt Ereton's arm around him, helping him back into the solidity ship, where they both lay down for the last time.

Well, Asmravaar, what do you think of that? A sad tale in some respects — but above all, I think, a triumphant victory for the spirit of intelligent life.

There is one tiny aspect of the narrative that may strike you as suspicious. I mean the part in which Erled and Ereton were turned aside from their course, and thereby enabled to find the new cavity, by the intervention of a rock quake. Did this smack of providence? Well, there, I confess, I failed to play fair and concealed the truth: — it *was* providence — *my* providence. The rock in which these creatures dwell is scattered with caverns at intervals too infrequent to hit upon by sheer luck, and the antronoscopes they use are so primitive that they are only effective over a range of two or three miles. So, seeing a suitable cavern lying quite close to their route, I could not resist helping them out a bit by causing a minor disturbance with an effector beam!

How the bipeds came to exist in their rock environment is something of a mystery. Since the surface of the planet, a thousand miles over their heads, is desolate and airless, I surmise that they might have retreated millennia ago from a natural catastrophe or, what amounts to the same thing, from a war of annihilation.

It might seem surprising that the bipeds have never guessed that they live in the interior of a spherical planet, until one remembers that there is nothing in their environment to suggest the fact. The rock stratum in which they live is a variety of basalt and is roofed over by a somewhat rare phenomenon— a five-hundred mile thick stratum of extremely hard carbon-bonded iron and granite. It would take some really advanced expertise to penetrate this particular lithosphere and when the bipeds took refuge below it, afterwards allowing their science to deteriorate, they effectively imprisoned themselves inside the planet forever.

The stories about the epic voyages of ancient times are literally true, by the way. They really *did* journey hundreds of thousands of miles, never suspecting that they were simply travelling round the planet's gravity radius (at that depth a circumference of roughly eighteen thousand miles) again and again.

In a way I feel glad that they never knew.

And where is my "philosophic victory", you want to know? As you are too blockheaded to see it yourself, I shall have to explain. I have discovered a solid universe of infinite rock! But, you protest, the bipeds only *think* they live in such a universe — in actuality they dwell in a completely unremarkable, average planet, leaving aside one or two details of geological interest.

Yet, Asmravaar, are imagination and reality so very much different, really? If the mind is able to entertain some state of affairs as though it were real, then perhaps somewhere in the transfinite universe it *is* real.

As it happens I have a little more than just fancy to support this contention of mine. There is a puzzling little coincidence in the tale I have just related. Ereton, the theoretician, made a calculation of the hypothetical ratio of "emptiness" to "solidity" in his (imaginary) universe. I was astonished when I realised that the figures he produced come close to describing the actually existing *converse* case in the real universe — namely the average ratio of *matter* to *empty space*. I cannot help wondering, therefore, whether this is something more than a coincidence.

Some years ago there used to be much talk about the universe possessing "matter/anti-matter symmetry", that is, that spatialities of our type might correspond to an equal number of spatialities where matter has its electrical charges reversed — the electron being positive and the proton negative. Since no anti-matter spatialities have been found one hears little about this idea nowadays. Well: Ereton's calculation has led me to construct, along somewhat similar lines, a theory of my own which I shall present to the Explorers' Club on my next return home. In my theory the universe exhibits "space/anti-space symmetry", or if you like, "emptiness-solidity symmetry" to use the bipeds' terminology, so that if one passes the "mid-point" of the universe, as it were (not a very accurate way to speak of transfinity, I know), then one enters a complementary series of spatialities where there is, not primarily void containing islands of matter, but primarily solid matter containing occasional bubbles of void.

I'm pretty confident that my theory will make quite a splash when I announce it. It's amusing to think how one might explore these solid spatialities. Just imagine me and my antronoscope as I bore endlessly through the rock in search of cavity-worlds!

Well, I think that's about enough for now, as I'm very tired. I'll burst this lot to you without delay, and then I'm going to get some much-needed sleep. Yours, and let me hear from you soon: Utz.

My poor Utz: While it was delightful to hear from you after so long, I'm afraid that your ravings about a "philosophic victory" only go to show that you are suffering from hysterical boredom. Your story, let me say at once, was most entertaining, but apart from that all you have done is to blow up a simple incident into some sort of cosmic hot air which you revealingly admit to be all in your imagination. As for your theory of anti-space it is purely hypothetical and has no solid evidence to support it (the pun was unintentional). These fanciful theories never do turn out to correspond to reality anyway.

I have warned you many times about the monotony of the universe at large and now I think it's beginning to get at you. Let me urge you to come directly home, for I think the rest will do you good. I might even find a part for you in my next play, since you obviously have a misplaced talent for the dramatic. Your ever-loving friend: Asmravaar.

:: :: :: Transfinite cable to Venerable Gob Slok Ok :: Please collect :: :: ::
DEAR REVERED Uncle,

I trust that the surprise and distaste you will feel on receiving this cable will be decreased when I tell you that I am sending it from the 10^{6248}th series. Since many, many infinities of solid rock and metal therefore separate us, you need not fear an attack of the disgust and revulsion which my presence seems to cause you.

I am contacting you because, whatever your feelings for me personally, you are still one of the most noted of scholars, whose professional opinion I value, and I cannot refrain from notifying you of a discovery of mine, even though I know how much you disapprove of my life as a cosmic explorer.

Having transmigrated myself into the 10^{6248}th series of solidities I proceeded to tunnel strongly through rock which proved, for an immense distance, to be unbroken. I was, I should add, in a region far removed from any of the cavity-clusters which usually abound in this series, a desolate region which would normally remain unexplored for all time. My reason for tunnelling in this direction, I say without shame (at the risk of enraging you, Uncle) was sheer caprice.

At any rate my antronoscopes registered the unexpected presence of a very large cavity so I hurried to investigate. It transpired that this cavity was the largest I have ever encountered or heard of. The mean diameter is ten million miles!

Let me repeat that, Uncle, in case you think there has been a mistake in transmission. Ten million miles! Not only that but the cavity contains a rich biological life and has several intelligent species scattered around its circumference, none of which I have made contact with yet, as I want to await your advice.

The fact is, Uncle, that so far I have investigated only one of these species and it entertains such an astonishing picture of the cosmos that I don't know quite how to proceed. Let me explain. In a cavity of this size centrifugal gravity works very efficiently. Consequently there is a film of atmosphere about two hundred miles deep upon the walls of the cavity, but the rest is void — pure emptiness.

I should also add that it is almost impossible to see as far as the opposite side of the cavity, for reasons rather too complicated to go into here. Anyway, the upshot is that these intelligent beings, who live, of course, within the atmosphere, are aware that a vacuum lies above them after the atmosphere peters out (being compressed, of course, by the excessive gravity). But their world is so large, and so impossible for them to explore fully on account of its size, that they possess no idea that it constitutes the inner surface of a sphere! (Or near-sphere.) They suppose that the void above them extends without limit — *that the cosmos is an infinity of vacuum with only islands of solid matter in it.*

It was some time before I was able to comprehend a belief so bizarre and inconceivable. And yet now that I have managed, after a fashion, to grasp it, I find the idea rather compelling and fascinating, and I can't help wondering whether there *might*, among all the solidities as yet unexplored, be one consisting of almost nothing but emptiness?

I hope, Uncle, that you can forget our differences for long enough to give your attention to this question. We are both, remember, animated by a love of knowledge and I would listen to your opinion most earnestly. Do you think that a nearly-empty solidity — one would, I suppose, have to call it a "spatiality" — is possible?

And apart from that, should I attempt to contact the beings in the giant cavity, or should I leave them alone with their delusion?

Your perplexed and respectful nephew,
Awm.

:: :: :: Transfinite Open Cable Receipt Awm Oosh Ok :: Transmit 10^{62} ⁻ ⁻ range :: Reply not prepaid :: :: ::

DEAR Nephew,

Not only is your idea of a vacuous infinity inconceivable, it is also downright silly and utterly impossible, as well you know.

In a way it's a pity we don't live in such a world because no type of propulsion could operate in a void, since there would be nothing on which to gain traction, and that would at least prevent you young grubs from gadding about the cosmos with all the irresponsibility of flame-flies.

I have placed on record your discovery of the curiosity, namely the giant cavity, and I suppose I should thank you for that trifle. However I feel it is amply repaid by my deigning to reply at all to your cable, which otherwise I would have ignored.

If you solicit my opinion then you must accept it on any subject I care to name. Let me be quite specific: your larvae, of which you seem to generate an indecent number with each visit to your long-suffering family, are hatching without the benefit of a father to guide them in the rituals of the swarm, and seem most unlikely to grow into decent, low-crawling worms. Your wives grow fat and lazy without the discipline which only a strict husband can provide, and the affairs of your estates are going to rack and ruin. I thank God that your father is not alive to see how his son has turned out.

A worm's place is at home — that is my opinion, and I strongly recommend that you repair hither post-haste. As for whether you should or should not communicate with ignorant savages, that is of absolutely no interest to me.

                                        Your most displeased uncle,
                                                      Gob.

All the King's Men

I saw Sorn's bier, an electrically driven train decorated like a fanfare, as it left the North Sea Bridge and passed over the green meadows of Yorkshire. Painted along its flank was the name HOLATH HOLAN SORN, and it motored swiftly with brave authority. From where we stood in the observation room of the King's Summer Palace, we could hear the hollow humming of its passage.

"You will not find things easy without Holath Holan Sorn," I said, and turned. The King of All Britain was directing his mosaic eyes towards the train.

"Things were never easy," he replied. But he knew as well as I that the loss of Sorn might mean the loss of a kingdom.

The King turned from the window, his purple cloak flowing about his seven-foot frame. I felt sorry for him: how would he rule an alien race, with its alien psychology, now that Sorn was dead? He had come to depend entirely upon that man who could translate one set of references into another as easily as he crossed the street. No doubt there were other men with perhaps half of Sorn's abilities, but who else could gain the King's trust? Among all humans, none but Sorn could be the delegate of the Invader King.

"Smith," he said, addressing me, "tomorrow we consign twelve tooling factories to a new armaments project. I wish you to supervise."

I acknowledged, wondering what this signified. No one could deny that the alien's reign had been peaceful, even prosperous, and he had rarely mentioned military matters, although I knew there was open enmity between him and the King of Brazil. Either this enmity was about to become active, I decided, or else the King forecast a civil uprising.

Which in itself was not unlikely.

Below us, the bier was held up by a junction hitch. Stationary, it supplemented its dignity by sounding its klaxon loudly and continuously. The King returned his gaze to it, and though I couldn't read his unearthly face I suppose he watched it regretfully, if he can feel regret. Of the others in the room, probably the two aliens also watched with regret, but certainly no one else did. Of the four humans, three were probably glad he was dead, though they may have been a little unsure about it.

That left myself. I was more aware of events than any of them, but I just didn't know what I felt. Sometimes I felt on the King's side and sometimes on the other side. I just didn't have any definite loyalties.

Having witnessed the arrival of the bier from the continent, where Sorn had met his death, we had achieved the purpose of the visit to the Summer Palace, and accordingly the King, with his entourage of six (two fellow beings, four humans including myself) left for London.

We arrived at Buckingham Palace shortly before sunset. Wordlessly the King dismissed us all, and with a lonely swirl of his cloak made his way to what was in a makeshift manner called the throne-room. Actually it did have a throne: but it also had several other kinds of strange equipment, things like pools, apparatus with what psychologists called threshold associations. The whole chamber was an aid to the incomprehensible, insectile mentality of the King, designed, I suspected, to help him in the almost impossible task of understanding a human society. While he had Sorn at his elbow there had been little need to worry, and the inadequacy of the chamber mattered so little that he seldom used it. Now, I thought, the King of All Britain would spend a large part of his time meditating in solitude on the enigmatic throne.

I had the rest of the evening to myself. But I hadn't gone far from the palace when, as I might have guessed, Hotch placed his big bulk square across my path.

"Not quite so fast," he said, neither pleasantly nor unpleasantly.

I stopped — what else could I have done? — but I didn't answer. "All right," Hotch said, "let's have it straight. I want nobody on both sides."

"What do you mean?" I asked, as if I didn't already know.

"Sorn's dead, right? And you're likely to replace him. Right?"

"Wrong," I told him wearily. "Nobody replaces Sorn. He was

the one irreplaceable human being."

His eyes dropped in pensive annoyance. He paused. "Maybe, but you'll be the closest to the King's rule. Is that so?"

I shrugged.

"It has to be so," he decided. "So which way is it going to be, Smith? If you're going to be another traitor like Sorn, let's hear it from the start. Otherwise be a man and come in with us."

It sounded strange to hear Sorn called a traitor. Technically, I suppose he was— but he was also a man of genius, the rarest of statesmen. And even now only the 0.5 per cent of the population roused by Hotch's super-patriotism would think of him as anything else. Britain had lived in a plentiful sort of calm under the King. The fact of being governed by an alien conqueror was not resented, even though he had enthroned himself by force. With his three ships, his two thousand warriors, he had achieved a near-bloodless occupation, for he had won his victory by the sheer possession of superior weapons, without having to resort much to their usage. The same could be said of the simultaneous invasion of Brazil and South Africa: Brazil by fellow creatures of the King, South Africa by a different species. Subsequent troubles in these two areas had been greater, but then they lacked the phlegmatic British attitude, and more important, they lacked Holath Holan Sorn.

I sighed. "Honestly, I don't know. Some human governments have been a lot worse."

"But they've been human. And we owed a lot to Sorn, though personally I loathed his guts. Now that he's gone — what? The King will make a mess of things. How do we know he really cares?"

"I think he does. Not the same way a man would care, but he does."

"Hah! Anyhow, this is our chance. While he doesn't know what he's doing. What about it? Britain hasn't known another conqueror in a thousand years."

I couldn't tell him. I didn't know. Eventually he stomped off in disgust.

I didn't enjoy myself that evening. I thought too much about Sorn, about the King, and about what Hotch had said. How could I be sure the King cared for England? He was so grave and gently ponderous, but did that indicate anything? His appearance could simply be part of his foreignness and nothing at all to do with his feelings. In fact if the scientists were right about him, he had no feelings at all.

But what purpose had he?

I stopped by Trafalgar Square to see the Green Fountains.

The hand of the invader on Britain was present in light, subtle ways, such as the Green Fountains. For although Britain remained Britain, with the character of Britain, the King and his men had delicately placed their alien character upon it; not in law, or the drastic changes of a conqueror, but in such things as decoration.

The Green Fountains were foreign, unimaginable, and un-British. High curtains of thin fluid curled into fantastic designs, creating new concepts of space by sheer ingenuity of form. Thereby they achieved what centuries of Terran artists had only hinted at.

And yet they *were* British, too. If Britons had been prompted to conceive and construct such things, this was the way they would have done it. They carried the British stamp, although so alien.

When I considered the King's rule, the same anomaly emerged. A strange rule, by a stranger, yet imposed so easily.

This was the mystery of the King's government: the way he had adopted Britain, in essence, while having no comprehension of that essence.

But let me make it clear that for all this, the invader's rule did not *operate* easily. It jarred, oscillated, went out of phase, and eventually, without Sorn, ended in disaster. It was only in this other, peculiar way, that it harmonised so pleasingly.

It was like this: when the King and his men tried to behave functionally and get things done, it was terrible. It didn't fit. But when they simply added themselves to All Britain, and lay quiescently like touches of colour, it had the effect I describe.

I had always thought Sorn responsible for this. But could Sorn mould the King also? For I detected in the King that same English passivity and acceptance; not just his own enigmatic detachment, but something apart from that, something acquired. Yet how could he be something which he didn't understand?

Sorn is dead, I thought, Sorn is dead.

Already, across one side of the square, were erected huge, precise stone symbols: HOLATH HOLAN SORN DIED 5.8.2034. They were like a mathematical formula. Much of the King's speech, when I thought of it, had the same quality.

Sorn was dead, and the weight of his power which had steadied the nation would be abruptly removed. He had been the operator, bridging the gap between alien minds. Without him, the King was incompetent.

A dazzling blue and gold air freighter appeared over the square and slanted down towards the palace. Everyone stopped to look, for it was one of the extraterrestrial machines, rarely seen since the invasion. No doubt it carried reinforcements for the palace defences.

Next morning I motored to Surrey to visit the first of the ten factories the King had mentioned.

The managers were waiting for me. I was led to a prepared suite of offices where I listened sleepily to a lecture on the layout and scope of the factory. I wasn't very interested; one of the King's kinsmen (referred to as the King's men) would arrive shortly with full details of the proposed conversion, and the managers would have to go through it all again. I was only here as a representative, so to speak. The real job would be carried out by the alien.

We all wandered round the works for a few hours before I got thoroughly bored and returned to my office. A visitor was waiting.

Hotch.

"What do you want now?" I asked. "I thought I'd got rid of you."

He grinned. "I found out what's going on." He waved his arms to indicate the factory.

"What of it?"

"Well, wouldn't you say the King's policy is . . . ill-advised?"

"You know as well as I do that the King's policy is certain to be laughably clumsy." I motioned him to a seat. "What exactly do you mean? I'm afraid I don't know the purpose of this myself."

I was apologetic about the last statement, and Hotch laughed. "It's easy enough to guess. Don't you know what they're building in Glasgow? *Ships* — warships of the King's personal design."

"Brazil," I murmured.

"Sure. The King chooses this delicate moment to launch a transatlantic war. Old Rex is such a blockhead he almost votes himself out of power."

"How?"

"Why, he gives us the weapons to fight him with. He's organising an armed native force which *I* will turn against him."

"You jump ahead of yourself. To go by the plans I have, no extraterrestrial weapons will be used."

Hotch looked more sober. "That's where you come in. We can't risk another contest with the King's men using ordinary arms. It would kill millions and devastate the country. Because it won't be the skirmish-and-capitulate of last time. This time we'll be in earnest. So I want you to soften things up for us. Persuade the King to hand over more than he intends: help us to chuck him out easily. Give us new weapons and you'll save a lot of carnage."

I saw his stratagem at once. "Quit that! Don't try to lay blood responsibility on my shoulders. That's a dirty trick."

"For a dirty man — and that's what you are, Smith, if you continue to stand by, too apathetic even to think about it. Anyhow, the responsibility's already laid, whatever you say. It depends on you."

"No."

"You won't help?"

"That's right."

Hotch sighed, and stared at the carpet for some seconds. Then he stared through the glass panels and down onto the floor of the workshops. "Then what will you do? Betray me?"

"No."

Sighing again, he told me: "One day, Smith, you'll fade away through sheer lack of interest."

"I'm interested," I said. "I just don't seem to have the kind of mind that can make a decision. I can't find any place to lay blame, or anyone to turn against."

"Not even for Britain," he commented sadly. "Your Britain as well as mine. That's all I'm working for, Smith, our country."

His brashness momentarily dormant, he was moodily meditative. "Smith, I'll admit I don't understand what it's all about.

What does the King want? What has he gained by coming down here?"

"Nothing. He descended on us and took on a load of troubles without profit. It's a mystery. Hence my uncertainty." I averted my eyes. "During the time I have been in contact with the King he has impressed me as being utterly, almost transcendentally unselfish. So unselfish, so abstracted, that he's like a — just a blank!"

"That's only how you see it. Maybe you read it into him. The psychos say he's no emotion, and selfishness is a kind of emotion."

"Is it? Well, that's just what I mean. But he seems — humane, for all that. Considerate, though it's difficult for him."

He wasn't much impressed. "Yeah. Remember that whatever substitutes for emotion in him might have some of its outward effects. And remember, he's not the only outworlder on this planet. He doesn't seem so considerate towards Brazil."

Hotch rose and prepared to leave. "If you survive the rebellion, I'll string you up as a traitor."

"All right!" I answered, suddenly irritable. "I know."

But when Hotch did get moving, I was surprised at the power he had gained for himself in the community. He knew exactly how to accentuate the irritating qualities of the invader, and he did it mercilessly.

Some of the incidents seemed ridiculous: Such as when alien officials began to organise the war effort with complete disregard for some of the things the nation took to be necessities — entertainment, leisure, and so on. The contents of art galleries and museums were burned to make way for weapons shops. Cinemas were converted into automatic factories, and all television transmissions ceased. Don't get the idea that the King and his men are all tyrannical automata. They just didn't see any reason for not throwing away priceless paintings, and never thought to look for one.

Affairs might have progressed more satisfactorily if the set-up had been less democratic. Aware of his poor understanding, the King had appointed a sort of double government. The first, from which issued the prime directive, consisted of his own men in key positions throughout the land, though actually their power had peculiar limitations. The second government was a human representation of the aboriginal populace, which in larger matters was still obliged to gain the King's spoken permission.

The King used to listen very intently to the petitions and pseudo-emotional barrages which this absurd body placed before him — for they were by no means co-operative — and the meetings nearly always ended in bewilderment. During Sorn's day it would have been different: he could have got rid of them in five minutes.

Those men caused chaos, and cost the country many lives in the Brazilian war which shortly followed. After Hotch gained control over them, they were openly the King's enemies. He didn't know it, of course, and now that it's all finished I often wish I had warned him.

I remember the time they came to him and demanded a national working week of twenty-five hours. This was just after the King's men had innocently tried to institute a sixty-hour working week, and had necessarily been restrained.

The petitioners knew how impossible it was; they were just trying to make trouble.

The King received them amid the sparse trappings of his Court. A few of his aides were about, and a few human advisers. And I, of course, was close at hand.

He listened to the petition in silence, his jewel eyes glinting softly in the subdued light. When it was over he paused. Then he lifted his head and asked for help.

"Advise me," he said to everyone present.

But the hostile influences in the hall were so great that all those who might have helped him shrugged their shoulders. That was the way things were. I said nothing.

"If the proposal is carried out," the King told the ministers, "current programmes will not go through."

He tried to reject the idea, but they amazingly refused to let it be rejected. They threatened and intimidated, and one gentleman began to talk hypocritically about the will and welfare of the people. Naturally there was no response: the King was not equipped. He surveyed the hall again. "He who can solve this problem, come forward."

There was a lethargic, apathetic suspension. The aliens were immobile, like hard brilliant statues, observing these dangerous events as if with the asceticism of stone. Then there was more shrugging of shoulders.

It speaks for the leniency of the extraterrestrials that this could happen at all. Among human royalty, such insolence would bring immediate repercussions. But the mood was contagious, because I didn't volunteer either. Hotch's machinations had a potential, unspoken element of terrorism.

Whether the King realised that advice was being deliberately withheld, I don't know. He called my name and strode to the back of the hall.

I followed his authoritatively gyrating cloak, reluctantly, like a dreading schoolboy. When I reached him, he said: "Smith, it is knowledge common to us both that my thinkings and human thinkings are processes apart. Not even Sorn could have both kinds; but he could translate." He paused for a moment, and then continued with a couple of sentences of the mixed-up talk he had used on Sorn, together with some of the accompanying queer honks and noises. I couldn't follow it. He seemed to realise his mistake, though, for he soon emerged into fairly sensible speech again, like this: "*Honk.* Environs matrix wordy. Int apara; is trying like light to; apara see blind, from total outside is not even potential . . . if you were king, Smith, what would you do?"

"Well," I said, "people have been angered by the impositions made on them recently, and now they're trying to swing the pendulum the other way. Maybe I would compromise and cut the week by about ten hours."

The King drew a sheaf of documents from a voluminous sash pocket and spread them out. One of them had a chart on it, and lists of figures. Producing a small machine with complex surfaces, he made what appeared to be a computation.

I wished I could find some meaning in those cold jewel eyes. "That would interfere with my armament programme," he said. "We must become strong, or the King of Brazil will lay Britain waste."

"But surely it's important not to foster a discontented populace?"

"Important! So often I have heard that word, and cannot understand it. Sometimes it appears to me, Smith, that human psychology is hilly country, while mine is a plain. My throne room contains hints that some things you see as high, and others as low and flat, and the high is more powerful. But for me to travel this country is impossible."

Smart. And it made some sense to me, too, because the King's character often seemed to be composed of absences. He had no sense of crisis, for example. I realised how great his effort must have been to work this out.

"And 'importance'," he continued. "Some mountain top?"

He almost had it. "A big mountain," I said.

For a few seconds I began to get excited and thought that perhaps he was on his way to a semantic break-through. Then I saw where I was wrong. Knowing intellectually that a situation is difficult, and *why* it is difficult, is not much use when it comes to operating in that situation. If the King had fifty million minds laid out in diagram, with all their interconnections (and this is perfectly possible) he would still be no better able to operate. It is far too complex to grasp all at once with the intellect; to be competent in an environment, one must live in it, must be homogeneous with it. The King does not in the proper sense do the former, and is not the latter.

He spent a little while in the throne room, peering through thresholds, no doubt, gazing at pools and wondering about the mountainous. Then he returned and offered the petitioners a concession of ten minutes off the working week. This was the greatest check he thought he could allow on his big industrial drive.

They argued angrily about it, until things grew out of hand and the King ordered me to dismiss them. I had to have it done forcibly. Any one of the alien courtiers could have managed it single-handed by mere show of the weapons on his person, but instead I called in a twenty-man human bodyguard, thinking that to be ejected by their own countrymen might reduce their sense of solidarity.

All the humans of the court exuded uneasiness. But they needn't have worried. To judge by the King and his men, nothing might have happened. They held their positions with that same crystalline intelligence which they had carried through ten years of occupation. I was beginning to learn that this static appearance did not wholly result from unintelligibility, but that they actually maintained a constant internal state irrespective of external conditions. Because of this, they were unaware that the scene that had just been enacted comprised a minor climax. Living in a planar mentality the very idea of climax was not apparent to them.

After the petitioners had gone, the King took me to his private chambers behind the courtroom. "Now is the time for consolidation," he said. "Without Sorn, the governing factions become separated, and the country disintegrates. I must find contact with the indigenous British. Therefore I will strike a closer liaison with you, Smith, my servant. You will follow me around."

He meant that I was to replace Sorn, as well as I could. Making it an official appointment was probably his way of appealing for help.

He had hardly picked the right man for the job, but that was typical of the casual way he operated. Of course, it made my personal position much worse, since I began to feel bad about letting him down. I was caught at the nexus of two opposing forces: even my inaction meant that somebody would profit. Altogether, not a convenient post for a neutral passenger.

Anyway, since the situation had arisen, I decided to be brash and ask some real questions.

"All right," I said, "but for whose sake is this war being fought — Britain's or yours?"

As soon as the words were out of my mouth I felt a little frightened. In the phantasmal human-alien relationship, such earthy examinations were out of place. But the King accepted it.

"I am British," he answered, "and Britain is mine. Ever since I came, our actions are inseparable."

Some factions of the British public would have disagreed with this, but I supposed he meant it in a different way. Perhaps in a way connected with the enigmatically compelling characters and aphorisms that had been erected about the country, like mathematics developed in words instead of numbers. I often suspected that the King had sought to gain power through semantics alone.

Because I was emotionally adrift, I was reckless enough to argue the case. "Well," I said, "without you there would be no war. The Brazilians would never fight without compulsion from their own King, either. I'm not trying to secede from your authority, but resolve my oponion that you and the King of

Brazil are using human nations as instruments . . . in a private quarrel."

For some while he thought about it, placing his hands together. He answered: "When the events of which I and the King of Brazil are a part moved into this region, I descended onto Britain, and he onto Brazil. By the fundamental working of things, I took on the nature of Britain, and Britain in reciprocation became incorporated in the workings of those events. And likewise with the King of Brazil, and with Brazil. These natures, and those events, are not for the time being separables, but included in each other. Therefore it is to defend Britain that I strive, because Britain is harnessed to my section of those outside happenings, and because I am British."

When I had finally sorted out that chunk of pedantry, his claims to nationality sounded like baloney. Then I took into account the slightly supra-sensible evidence of his British character. After a little reflection I realised that he had gone halfway towards giving me an explanation of it.

"What kind of happenings," I wondered, "can they be?"

The King can't smile, and he can't sound wistful, and it's hard for him to convey anything except pure information. But what he said next sounded like the nearest thing to wistfulness he could manage.

"They are very far from your mind," he said, "and from your style of living. They are connected with the colliding galaxies in Cygnus. More than that would be very difficult to tell you. . . ."

There was a pause. I began to see that the King's concern was with something very vast and strange indeed. England was only a detail. . . .

"And those outsiders who took over South Africa. What's their part in this?"

"No direct connection. Events merely chanced to blow this way."

Oddly, the way he said it made me think of how neat the triple invasion had been. In no instance had the borders of neighbouring states been violated, and the unmolested nations had in turn regarded the conquests as internal matters. Events had happened in discreet units, not in an interpenetrating mass as they usually do. The reactions of the entire Terrestrial civilisation had displayed an unearthly flavour. Maybe the incompatibility of alien psychology was not entirely mental. Perhaps in the King's native place not only minds but also events took a different form from those of Earth. What is mentality, anyway, but a complex event? I could imagine a sort of transplanting of natural laws, these three kings, with all their power, bringing with them residual influences of the workings of their own worlds. . . .

It sounded like certain astrological ideas I had once heard, of how on each world everything is different, each world has its own basic identity, and everything on that world partakes of that identity. But it's only astrology.

As the time for war drew nearer, Hotch became more daring. Already he had made himself leader of the unions and fostered general discontent, as well as organising an underground which in some ways, had more control over Britain than the King himself had. But he had a particular ambition, and in furtherance of this he appeared one day at Buckingham Palace.

Quite simply, he intended to do what I had refused to do for him.

He bowed low before the King, ignoring me, and launched into his petition.

"The people of Britain have a long tradition of reliability and capability in war," he proclaimed. "They cannot be treated like children. Unless they are given fighting powers equal to those of the extraterrestrials — for I do not suppose that your own troops will be poorly armed — their morale will relapse and they will be defeated. You will be the psychological murderer of Britain."

When he had finished, he cast a defiant glance at me, then puffed out his barrel chest and waited for a reply.

He had good reason to be afraid. One word from me, and he was finished. I admired his audacity.

I was also astounded at the outrageous way he had made the request, and I was at a loss to know what to do.

I sank onto the throne steps and slipped into a reverie. If I kept silent and showed loyalty to my country I would bring about the downfall of the King.

If I spoke in loyalty to the King, I would bring about the downfall of Hotch.

And really, I couldn't find any loyalty anywhere. I was utterly adrift, as if I didn't exist on the surface of the planet at all. I was like a compass needle which failed to answer to the magnetic field.

"Psychological murderer of Britain," I repeated to myself. I was puzzled at the emotional evocation in that phrase. How could a human administer emotion to the King? But of course, it wasn't really an emotion at all. In the King's eyes the destruction of Britain was to be avoided, and it was this that Hotch was playing on.

Emerging from my drowsy thoughts, I saw Hotch leave. The King had not given an answer. He beckoned to me.

He spoke a few words to me, but I was non-committal. Then I waited outside the throne room, while he spent an hour inside.

He obviously trusted Hotch. When he came out, he called together his full council of eight aliens, four humans and myself, and issued directives for the modification of the war. I say of war, and not of preparations for the war, because plans were now sufficiently advanced for the general outlines of the conflict to be set down on paper. The way the aliens handled a war made it hardly like fighting at all, but like an engineering work or a business project. Everything was decided beforehand; the final outcome was almost incidental.

And so several factories were retooled to produce the new weapons, the military hierarchy readjusted to give humans a greater part, and the focus of the main battle shifted five hundred miles further west. Also, the extrapolated duration of the war was shortened by six months.

Hotch had won. All Britain's industries worked magnificently for three months. They worked for Hotch as they had never worked, even for Sorn.

I felt weary. A child could have seen through Hotch's trick, but the King had been taken in. What went on in his head, after all? What guided him? Did he really care — for anything?

I wondered what Sorn would have thought. But then, I had never known what went on in Sorn's head, either.

The fleet assembled at Plymouth and sailed west into a sunny, choppy Atlantic. The alien-designed ships, which humans called swan-boats, were marshalled into several divisions. They rode high above the water on tripod legs, and bobbed lightly up and down.

Aerial fighting was forbidden by treaty, but there was one aircraft in the fleet, a wonderful blue and gold non-combatant machine where reposed the King, a few personal servants and myself. We drifted a few hundred feet above the pale green watership, matching our speed with theirs.

That speed was slow. I wondered why we had not fitted ourselves out with those steel leviathans of human make, fast battleships and destroyers, which could have traversed the ocean in a few days whereas our journey required most of a month. It's true the graceful swarm looked attractive in the sunlight, but I don't think that was the reason. Or maybe it was a facet of it.

The Brazilians were more conventional in their combat aesthetics. They had steamed slowly out of the Gulf of Mexico to meet us at a location which, paradoxically, had been predetermined without collusion. We were greeted by massive grey warships, heavy with guns. Few innovations appeared to have been introduced into the native ship-building, though I did see one long corvette-shape lifted clean out of the water on multiple hydroplanes.

Fighting began in a casual, restrained manner when the belligerents were about two miles apart. There was not much outward enthusiasm for some hours. Our own ships ranged in size from the very small to the daintily monstrous, and wallowed prettily throughout the enemy fleet, discharging flashes of brilliant light. Our more advanced weapons weren't used much, probably because they would have given us an unfair advantage over the Brazilian natives, who had not had the benefit of Hotch's schemings.

Inside me I felt a dull sickness. All the King's men were gathered here in the Atlantic; this was the obvious time for Hotch's rebellion.

But it would not happen immediately. Hotch was astute enough to realise that even when he was rid of the King he might still have to contend with Brazil, and he wanted to test his future enemy's strength.

The unemphatic activity on the surface of the ocean continued, while one aircraft floated in the air above. The King watched, sometimes from the balcony, sometimes by means of a huge jumble of screens down inside, which showed an impossible montage of the scene viewed from innumerable angles, most of which had no tactical usefulness that I could see. Some were from locations at sea-level, some only gave images of rigging, and there was even one situated a few feet below the surface.

I followed the King around, remembering his warning of the devastation which would ensue from Britain's defeat. "But what will happen if we win?" I asked him.

"Do not be concerned," he told me. "Current events are in the present time, and will be completed with the cessation of the war."

"But something must happen afterwards."

"Subsequent events are not these events." A monstrous swinging pattern, made of bits and pieces of hulls and gunfire, built up mysteriously in the chaos of the screens, and dissolved again. The King turned to go outside.

When he returned, the pattern had begun again, with modifications. I continued: "If you believe that, why do you talk about Britain's welfare?"

He applied himself to watching the screens, still showing no deviation from his norm, in a situation which to a normal man would have been crisis. "All Britain is mine," he said after his normal pause. "Therefore I make arrangements for its protection. This is comprehensible to us both, I think."

He swivelled his head towards me. Why do you enquire in this way, Smith? These questions are not the way to knowledge."

Having been rebuked thus — if a being with a personality like atonal music can be said to rebuke — I too went outside, and peered below. The interpenetrated array seemed suddenly like male and female. Our own more neatly shaped ships moved lightly, while the weighty, pounding Brazilians were more demonstratively aggressive, and even had long gun turrets for symbolism. Some slower part of my mind commented that the female is alleged to be the submissive, receptive part, which our fleet was not; but I dismissed that.

After two hours the outcome still looked indefinite to my mind. But Hotch decided he had seen enough. He acted.

A vessel which hitherto had kept to the outskirts of the battle and taken little part, abruptly opened up its decks and lifted a series of rocket ramps. Three minutes later, the missiles had disappeared into the sky and I guessed what war-heads they carried.

Everything fitted neatly: it was a natural decision on Hotch's part. In such a short time he had not been able to develop transatlantic rockets, and he might never again be this close to the cities of Brazil. I could see him adding it all up in his mind.

Any kind of aeronautics was outlawed, and the Brazilians became enraged. They used their guns with a fury such as I hope never to see again. And I was surprised at how damaging a momentum a few thousand tons of fast-moving steel can acquire. Our own boys were a bit ragged in their defence at first, because they were busy butchering the King's men.

With the new weapons, most of this latter was over in twenty minutes. I went inside, because by now weapons were being directed at the aircraft, and the energies were approaching the limits of its defensive capacity.

The hundred viewpoints adopted by the viewing screens had converted the battle-scene into a flurry too quick for my eyes to follow. The King asked my advice.

My most immediate suggestion was already in effect. Slowly, because the defence screens were draining power, we ascended into the stratosphere. The rest of what I had to say took longer, and was more difficult, but I told it all.

The King made no comment on my confession, but studied the sea. I withdrew into the background, feeling uncomfortable.

The arrangement of vision screens was obsolete now that the battle-plan had been disrupted. Subsidiaries were set up to show the struggle in a simpler form. By the time we came to rest in the upper air, Hotch had rallied his navy and was holding his own in a suddenly bitter engagement.

The King ordered other screens to be focused on Brazil. He still did not look at me.

After he had watched developments for a short time, he decided to meditate in solitude, as was his habit. I don't know whether it was carelessness or simple ignorance, but without a pause he opened the door and stepped onto the outside balcony.

Fortunately, the door opened and closed like a shutter; the air replenishers worked very swiftly, and the air density was seriously low for less than a second. Even so, it was very unpleasant.

Emerging from the experience, I saw the King standing pensively outside in the partial vacuum of the upper air. I swore with surprise: it was hot out there, and even the sunlight shining through the filtered windows was more than I could tolerate.

When he returned, he was considerate enough to use another door.

By this time the monitor screens had detected the squadrons of bombers rising in retaliation from Brazil's devastated cities. The etiquette of the old war was abandoned, and there was no doubt that they too carried the nuclear weapons illegally employed by Hotch.

The King observed: "When those bombers reach their delivery area in a few hours' time, most of Britain's fighting power will still be a month away in the Western Atlantic. Perhaps the islands should be warned to prepare what defences they have." His gem eyes lifted. "What do you say, Smith?"

"Of course they must be warned!" I replied quickly. "There is still an air defence — Hotch has kept the old skills alive. But he may not have expected such quick reprisals, and early interception is essential."

"I see. This man Hotch seems a skilful organiser, Smith, and would be needed in London." With interest, he watched the drive and ferocity of the action on the sea-scape. "Which is his ship?"

I pointed out the large swan-boat on which I believed Hotch to be present. Too suddenly for our arrival to be anticipated, we dropped from the sky. The servants of the King conducted a lightning raid which made a captive of Hotch with thirty per cent casualties.

We had been absent from the stratosphere for two minutes and forty-five seconds.

Hotch himself wasn't impressed. He accused me of bad timing. "You may be right," I said, and told him the story.

If he was surprised he didn't show it. He raised his eyebrows, but that was all. No matter how grave the situation might be, Hotch wouldn't let it show.

"It's a native war from now on," he acclaimed. "There's not an alien left in either fleet."

"You mean the Brazilians rebelled too?"

"I wish they would! The green bosses hopped it and left them to it."

The King offered to put Hotch down at Buckingham Palace, the centre of all the official machinery. Hotch greeted the suggestion with scorn.

"That stuff's no good to me," he said. "Put me down at my headquarters in Balham. That's the only chance of getting our fighter planes in the air."

This we did. The pilots had already set the aircraft in silent motion through the stratosphere, and within an hour we slanted downwards and flashed the remaining five hundred miles to England.

London was peaceful as we hovered above it three hours in advance of the raiders. Only Hotch's impatient energy indicated the air of urgency it would shortly assume.

But what happened on Earth after that, I don't know. We went into space, so I have only a casual interest.

It's like this: the King showed me space.

To see it with the bare eyes is enough, but on the King's set of multi- and null-viewpoint vision screens it really gets hammered in. And what gets knocked into you is this: nothing matters. Nothing is big enough to matter. It's as simple as that.

However big a thing is, it just isn't big enough. For when you see the size of totality — I begin to understand now why the King, who has seen it all the time, is as he is.

And nothing is important. There is only a stratified universe, with some things more powerful than others. That's what makes us think they are important — they're more powerful, but that's all. And the most powerful is no more significant than the least.

You may wonder, then, why the King bothers with such trivial affairs as Britain. That's easy.

When I was a young man, I thought a lot of myself. I thought myself valuable, if only to myself. And, once, I began to wonder just how much it would take for me to sacrifice my life, whether if it came to it I would sacrifice myself for a less intelligent, less worthwhile life than my own. But now I see the sacrifice for what it is: simply one insignificance for another insignificance. It's an easy trade. So the King, who has ranged over a dozen galaxies, has lost his war, his army, and risks even his own life, for Britain's sake. It's all too tiny even to hesitate over. He did what he could: how could he do anything else?

Like the King, I am quickly becoming incapable of judgement. But before it goes altogether, I will say this of you, Hotch: It was a low trick you played on the King. A low, dirty trick to play on a good man.

An Overload

They always met by television. Usually it was once every three months. Always it was with much argument. The meeting chamber, though in a secret location and possessing neither door nor windows, had a dignity wholly befitting its role. Its walls were panelled with ancient, grained oak. The floor was deeply carpeted. Mahogany, another near-extinct and much-valued wood, had been used to make the incomparable boardroom table. On its dark shining surface rested six holo television sets arranged so that the stage-screen of each could view all the others.

Today Sinatra was sour. "You know what I think?" he said, stubbing out a cigarette with a derisory gesture. "I'll tell you: I think this thing's not worth talking about."

Bogart gave a typical puzzled frown, his shrewd preoccupied eyes shifting from side to side as he spoke. "If it bothers us it's worth talking about. This guy Karnak seems to be making progress."

"Aw, nuts." Sinatra's blue and disturbingly hot eyes came to rest on Bogart; his lean face was sardonic, his wide mouth wryly twisted. "He's just another bum."

"Remember Reagan," Bogart continued defensively. "Not so long ago he was sitting right here with us. Until, that is, he got over confident, began over-extending, thinking he could get into SupraBurgh. Suddenly there he was, dying on a rising curve."

Cagney shook his head sadly. "Not even viable for the voters any more."

"I remember what it was like seeing him go. Spooky."

Sinatra chuckled. "Sure I remember Reagan. He had it coming: that's what you get for messing with SupraBurgh. None of us will make that mistake again." He paused reflectively, a cigarette held midway to his lips. "You know, sometimes when I go over my piece of his holdings I think I can hear him whining through the circuits."

"We all can," Raft said shortly, in a flat gravelly voice,

"because we all took a piece of him. I like to think he'd be happy knowing we profited by his fall. But I'd also like to think it can't happen to me." The grisly crack came deadpan out of Raft's poker face. Cagney and Schultz grinned slightly.

"It can't," Sinatra affirmed. "We've got things sewn up too tight now."

"If we stick together it can't," Bogart corrected. "Maybe Reagan wouldn't have hit the dust if some of you guys hadn't been so quick to pull the rug from under him."

"Yeah, okay, that's right," said Sinatra hastily, cutting off the angry protests from the others. "If things get rough we stick together, okay? Karnak has only taken one ward so far. That's a long way from being a threat. Now let's get on to other business. Take a look at this."

An oak panel slid aside to reveal a holo stage. A simple sine wave moved slowly across it, was momentarily transformed into a stationary bell-shaped probability curve, and then broke up into a dizzying sequence of graph curves, the axes standing out in contrasting colours.

Filling in with a terse commentary, Sinatra watched the flickering curves calmly. "I guess you can get the picture from this. Intricative Products, working in harness with Stylic Access Services, are on their way to capturing the whole of the design-percept market. This will mean that a lot of smaller businesses not currently in syn will be brought in syn. Now here are the production breakdowns leading through to maybe four months' time."

A new set of dancing, swinging curves appeared, at the rate of two a second. Sinatra held one of them for a few moments.

"Here's the aesthetic/inventive index of the stuff we'll be releasing in a short while now."

The display went into motion again. "I'm giving you the picture because I don't want you to go upsetting the caper. Putting smaller people out of business isn't just a matter of seizing their markets, it's also a matter of denying them operating capital. Now for a short while my activities will create something of a vacuum in the field of property in-decor, an associated area of commerce. Some of you, particularly Lancaster and Cagney, might be tempted to pour money into it. But it's a fact that capital flows easily from property in-decor to design-percept. So back off, willya? Otherwise you might louse up my operation."

The display ended and the holo stage showed an indefinite empty depth, tinted pale lilac.

Raft grunted.

"And why should we want to do you such a favour?" he asked.

"Oh, I wouldn't ask you to do it as a favour," Sinatra replied mildly. "Just so as to be open and above board, I'll show you the current programme of another of my properties, Up-Supra-Burgh Road Mercantile." The holo started up again, dazzling in its rapid disclosure of professional information. "If this doesn't give some of you cardiac arrest, it should. It shows just how ready I am to start forcing the pace in the Up-SupraBurgh outlets. Before long I could — if I wanted — squeeze you out of some of these routes altogether. You wouldn't like that. So it's a straight deal. I'll back off SupraBurgh if you'll back off property in-decor."

"We all agreed not to try to monopolise the upgoing routes," Raft said without expression.

"I hope I won't have to," Sinatra told him affably.

"What are you trying to put over on us, Frank?" It was Lancaster who spoke now, anger edging into his softly incisive, muscular voice. "Let's take another look at that crap you just handed us." And he projected Sinatra's own graphs back on the wall holo. "It's kind of funny how it compares with what *I'm* doing in Up-SupraBurgh."

More curves, Lancaster's graphs this time, glittered out at them in quick succession, like spitting out pips. "Get that, Frank? Put it together, all of you. Frank is telling us he and I share seventy-three per cent of the upgoing trade. Add your own business to it, and how do you explain a total of *one hundred and eighteen* per cent?"

"Are you calling me a liar, you — ?" Sinatra lunged towards Lancaster, an incredulous, outraged look on his face. He gesticulated at the wall holo. *"This* is how you put those figures together, and *this* is what it means in a year's time." And while he spoke he shot an even faster display at the holo stage.

Cagney spoke up lazily. "Frank is always talking about bringing out-of-syn business into syn. What for? I notice most of these properties seem to wind up in his own stable. What are you gonna do, Frank? Bring the whole of UnderMegapolis into syn?"

"Sure!" bellowed Sinatra. "I'd like it that way!"

Bogart lit a cigar, blowing aromatic smoke that appeared to drift out of the holo and into the room. "Great," he observed. "So whenever anything goes wrong the voters have nobody to blame but us."

"Yeah, that would be great all right, wouldn't it?" Lancaster echoed.

There was a moment's silence. Sinatra calmed himself, glancing around him at the hexagon of power that made up the syndicate: himself, Bogart, Lancaster, Raft, Cagney, and on Sinatra's left, Schultz, a furtive, dour figure who spoke but seldom.

"Nothing ever does go wrong in the outfits *I* run," he declared.

"Nothing except the credibility of your own accounts," Lancaster answered tightly. "Let's put your figures to the test, Frank. How about if we analyse them *this* way?"

The argument raged back and forth. The graph displays flickered so fast as to be on the edge of visibility, merging into a rainbow blur.

As the vert-tube dropped for mile after mile the golden glitter of SupraBurgh vanished. There was a brief, limbo-like transit through the abandoned area of Central Authority; then Obsier was plunged deep into the planet and entered UnderMegapolis.

Forms, hues and vistas slid into one another as the level-within-level mightiness of Obsier's home supercity swung past. This was the kind of immensity, the kind of power, he was familiar with: ancient yet eternally modern, below reach of the sun, a deep thrusting place of hegemonies. It impressed him anew to return to it in this fashion, falling like a bullet in the v-tube.

Obsier had to admit that SupraBurgh, perched above it, using it as a foundation, was stunning — but in a way that was alien and frightening, spreading up and out like a great tree to glory in the sunlight that struck, unnaturally to Obsier's mind, out of a naked sky. Equally unnatural were the interstellar ships that occasionally arrived to settle like birds in that tree, or, again like birds, winged up to depart from it. The spectacle of those vanishing craft was most unnerving; Obsier found it a tremendous relief to escape from that oppressive feeling of vast expanses of air and sunlight.

It was even a relief, despite the failure of his mission, to know that he had seen SupraBurgh's horrors for the last time. Thankfully blotting out the repellent images from his mind, Obsier thought it almost incredible to reflect that at their founding the two conurbations had been governed as a single city: Megapolis; and that only gradually had the functions of Central Authority withered away as disparate physical environments (one underground, one up in the air) inevitably gave rise to divergent social and economic forms: divergent traditions, divergent languages, and finally divergent governments.

Just how long ago that had been could be judged from the fact that the deserted section where Central Authority had functioned (even now its empty corridors were left tactfully undisturbed by both sides) had originally been at ground level and now was half a mile into the Earth. Megapolis, a huge plug drilled into the planet's skin, had sunk by its own weight. Its floor was now so close to the mohorivic discontinuity that UnderMegapolis was able to tap heat from the basaltic mantle beneath.

The v-tube decelerated fiercely, and shortly came to a halt. Ahead, the greenish radiance of serried strip-lights stretched away into the distance. Clutching a sheaf of documents, Obsier made his way towards a nearby Schultz In-Town Transit Services station.

"So they wouldn't wear it?" Mettick asked.

"No," Obsier told him. "And I guess that will be my last trip to SupraBurgh. In a way I'm glad of it. I don't like it up there."

"Did you get *any* offers out of them?"

"Not one. They're not interested."

"Is it because they don't use ipse holo up there?"

"That's true, they don't, but I don't think that's it. They must have all the technical data available. We could get it built ourselves, perhaps, if they'd fund it. They're just not interested. They don't want to know us down here."

"It's hard to understand. If an offer like that was made to any of the syn bosses they'd grab it like an alligator grabbing meat."

"Their system is different from ours. They're not democratic, and not oligarchic. They have some sort of elitist social structure. They act as though we don't exist. . . ."

Mettick shrugged. "*We* act as though *they* don't exist. . . . You know why I think they won't play? They're afraid of the syn. Do you think that's right?"

Obsier placed his papers in a desk drawer. "Maybe. It's more likely that they have an agreement with them: no interference in each other's pitch. But it's more than that, too. There's a difference in mentality we could never cross. It was a mistake to think we could."

"Yes, I suppose so." Mettick was reflective for a moment. "Well, we'd better tell Karnak."

They went through a door into an inner office where the campaign team was working. Girls with tabulators were feeding in data for the prediction polls. If Karnak could gain this second ward in the imminent local election he would be riding high.

Mettick paused by the supervisor's desk. "Is the Man in?"

She nodded. Mettick knocked on a door and they entered. Karnak was surrounded by his aides, hard at it as usual.

Karnak was the epitome of the tireless, hard-working politician. When he wasn't actively campaigning he was busy on some side project, as now: trying to analyse the syn — the vast business syndicate whose bosses ruled UnderMegapolis by reason of holding all the seats on the Magisterial Council. To gain such a seat for himself — to be a magister — and break the syn's monopoly was his life's ambition.

A small holo screen was reeling off a list of the properties owned by one of the syn tycoons, Sinatra. Momentarily Obsier let his eye run through the exotic language of present-day business: Intricative Products; Non-Linear Machinations Composited; Stylic Access Services; Up-SupraBurgh Road Mercantile; Andromatic Enterprises; Andromatic On-Return Hook-Up . . . and on and on.

Karnack killed the holo and turned to face the newcomers. Straight away Obsier could feel the man's charisma. The force of it struck him anew every time he came into Karnak's presence, like an enveloping field of magnetism. That magnetism was a necessary prerequisite: all the magisters had it.

"I'm sorry," Obsier said immediately. "SupraBurgh won't finance an ipse holo set-up."

Karnak took the news as a great man should. He paced the room, his long-jawed, handsome features briefly turned inward in concentration. "Okay, so that avenue is closed," he said firmly. "We shall just have to find another way."

He stopped in front of the campaign charts that covered one wall. "I'm confident we're going to win this ward. That will give me the right to contest the supercity general election in a month's time."

He swung round to face them again. "But let's not kid ourselves: ipse holo is the key to success on a supercity scale. We can do quite a lot with ordinary holo in a ward election, because it can be backed up with personal appearances. But in a population of a hundred million, where holocom is of the essence—" He made a gesture. "Just imagine me coming over like a shadow and Sinatra or Lancaster sitting right there in the room, with all the spiel they're able to put over."

There was a short silence. "If we sank all our assets maybe we could come up with the needed amount, though I doubt it," one of the aides said tentatively. "But we'd be really out on a limb."

Karnak nodded.

"It isn't just that," Mettick injected. "There's the technical data too. I've done some research in the library. It isn't all there: the syn has kept some of it private. Which means that businesses capable of artifactoring ipse equipment are all syn-owned, too."

Another of the aides slapped his fist in his palm. "They've really got it sewn up," he said savagely.

"It's getting so they're sewing everything up," said the aide who had first spoken. The rate of absorption of businesses taken over by the syndicate — brought into syn, in the jargon — was one of the things Karnak's team liked to grouse about.

"*Right*: this is what we'll do," said Karnak, cutting into their talk like a hand cutting through smoke. Their attention snapped on to him: the Man had made a Decision.

"We'll make an election issue of it, starting as of right now," he told them. "The syn has a monopoly of ipse holo. That's undemocratic — it should be available to *all* magisterial candidates. We'll push the idea that the owners of ipse equipment should lease it, or even loan it, to anyone on the elective list. Wrap it up in a package — the ever-increasing hold the syn is having on our lives, the stricture on routes to the top in our society, and so forth. But press it hard."

"Hmm." An aide nodded thoughtfully. "The syn's reply will be that we are trying to subvert the plutocratic principle — anybody not successful enough to have their own ipse apparatus doesn't deserve to have it, dig? But it will definitely put them on the defensive. They might even have to let us use their ipse to avoid looking mean and brutish. It's good, K, it's good." He nodded again, enthusiastically.

"Maximum publicity," Karnak intoned. "Get to work on it, there isn't much time." He waved his arms; the aides began to leave the room. "You two stay," he said to Obsier and Mettick. "I've another little job for you."

When the three of them were alone Karnak settled himself in his plush black swivel chair and leaned back, placing his finger-tips together.

"Did you have a hard time in SupraBurgh?" he asked, shooting a glance at Obsier.

Obsier shrugged. "A little."

"It makes me wonder — you know, everything's so different up above. If it changes your outlook at all when you come back."

Obsier frowned. The question was interesting. He had been to SupraBurgh five times in all, each time with a view to setting up some kind of arrangement for Karnak. He had tried to identify the unnamed feelings it stirred up in him, but had always failed.

"It gives you an outside view of UnderMegapolis, as it were," he said, "but that soon fades once you return. Frankly I wouldn't advise anyone to make the trip."

"So it *does* change you?" Mettick asked.

"Well, it arouses peculiar sensations, like ideas that drift through your mind. As if you're resentful that — that we're living down here, subterranean, and can't get out, while they're. . . ."

The other two looked at him in blank incomprehension, as if he had suddenly begun to speak gibberish.

"But it's just some sort of illusion, I guess," he resumed. "Some of the things you see in SupraBurgh would unnerve anyone. I saw an interstellar ship taking off once, just disappearing up and up into the blue sky without limit—" He broke off, attacked by sudden nausea.

"My God," said Mettick quietly.

"It was too much," Obsier said. "Luckily I had tranquillisers. I was under sedation for six hours."

There was an embarrassed silence at this description of foreign perversions. Karnak changed the subject.

"Well, you can forget all about that now. But I appreciate your sacrifices, I truly do. I wouldn't relish going up there myself. Now to more immediate matters. Our campaign for the use of ipse holo will probably turn out to be the most crucial issue of recent times. You and Mettick make a good team, especially where historical research is concerned. I'd like you to spend some time in the library."

"What are we supposed to be looking for?"

Karnak placed his hands flat on the desk top, his expression distant, slightly puzzled. "I just can't help feeling there's an angle on the syn bosses we could use. I've got an itch up here." He tapped his cranium. "The trouble is, I don't know what it is. Do you realise how hard it is to get close to the syn bosses datawise?"

"They are shielded, naturally," Obsier admitted. "That makes sense. But there are the official biographies."

"Yes, detailed but . . . artificial, somehow. Business, business, business. One long story of public service, private life coming off second best."

"It would be hard to sort out the man from the commercial empire in the jobs they are doing." Mettick pointed out.

"True, boys, true. You know, I've spent hours studying their holocom talks. After a while I get the feel of their style. You know something? It's as if they've all been to the same school. There's something in their approach to spiel that's the same in each of them, despite their being such distinctive characters."

Obsier and Mettick looked at one another. "Perhaps they've been coached by the same expert," Mettick suggested.

"Except Schultz," Karnak added. "He's different. But of course he doesn't appear on holo nearly as much as the others. He rides in on Sinatra's ticket, everybody knows that. And his network is a subsidiary of Sinatra's, we know that too. As a matter of fact if I get on the magisterial council it's Schultz I expect to be replacing."

Obsier mulled it over but came up with nothing.

"Just give your imagination free play and browse around. Probably you won't come up with anything, but again you might." Karnak smiled ruefully. "We'll soon be in the thick of it. This is a mountain we're tackling, and it's as well to know all the slopes."

Cybration.

Cybration was the key to modern business.

Cybration was the key to how UnderMegapolis was able to exist.

As the transit pod swept across the supercity advertising flashes swung by and receded like star systems undergoing doppler effect, composing a cityscape of endless dimensions; internal hormones of the business world.

RAFT ENTERPRISES ARE HERE TO SERVE YOU
EX-TYPE INTRACTIONS OFFER 100% BIREFRINGENCE
WANT IT? STYLIC ACCESS *HAS* IT

Having researched the inane selling promotions of an earlier age, Obsier admired modern advertising for its muscular simplicity, its impression of underlying power and reliability. It was functional. It didn't insult the intelligence. And it was effective.

"May as well split into two departments," Mettick was saying. "I'll research the personalities. You go into the technical side."

"Right."

The pod deposited them ten miles from Karnak's headquarters. Ahead of them was the towering frontage of the central library. Obsier left Mettick and went wandering through interminable sepulchral galleries. Eventually he settled down before a terminal in the Useful Hardware section. He ruminated; he had no lead, no idea of what he was looking for.

Idly, for the sake of making a move, he called on a subject.

"CYBRATION: The history of cybration goes back in a realistic sense to the year circa minus 780, when the first genuine cybrators were constructed. The name used for these early machines was 'computer', which was an accurate term since they were in fact little more than high-speed counters. Round about the year minus 700 the term cybration was coined to describe all types of automatic data processing both electronic and laseronic and covering computer, executive and andromatic modes.

"The modern business corporation is largely a cybrated system where personnel are used to fill particular positions requiring 'personalisation'. But for this method UnderMegapolis could not exist, since the complexity of a modern society within a closed environment is beyond the capacity of an individual or group."

Pictures of early computers and later installations. The account continued, becoming increasingly technical. Obsier quickly lost interest. He called on another subject.

"IPSEIC HOLOCOM: The introduction of ipseic transmission must be admitted to be the last word in image reproduction at a distance, unless the waveform transmission of actual physical objects one day becomes possible. The first workable ipseic transmitting apparatus was tested in United Laserelec Laboratories (owned by the now defunct Megac RD Consolidated) in year 421.

"For a number of centuries it had been considered that the standard holo television system provided absolute perfection since it can reproduce images, with full colour and full parallax, that are indistinguishable from the original. United Laserelec drew attention to a deficiency, soon confirmed by psychological tests, that had long been overlooked: holocom, like earlier television systems before it, does not convey charisma. It is easy to ignore someone speaking on an ordinary holo stage, and no display of emotion or insistence on the part of the performer can force attention out of the viewer if he does not feel like giving it.

"It would be simple to attribute this lack to the viewer's knowledge that the performer is not actually present and that he is confronting only an insubstantial image. By means of careful experimentation United Laserelec destroyed this myth. Later it was discovered that 'presence' — the effect of 'being there' that one person has on another — is not a mental supposition but an actual, though subtle, force transmitted between people at short range. Further research showed that this force is an emanation radiated on a frequency of the order of 23 trillion trillion cycles per second. When a transmitter capable of adding this waveform to the normal holocom waveband was developed it was found that the transmitted image of a person carried the full force of his presence. It achieved *ipseity*: 'he himself'.

"Ipseic holocom has not come into general use. Although the modifications enabling an ordinary holo receiver to pick up ipseity are inexpensive — and in fact all holo sets are now so adapted — the cost of ipseity transmission is prohibitive. A number of transmitters are owned by the leading conglomerates of UnderMegapolis and are used for political purposes."

Mettick was on a different tack. He had before him the names and images of all six syn leaders — six heads of colossal business conglomerates. He had decided to investigate their family backgrounds.

Surprisingly, although their biographies detailed brief family histories in each case, these families were difficult to track down. Accordingly Mettick set the library unit he had been allotted to engage on a lineal-and-likeness hunt.

This was on the third day of his somewhat aimless hit-and-miss tactics. Mettick sat back daydreaming as the unit hummed faintly. He dozed, and awoke with a start to find that the unit had been working for several hours.

There was a quiet clatter as a sheet slid out of the copy slot. Mettick picked it up and stared in bemusement.

A picture of Sinatra stared back at him. It was the same face he knew from many appearances on ipse holo — of all the magisters, Sinatra was probably the most sedulous where his public image was concerned.

Beneath the picture there was a caption. "Frank Sinatra, years circa minus 790-740 (mid 20th Century, contemporary reckoning), singer and actor on 'cinema' (primitive image reproduction system)." There followed a list of dramas in which the long-dead actor had appeared. The library, apparently, had recordings of a few of them.

Mettick shook his head in wonderment. The library unit had found an individual, far back in history, of the same name as the syn boss — and of exactly the same appearance. It was all there: the smiling blue eyes, the lean, rubbery, wide-mouthed face, the mixture of candour and astuteness, the toughness within the geniality. The amazing resemblance could only represent a centuries-ago emergence of very strong family traits that were still active. Sinatra's ancestors *could* be traced, after all.

Mettick folded up the picture and put it in his pocket. Then he leaned towards the terminal and started work again.

Frank Sinatra leaned forward with one arm resting on his knee, sitting relaxed and easy on an upright chair. His life-size form filled the holo stage. In almost the same way, the force of his personality seemed to fill and dominate the entire room.

"Sometimes I think it's possible to lose sight of the obvious, just because it is so obvious," he was saying to the family in the room — the average, healthy-minded family, like the millions of average families listening to Sinatra at this moment, who were watching the holo stage.

Sinatra gave a wry smile. "After all, that's a natural human failing and we are all prey to it, just as everybody sooner or later drops a hammer on his foot. But sometimes a character will come along and try to take advantage of our momentary inattention. He'll suggest it would be a good idea if the principles we've lived by for so long were to be laid aside. Well, whether that's so or not is something the whole city will decide, practising the best-established principle of all, the principle of elective democracy. All I'm saying is that before we accept any changes we should think good and hard about it, because the freedoms and the affluence we enjoy today didn't come about all at once, and they didn't come about by themselves, either. They needed the right system, and that took a long period of time to evolve."

Sinatra stopped speaking. He rubbed his jaw reflectively, more serious now, and then turned his warm, steady eyes back on his spellbound audience. "If this is beginning to sound like a sales pitch, you're dead right— that's just what it is. For my money it will be a sad day for UnderMegapolis if we ever lose sight of the principle of plutocratic democracy. It's given us everything we have, and I believe it's the best system of government there is. It ensures that only men rule who have already proved their ability to administrate on a large scale, their ability to increase wealth and to provide the community with goods and services. It means efficiency, intelligence and prowess in the high offices of government. And UnderMegapolis proves it by voting in the biggest and most successful corporation heads — the captains of industry, if you want to call it that — for term after term. Well, it now appears that there are some people who want to subvert this principle. Not having what it takes to make it big by their own efforts, they see the Magisterial Council as an easy way of getting to the top." Sinatra shook his head sadly. "They just don't know what they'd be letting themselves in for. Running a supercity is no job for anyone who hasn't been right through the whole school. The community would soon realise it, too. But that won't happen, because the voters have got too much sense. They realise what plutocratic democracy is for."

A red light glowed suddenly on the left of the holo stage. A thrill of unbelieving excitement ran through the listening family. Sinatra was inviting a question from *them*!

On-the-spot questioning was a regular feature of the fairly frequent magisterial holocasts, but in a population of a hundred million the chances of the red light going on in *their* household had always seemed, well, infinitesimal.

Sinatra was gazing at the head of the family, waiting. The middle-aged man rose nervously. He could have pressed the "no question" button on the ipseity unit, but he now understood why almost no one ever did. It would have been an insult to so commanding a presence.

"I have a question, sir. Why not let the new candidate, Karnak, use ipse holo if he wants to? It doesn't mean we're going to vote for him, but I can't see any reason why he shouldn't."

Sinatra's eyes clouded over ever so slightly. "There isn't any reason why he shouldn't use it," he said. "Who's stopping him? But he's not much of a candidate if he wants it handed to him on a plate. That's not how I got *my* equipment, and I didn't go around asking for anyone else's, either."

The family head nodded. It made sense. A man ought to be able to stand on his own feet, especially if he was to help rule UnderMegapolis. But a half-frown remained on his face.

Mutely the darkly shining mahogany reflected six holo images in agitated altercation. Raft took the lead, arguing in clipped, deadpan statements, deriding his colleagues' concern.

Sinatra, for once, seemed shaken, however. "I've changed my mind, something's gotta be done. I was on ipse tonight. You know what ninety per cent of the questions I got were? Why don't we put ipse holo at Karnak's disposal?"

"Nobody asked me that when I went on yesterday," Raft said.

Sinatra's face twisted sardonically. "You don't have a sympathetic manner."

"They'd have got a short answer if they had. The voters admire a guy who's tough but straight."

Cagney turned to look directly at Sinatra, his head tilted calculatingly. "What gives with this Karnak? What's his secret?"

Sinatra raised two fingers placed together. "He's got *it*. Ipseity. Charisma."

"Huh-huh. He's got ipseity, huh? So how's he going to put it over, huh?" Cagney chuckled. "On ipse holo, maybe?"

"Come together, you guys!" Sinatra pleaded. "We can't afford to let this kind of situation develop any further. You never know what it can do in future generations."

Lancaster clenched his fists and raised his face, lips drawn back over strong white teeth. He spoke in a voice that was low and intense, little more than a muscular whisper. "I say when you are threatened, *strike*! We should kill, kill, *kill*!"

"No!" Sinatra yelled. "We agreed before: no assassinations."

"Say," said Bogart suddenly, looking sidewise at Schultz as if hit by a crafty inspiration. "What if this Karnak guy *did* become a magister? Schultz is the one who'd get pushed out, that's for sure. We can do without him. Karnak wouldn't last long anyhow."

"No!" Schultz protested hoarsely.

"Leave Schultz alone!" Sinatra ordered loudly. "He's my buddy." But he, too, looked at Schultz speculatively.

A shiver ran through the room and the holo images flickered and seemed about to melt into something indefinable.

"One sign of trouble and you're all falling apart," Raft said disgustedly. "Sometimes I think I'm in crummy company. If you're so steamed up about it, let Karnak put himself on ipse. What does it matter? Let him take the consequences."

They all looked at one another, considering.

"Fact Number One: UnderMegapolis is run on personal charisma," said Mettick. "It's as real as the electricity in your holo set. And I'll tell you something I've found out that shows just how seriously the syn leaders themselves take it. Every one of them has onput recognition gates on his comlines, to stop the others from beaming their images into his conglomerates. They're afraid someone will subvert their managers by sheer charge of personality."

"Isn't that overcautious?"

"Not at all. One of their regular tactics is to call a non-syn enterprise and start giving orders to the underlings. You'd be surprised how often those orders are obeyed."

A disturbing picture formed in Obsier's mind of distrust and conspiracy in the highest echelon. "Then how do they communicate with one another?"

"Only privately, by direct face-to-face holo."

"You know, when I'm with Karnak I feel confidence in him," Obsier pondered slowly, "but when I see one of the syn bosses on holo I don't feel so sure of him, and I almost feel like giving up. Do you really think he has enough personal charge?"

"Only one person in millions has as much, but honestly I don't know. I keep trying to imagine how he'd make out in a confronation with Lancaster, say, or Raft. Those people have so much of it, it's frightening — almost unnatural. Not to speak of their having a monopoly of it, in supercity terms, since only they can use ipseity apparatus."

"Not any more. Haven't you heard? The syn has relented. Karnak is going on ipse holo tonight."

Mettick's quest for a believable human profile to the syn bosses had led him into labyrinths of the library that had been unpaced for decades. He walked through dusty low-vaulted galleries past rows of disused terminal units, each of which gave access to some obscure facet of the past. He knew the answer was here somewhere. The facts he had discovered so far were too puzzling, too extraordinary, not to have an answer.

There had been some fascinating sidelines, too, in his search into the past. Even as far back as the minus eighth century there seemed to have been some sort of premonition of more modern history. Mettick had found references to "the withering away of the state" and "the abolition of central authority" that was supposed to come about in the future. He wondered how the ancients could have guessed about the fate of the empty government levels that separated UnderMegapolis from SupraBurgh.

An age-old silence enveloped him. The nearest girl librarian was at least half a mile away, in the better-frequented upper floors. Mettick consulted some reference numbers on a list he carried and keyed on one of the terminal units. An ancient "cinema" comedy began to unreel, fascinating him with its extraordinary grimaces and quite ugly songs. He abandoned the unit after a couple of minutes and wandered on.

He entered a side passage where the lighting, for some unknown reason, was dimmer. To his amazement the material of the walls gave way to stone and wood in archaic, rotting panels. And while he stood there one of those panels gave a little squeak and swung open.

Behind it was a flat glass screen with a picture on it. Mettick had difficulty in recognising the image at first: it was not in holo but flat. There was something else wrong with it, too: it was made up, unnaturally, of only two colours, white and greyish black in various tones.

The picture had a graininess that, peering closer, he saw resulted from its being composed of hundreds of parallel horizontal lines. But, when he finally recognised what it was, he jumped back in shock.

It was the face of Magister Dutch Schultz.

He began to tremble and then calmed himself as he realised that the picture carried no charismatic charge. The screen was some unbelievably primitive kind of television which could not possibly convey ipseity. God knew how old it was — it was a wonder it was still functioning.

"Hello, citizen," Schultz said in a husky voice. "So you're tryin' to find out the truth? Okay, I'll tell you the truth. . . ."

Karnak strode into the transmitting studios feeling ten feet tall. This was to be his night. By the pressure of democracy — *pure* democracy, not the plutocratic variety — the magisters had been forced to concede an elementary right.

The studio producers were deferential. He waited in a cool blue chamber while the announcements were made. Then he was ushered into the transmitting cubicle. In front of him was the holo camera. Around him were the sensors that, with a faint hum, began to pick up his ipseity emanations at a frequency of 23 trillion trillion per second and feed them through the com-lines. . . .

The producer signalled to him through the side of the cubicle. He was on.

"Fellow citizens," he began, "tonight. . . ."

And then the impressions began to hit him. It was merely like a tidal wave at first and he was able to ride with it. But in the next few seconds it became stronger. Millions upon millions of scenes, tens of millions of human consciousnesses, were forcing themselves into *his* consciousness, which like a balloon expanded, expanded, expanded—

And burst.

Sinatra had cornered Schultz in a small, narrow room with drab brown walls. It had no furniture, no means of escape.

"You goddam stool pigeon," Sinatra raged. "You ratted on us all."

"Whaddya want me to do, Frank?" Schultz screamed in terror. "You were gonna bump me off. I could see it coming." He had run and run and fought for his life, but now there was nowhere left to go.

"I put you on the council," Sinatra said, "and if I want it's my right to take you off or do what the hell I like with you."

"No, Frank, no!"

Sinatra leaped at Schultz. His fists smashed into him again and again, throwing him cowering to the floor. Then he attacked him with a crowbar that appeared in his hand, bringing the weapon down in three savage strokes. Soon there was blood everywhere.

Mettick burst into campaign headquarters looking desperate. "Get hold of Karnak," he demanded. "Don't let him go on ipse."

Obsier looked up tiredly. "Why?" he said mildly. "Actually you're too late. Karnak was taken ill at the start of the programme. We're waiting for news now."

Mettick sank down on to a chair. "He's dead, isn't he?"

"Should he be?" Obsier stared at him perplexed. "I hear he's in a coma. We're waiting for the doctor's report."

"He'll be dead," Mettick said in despair.

Suddenly Obsier became alert, matter-of-fact. "Tell me what you found out," he said rapidly.

"Two things, chiefly." Mettick fished in his pocket and came out with a sheaf of pictures. "Take a look at these. They're portraits of world-famous actors living about a thousand years ago. They were known colloquially as 'Hollywood stars'. Notice the resemblance?"

Obsier leafed through them. He saw the familiar, compelling faces of the Magisters of UnderMegapolis, captioned with their names. Burt Lancaster, James Cagney, Humphrey Bogart, and so on. Some were wearing characteristic expressions; others were in strange, surprising poses. Lancaster had his head tilted, favouring the viewer with a most uncharacteristic glossy smile.

"Absolutely incredible!" he exclaimed. "What is it? Some fantastic coincidence of genetic reconstitution? Or — " His voice sank. Unwelcome, irrepressible thoughts were going through his brain. "Or. . . ."

"You've guessed it." Mettick pushed away the pictures and slumped down in his chair. "The change must have come fairly recently, certainly within the last hundred years. The cybration of big business reached a point where human beings were eliminated at the top. The cybration system became the actual, effective owner of the capital."

"Without anyone knowing?"

"Why not? It was so complicated, data processing gives such opportunities for mystery. . . . Besides, it only happened with the five biggest conglomerates — no, six, counting Reagan. Remember him? Each of these conglomerates became the property of a single mass of automatic data processing. Much cleverer, much more efficient than a human being."

"Yes, but why? . . ."

"Don't you see it? There was still the problem of the interface, to use a piece of cybration jargon. The cybrators needed *personae* so as to be able to deal with human beings and to help them find their bearings in a human world. So they went back through history looking for the most charismatic personalities they could find, the ones with greatest mass appeal. There must have been other considerations, too. I mean, the cybrators must have had some kind of affinity — anyway, they found them among the cinema stars of the minus eighth century. And they reconstructed those personalities in their data banks. Totally. You couldn't call those personae puppets by now. The identification must be complete."

"So we're ruled by ghosts," Obsier said woodenly.

"Yes. Or eighth-century Hollywood film stars. Whichever you prefer."

"But on ipse holo they come over . . . they're *real*."

"So what? They generate the ipseity just as they build up a *persona*. That's why they have so much of it. More, probably, than the original film stars had."

"How did you find out all this?"

"Schultz told me. He got in touch with me in the library. He's the odd one out, by the way — he never was a film star but a genuine gangster, the type that the actors were supposed to portray. That's why there are no good pictures of him." He touched a blurred photo of a round, indistinct face. "He wasn't in the original set. Sinatra created him for convenience, to look after some subsidiaries and give him added weight on the council. That's why he chose a real gangster, I guess: it amused him somehow. But something went wrong. Schultz has developed in his own direction, has become separated from Sinatra and wants to break away from him. He tried to do a deal with me; said he'd help me break open the syn. And he told me—" Mettick slammed his fist on the desk. "But too late!"

"Told you what?" Obsier pressed anxiously, leaning forward.

"About ipse holo! The real reason why it's never used, except by the syn. It's a killer!"

"What are you talking about?" Obsier stared at him.

"Ipseity transmission is a reciprocal process. It can't work one way. The sender becomes aware of the receiver, too. When you're broadcasting to millions of people they not only become aware of *your* presence, but you at the same time receive the presence of all those millions. The consciousness can't take it. It overloads."

Noting the other's expression, Mettick continued:

"That datum has been removed from the library. Everybody thinks it's just too expensive, not too dangerous."

"But the syn bosses. They don't —"

"They're not alive!" cut in Mettick savagely. "They're what you said, ghosts animated by electricity. You know that 'question time' technique they use on ipse holo? I learned today they handle thousands of questions at the same time, calculated on a scatter pattern so nobody ever suspects anything."

They sat silently for a while. Finally Obsier forced his brain into motion again.

"Maybe this is the beginning of something new after all," he said uneasily. "If Schultz really is going to help break the syn, it will all have been worth it."

"I don't think there's any hope there. Schultz can't be too bright, or he wouldn't have left it so late to warn me. And remember, he's really part of Sinatra. He'll never be able to hide what he's done. I imagine the Schultz *persona* has been washed right down the drain by now."

"And where does that leave us? We're the ones who know."

"We're in a spot. It's no good thinking anybody can fight the syndicate. They've got the means to power nobody else can use: ipseic holocom. We could go into hiding but they'd always be able to find us. We might be able to flee to SupraBurgh but —" He shuddered.

"I can't face SupraBurgh," said Obsier definitely, thinking of the obscene sight of a starship riding up into the endless blue.

"No, me neither. And that's something else we have to thank them for—"

The desk holo chimed behind Obsier. He turned, spoke quietly to it, then swung back to Mettick.

"Karnak's dead."

"The syndicate murdered him by his own hand."

"Yes."

Again they were silent, until Obsier said sombrely, "What were you saying about SupraBurgh?"

"There's one thing that obsesses the syn. The stars. They have a psychotic resentment about them. Remember Reagan? They wiped him out, too. He was the last one to make a bid for the stars, which was what he was doing when he tried to extend into SupraBurgh. But he couldn't make it and they know they can never make it, either. They're machines, imprisoned down here and keyed into this subterranean supercity. So they hate the stars and the open sky. And that's why, over the generations, they've conditioned us to hate them too."

Mutation Planet

Filled with ominous mutterings, troubled by ground-trembling rumblings, the vast and brooding landscape stretched all around in endless darkness and gloom. Across this landscape the mountainous form of *Dominus* moved at speed, a massed, heavy shadow darker than the gloom itself, sullenly majestic, possessing total power. Above him the opaque sky, lurid and oppressively close, intermittently flared and discharged sheets of lightning that were engulfed in the distant hills. In the instant before some creature fed on the electric glare the dimness would be relieved momentarily, outlining uneven expanses of near-barren soil. *Dominus*, however, took no sensory advantage of these flashes; his inputs covered a wider, more reliable range of impressions.

As he sped through his domain he scattered genetic materials to either side of him to dampen down evolutionary activity, so ensuring that no lifeform would arise that could inconvenience him or interfere with the roadway over which he moved. This roadway, built by himself as one of the main instruments of his control over his environment, spanned the whole eight thousand miles of the planet's single continent, and was a uniform quarter of a mile wide; at irregular intervals side roads diverged into the larger peninsulas. Since the substance of the roadbed was quasi-organic, having been extruded by organs he possessed for that purpose, *Dominus* could, moreover, sense instantly any attack, damage, or unacceptable occurrence taking place on any part of it.

After leaving the interminable plain the road undulated over a series of hills, clinging always to the profile of the land, and swept down into a gigantic bowl-like valley. Here the gloom took on the darkness of a pit, but lifeforms were more copious. By the light of the flickering lightning flashes, or by that of the more diffuse radiations employed by *Dominus*, they could be seen skulking out there in the valley, a scattering of unique shapes. They were absolutely motionless, since none dared to move while

Dominus passed by. Leagues further afield lights winked and radio pulses beamed out as the more powerful entities living up the slopes of the valley signalled their submission.

Dominus dosed the valley heavily with genetic mist, then surged up the opposite wall. As he swept over onto a table-land a highly-charged lightning bolt came sizzling down, very close; he caught it in one of his conductors and stored the charge in his accumulators. It was then, while he raced away from the valley, that his radar sense spotted an unidentifiable object descending through the cloud blanket. Puzzled, *Dominus* slowed down to scarcely a hundred miles per hour. This was the first unusual event for several millennia. He could not, at first, account for it.

The strangeness lay in the fact that the object was so large: not very much smaller than *Dominus* himself. (Its shape, though new to him, was of no account — even at the low, controlled level of mutation he permitted thousands of different lifeforms continued to evolve.) Also, it was moving through the air without the visible benefit of wings of any kind. Come to that, a creature of such bulk could not be lifted by wings at all.

Where had it evolved? In the sky? Most unlikely. The plethora of flying forms that had once spent their lives winging through the black, static-drenched cloud layer had almost — thanks to *Dominus* — died out. Over the ages his mutation-damping mist, rising on the winds, had accumulated there, and without a steady mutation rate the flying forms had been unable to survive the ravages of their environment and each other.

Then from where? Some part of the continent receiving only scant surveillance from *Dominus*? He was inclined to doubt this also. The entity he observed could not have developed without many generations of mutation, which would have come to his notice before now.

Neither was the ocean any more likely a source. True, *Dominus* carried out no surveillance there. But a great deal of genetic experience was required to survive on the land surface. Emergent amphibia lacked that experience and were unable to gain a foothold. For that reason oceanic evolution seemed to have resigned itself to a purely submarine existence.

One other possibility remained: the emptiness beyond the atmospheric covering. For *Dominus* this possibility was theoretical only, carrying no emotional ambience. Up to now *this* world had absorbed his psychic energies: *this* was life and existence.

Due to this ambiguity *Dominus* did not act immediately but kept in check the strong instinctive urges that were triggered off. Interrupting his pan-continental patrol for the first time in millennia, he followed the object to its landing place. Then he settled down patiently to await developments.

Eliot Harst knew exactly where to find Balbain. He climbed the curving ramp to the upper part of the dome-shaped spaceship and opened a door. The alien was standing at the big observation window, looking out on to Five's (whatever system they were in, they always named the planets in order from their primary) blustering semi-night.

The clouds glowed patchily as though bombs were being let off among them; the lightning boomed and crashed. The tall, thin alien ignored all this, however. His attention was fixed on the gigantic organism they had already named *Dominus*, which was slumped scarcely more than a mile away. Eliot had known him to gaze at it, unmoving, for hours.

"The experiment has worked out after all," he said. "Do you want to take a look?"

Balbain tore his gaze from the window and looked at Eliot. He came from a star which, to Eliot, was only a number in Solsystem's catalogues. His face was partly obscured by the light breathing mask he wore to supplement ship atmosphere. (The aliens all seemed to think that human beings were more sensitive to discomfort than themselves: everything on the ship was biased towards the convenience of Eliot and his assistant Alanie.) But over the mask Balbain's bright bird-like eyes were visible, darting from his bony, fragile and quite unhuman skull.

"The result is positive?" he intoned in an oddly hollow, resonant voice.

"It would seem so."

"It is as we already knew. I do not wish to see the offspring at present, but thank you for informing me."

With that he returned to the window and seemed to become abruptly unaware of Eliot's presence.

Sighing, the Earthman left the chamber. A few yards further

along the gallery he stopped at a second door. Jingling a bell to announce his presence, he entered a small bare cell and gave the same message as before to its occupant.

Abrak came from a star as far from Balbain's as the latter was from Solsystem. When fully erect he stood less than five feet in height and had a skin like corded cloth: full of neat folds and wavy grains. At the moment he squatted on the bare floor, his skeletal legs folded under him in an extraordinary double-jointed way that Eliot found quite grotesque.

Abrak's voice was crooning and smooth, and contained unnerving infra-sound beats that made a human listener feel uneasy and slightly dizzy — Eliot already knew, in fact, that Abrak could, if he wished, kill him merely by speaking: by voicing quiet vibrations of just the right frequency to cripple his internal organs.

"So the picture we have built is vindicated?" he replied to Eliot's announcement, pointing a masked, dog-like face towards the Earthman.

"There can be little doubt of it."

"I will view the offspring." The alien rose in one swift motion.

Eliot had already decided that there was no point in reporting to the fifth member of the team: Zeed, the third of the non-humans. He appeared to take no more interest in their researches.

He led the way back down the connecting ramps, through the interior of the spaceship which he had been finding increasingly depressing of late. More and more it reminded him of a hurriedly-built air-raid shelter, devoid of decoration, rough-hewn, dreary and echoing.

Balbain's people had built the ship. Eliot could recall his excitement on learning of its purpose, an excitement that doubled when it transpired he had a chance of joining it. For the ship was travelling from star to star on a quest for knowledge. And as it journeyed it occasionally recruited another scientist from a civilisation sufficiently advanced, if he would make a useful member of the team. So far, in addition to the original Balbain, there had been Zeed, Abrak (none of these being their real, unpronounceable names, but convenience names for human benefit: transliterations or syllabic equivalents), and, of course, Eliot and Alanie.

Alanie had been, for Eliot, one of the fringe benefits of the trip — another being that when they returned to Solsystem they would take back with them a prodigious mass of data, a sizeable number of discoveries, and would gain immortal fame. The aliens, recognising that human sexuality was more than usually needful, had offered to allow a male-female pair as Solsystem's contribution. Eliot had found that his prospect of a noble ordeal was considerably mitigated by the thought of spending that time alone with his selected team-mate: Alanie Leitner, vivacious, companionable, with an I.Q. of 190 (slightly better than Eliot's own, in fact) and an experienced all-round researcher. The perfect assistant for him, the selection board had assured him, and he had found little in their verdict to disagree with, then or since.

But the real thrill had been in the thing itself: in being part of a voyage of discovery that transcended racial barriers, in the uplifting demonstration that wherever intelligence arose it formed the same aspiration: to know, to examine, to reveal the universe.

Mind was mind: a universal constant.

Unfortunately he and Alanie seemed to be drifting apart from their alien travelling companions, to understand them less and less. The truth was that he and Alanie were doing all the work. They would arrive at a system and begin a survey; yet very quickly the interest of the others would die off and the humans would be left to carry out all the real research, draw the conclusions and write up the reports completely unaided. As a matter of fact Zeed now took scarcely any interest at all and did not stir from his quarters for months on end.

Eliot found it quite inexplicable, especially since Balbain and Abrak, both of whom had impressed him by the strength of their intellects, admitted that much that was novel had been discovered since leaving Solsystem.

At the bottom of the ramp he led Abrak into the laboratory section. And there to greet them was Alanie Leitner: a wide, slightly sulky mouth in a pale face; a strong nose, steady brown eyes and auburn, nearly reddish hair cut squarely at the nape of her neck. And even in her white laboratory smock the qualities of her figure were evident.

Though constructed of the same concrete-like stuff as the rest of the spaceship, the laboratory was made more cheerful by being a place of work. At the far end was the test chamber. Abrak made his way there and peered through the thick window. The parent specimen they had begun with lay up against the wall of the circular chamber, apparently dying after its birth-giving exertions. It was about the size of a dog, but was spider-like, with the addition of a rearward clump of tissue that sprouted an untidy bunch of antennae-like sensors.

Its offspring, lying inert a few yards away, offered absolutely no resemblance to the spider-beast. A dense-looking, slipper-shaped object, somewhat smaller than the parent, it might have been no more than a lump of wood or metal.

"It's too soon yet to be able to say what it can do," Alanie said, joining them at the window.

Abrak was silent for a while. "Is it not possible that this is a larval, immature stage, thus accounting for the absence of likeness?" he suggested.

"It's conceivable, certainly," Eliot answered. "But we think the possibility is remote. For one thing we are pretty certain that the offspring was already adult and fully grown, or practically so, when it was born. For another, the fact that the parent reproduced at all is pretty convincing confirmation of our theory. Added to everything else we know, I don't feel disposed towards accepting any other explanation."

"Agreed," Abrak replied. "Then we must finally accept that the Basic Polarity does not obtain here on Five?"

"That's right." Although he should have become accustomed to the idea by now Eliot's brain still went spinning when he thought of it and all it entailed.

Scientifically speaking the notion of the Basic Polarity went back, as far as Solsystem was concerned, to the Central Dogma. In a negative sense, it also went back to the related Koestler's Question, posed late in the twentieth century.

The Central Dogma expressed the keystone of genetics: that the interaction between *gene* and *soma* was a one-way traffic. The genes formed the body. But nothing belonging to the body, or anything that it experienced, could modify the genes or have any effect on the next generation. Thus there was no inheritance of acquired characteristics; evolution was conducted over immensely long periods of time through random mutations resulting from cosmic radiation, or through chemical accidents in the gene substance itself.

Why, Koestler asked, should this be so? A creature that could refashion its genes, endowing its offspring with the means to cope with the hazards *it* had experienced, would confer a great advantage in the struggle for survival. Going further, a creature that could lift itself by its bootstraps and produce a superior type in this way would confer an even greater advantage. Furthermore, Koestler argued that direct reshaping of the genes should be perfectly within the capabilities of organic life, using chemical agents.

So the absence of such a policy in organic life was counter-survival, a curious, glaring neglect on the part of nature. The riddle was answered, by Koestler's own contemporaries, in the following manner: if the *soma*, on the basis of its experiences, was to modify the gene-carrying DNA, then the modification would have to be planned and executed by the instinctive functions of the nervous system, or by whatever corresponded to those functions in any conceivable creature. But neither the instinctive brains of the higher orders, nor the primitive ganglia of the lower orders, had the competence to carry out this work: acting purely by past-conditioned responses, they had no apprehension of the future and would not have been able to relate experience to genetic alteration. Hence life had been dependent on random influences: radiation and accident.

For direct gene alteration to be successful, Koestler's rebutters maintained, some form of intellect would be needed. Primitive animals did not have this; if the gene-changing animal existed, then that animal was man, and man worked not through innate bodily powers but by artificial manipulation of the chromosomes. Even then, his efforts had been partial and inept: the eradication of defective genes to rectify the increasing incidence of deformity; the creation of a few new animals that had quickly sickened and died.

And with that the whole matter of Koestler's Question had been quietly forgotten. The Central Dogma was reinstated, not merely as an arbitrary fact but as a necessary principle. If Koestler's Question had any outcome, then it was in the recognition of the Basic Polarity: the polarity between individual and species. Because the species, not the individual, had to be the instrument of evolution. If the Central Dogma did not hold, then species would not need to exist at all (and neither, incidentally, would sex). The rate of change would be so swift that there would be nothing to hold them together — and any that did exist, because of some old-fashioned immutability of their genes, would rapidly be wiped out. And indeed the Basic Polarity seemed to be the fundamental form of life everywhere in the universe, as Balbain, Abrak and Zeed all confirmed.

Eliot was thinking of renaming Five "Koestler's Planet".

On a world where all traces of the past could be wiped out overnight, they would probably never know exactly what had happened early in Five's biological evolution to overthrow the Central Dogma. Presumably the instinctive functions had developed, not intelligence exactly, but a unique kind of telegraph between their experience of the external world and the microscopic coding of the germ plasm. It would, as Alanie pointed out, only have to happen once, and that once could even be at the bacterial level. The progeny of a single individual would rapidly supplant all other fauna. In the explosion of organic development that followed it would be but a short step before gene alteration became truly inventive; intellectual abilities would soon arise to serve this need.

It had been some time before the idea had dawned on them that Five might be a planet of single-instance species; in other words, of no species at all. There was one four-eyed stoat; one elephantine terror; one leaping prong; one blanket (their name for a creature of that description which spent most of its time merely lying on the ground). In fact there was a bewildering variety of forms of which only one example could be found. But there were one or two exceptions to the rule — or so they had thought. They had videotaped six specimens of a type of multi-legged snake. Only later had they discovered that the resemblance between them was a case of imitation, of convergent evolution among animals otherwise unrelated.

So they had been forced, reluctantly, to accept the evidence of their eyes, and later, of the electron microscope. But only now, in the last hour, was Eliot one hundred per cent convinced of it.

Another thing that had made him cautious was the sheer degree of knowledge and intelligence consistent with this level of biological engineering. He would have expected every creature on the planet to display intelligence at least equivalent to the human. Instead the animals here were just that — animals. Clever, ferocious animals, but content to inhabit their ecological niches and evincing no intellectual temperament.

All, that is, except *Dominus*.

They called him *Dominus* because he had the aspect of being king of all he surveyed. He must have weighed a thousand tons at least. He was also owner of the road system, which at first they had taken to be evidence of a civilisation, or at least the remains of one. It was now clear, however, that the road had been *Dominus*'s own idea — or, more probably, his parents' idea.

The great beast had demonstrated his understanding when they had gone out and tried to trap specimens for laboratory study. The exercise had proved to be dangerous and nearly impossible. Five's fauna were the universe's greatest experts at not getting killed, caught or trapped, and had responded not merely with claw, fang and evasive speed, but with electricity, poison gas, infra-sound (Abrak's own speciality), corrosives of various types they had still not classified but which had scared them very much, thick strands of unknown substance spun swiftly out from spinnerets and carried on the wind, slugs of pure iron ejected from porcupine-like quills with the velocity of rifle bullets, and — believe it or not — organically generated laser beams.

Retreating after one of their sorties to the shelter of their space-ship's force shield, the hunters had been about to give up and go back inside.

Alanie had said: "Let's get off this planet before one of those things throws a fusion beam at us."

And then *Dominus* had acted. Rushing down, like a smaller hill himself, from the hill where he had parked himself, he had advanced driving several smaller animals before him. Finally they had delivered themselves almost at the scientists' feet and promptly fallen unconscious. *Dominus* had then returned to the hill-top, where he had squatted motionless ever since. And Eliot, blended with his amazement, had felt the same thrill and transcendence that had overwhelmed him at the first arrival of Balbain's starship.

Dominus understood their wants! He was helping them!

Conceivably he could be communicated with. But that problem

had to wait. They got the creatures inside and put them under adequate restraint. Then Eliot and Alanie went immediately to work.

The creatures' genes followed the standard pattern produced by matter on planetary surfaces everywhere: coded helices forming a group of chromosomes. The code was doublet and not triplet, as it was on Earth, but that in itself was not unusual: Abrak's genes also were in doublet code. More significantly, the single gonad incorporated a molecular factory, vast by microscopic standards, able to dispatch a chemical operator to any specific gene in a selected germ cell. And, furthermore, a chain of command could be discerned passing into the spinal column (where there was a spinal column) and thence to the brain (where there was a brain).

Eliot had written in his journal:

> I get the impression that we are witness to a fairly late stage of Five's evolutionary development. For one thing, life here is relatively sparse, as though fierce competition has thinned down numbers rather than increased them, leading to a more subdued mode of existence. There are no predators; defensive mutations on the part of a potential prey would no doubt make it unprofitable to be a carnivore. The vegetation on Five conforms to the Basic Polarity and so presumably predates the overthrow of the Central Dogma, but it survives patchily in the form of scrub savannahs and a few small forests, and in many areas does not exist at all. The majority of animals own a patch of vegetation which they defend against all comers with an endless array of natural weapons, but they eat only in order to obtain body-building materials — proteins and trace elements — and not to provide energy, which they obtain by soaking up the ubiquitous lightning discharges. Some animals have altogether abandoned any dependence on an external food chain: they carry out the whole of the anabolic process themselves, taking the requisite elements and minerals from soil and air and metabolising all their requirements using the energy from this same lightning.
>
> It has occurred to us that all the animals here are potentially immortal. Ageing is a species-characteristic, the life-span being

adjusted to the maximum benefit of the species, not of the individual. If all our conclusions are correct, an organism on Five would continue to live a self-contained life until meeting some pressing exigency it was not able to master; only then would it reproduce to create a more talented version of itself and afterwards, perhaps, permit itself to die. This notion suggests that a test may be possible.

The slipper organism was the outcome of that test. They had placed the spider-thing in a chamber and subjected it to stress. They had bombarded it with pressure, heat, missiles, and various other discomforts suggested by the details of its metabolism. And they had waited to see whether it would react by "conceiving" and ultimately giving birth to another creature better than itself.

Of course, the new organism would be designed to accomplish one thing above all: escape. Eliot was curious now to see how the slipper would attempt it.

"Might it not be dangerous?" Abrak questioned mildly.

Eliot flipped a switch. A thick slab of dull metal slid down to occlude the window. Instead, they could continue to watch through a vidcamera.

"I'd like to see it get through that," he boasted. "Carbon and titanium alloy a foot thick. It's surrounded by it."

"You are being unsubtle," said Abrak. "Perhaps the beast will rely on trickery."

Alanie gave a deep sigh that strained her full breasts voluptuously against the fabric of her smock. "Well, what now?" she asked. "We've been here six months. I think we've solved the basic mystery of the place. Isn't it time we were moving on?"

"I'd like to stay longer," Eliot said thoughtfully. "I want to see if we can get into communication with *Dominus.*"

"But how?" she asked, sitting down at a bench and waving her hand. "Communication is a species-characteristic. He probably would never understand what language is."

"And yet already he's given us help, so we *can* communicate after a fashion," Eliot argued.

A warning sound came from Abrak. Something was happening on the screen looking into the test chamber.

The slipper organism had decided to act. Gliding smoothly to the far side of the chamber, the one nearest the skin of the ship, it pressed its tapered end against the wall. Abruptly the toe of the slipper ignited into an intense glare too bright for the vidcamera to handle. An instant later fumes billowed up and filled the chamber, obscuring everything.

By the time the fumes cleared sufficiently for the onlookers to see anything, the slipper had made its exit through the wall of the chamber, and thence through the ship's skin, by burning a channel whose edges were still white-hot.

"I think," said Eliot sombrely, "it might just have been a fusion beam, or something just as good."

He paused uncertainly. Then he flung open a cupboard and began pulling out gear. "Come on," he said. "We're going after our specimen."

"But it will kill us," Alanie protested.

"Not if *Dominus* helps us again. And somehow I think he will."

Dominus is an intelligent being, he told himself. Intelligent beings are motivated by curiosity and a sense of co-operation with other intelligent beings. His hunt for the slipper was, in fact, impelled more by the desire to prompt *Dominus* into co-operating with them again than by any interest in regaining the slipper itself, which could well be far away by now.

"But, once having recaptured the creature, how will you retain it?" inquired Abrak, looking meaningfully at the gaping hole in the chamber.

"We'll keep it under sedation," Eliot said, buckling on a protective suit.

Minutes later he stood at the foot of the spaceship. Besides the protective suit he was armed with a gun that fired recently prepared sleep darts (they had worked on the slipper's parent, following a biochemical analysis of that creature) and a cylinder that extruded a titanium mesh net.

Though evincing less enthusiasm, Alanie and Abrak had nevertheless followed him, despite his waiver to the girl. Abrak was unprotected, carried no weapons, and relied on his flimsy ship mask to take care of Five's atmosphere.

The environment boomed, flickered and flashed all around them. To Eliot's surprise the slipper could be seen less than a hundred yards away, lying quietly in the beams of their torches.

He glanced up towards the bulk of *Dominus*, then stepped resolutely forward, aware of the footsteps of the others behind him.

Up on the hill, *Dominus* began to move. Eliot stopped and stared up at him exultantly.

"Eliot," Abrak crooned at his elbow, "I strongly recommend caution. Specifically, I recommend a return to the ship."

Eliot made no answer. His mind was racing, wondering what gesture he could make to *Dominus* when the vast beast recaptured the slipper and returned it to them.

He was quite, quite wrong.

Dominus halted some distance away, and extended a tongue, or tentacle, travelling at ground level almost too fast for the eye to follow. In little more than a second or two it had flashed across the sandy soil and scrubby grass, seized on Alanie, lifted her bodily from the ground and whisked her away before a scream could form in her throat. Eliot noticed, blurrily, that the entire length of the tentacle was covered with wriggling wormy protuberances.

Even as Alanie was withdrawn into the body of *Dominus* Eliot was running forward, howling wildly and firing his dart gun. Light footsteps pattered to his rear; surprisingly strong, bony arms restrained his.

"It is no use, Eliot. *Dominus* has taken her. He is not what you thought."

Early on *Dominus* had perceived that the massy object, which he now accepted came from beyond the atmosphere, was not itself a lifeform but a lifeform's construct. The idea was already a familiar one: artifacts were rare on his planet — biological evolution was simpler — but there had been a brief period when they had proliferated, attaining increasing orders of sophistication until they had nearly devastated the continent. Stored in his redundant genes *Dominus* still retained all the knowledge of his ancestors on that score.

From the construct emerged undoubtedly organic entities, and it was in this that the mystery lay: there were several of them. *Dominus* spent some time mulling over this inexplicable fact.

Who, then, was owner of the construct? He noted that, within limits, all the foreign lifeforms bore a resemblance to one another, and reminded himself that ecological convergence was an occasional phenomenon within his own domain. Could this convergence have been carried further and some kind of *ecological common action* (he formed the concept with difficulty) have arisen among entities occupying the same ecological niche? He reasoned that he should entertain no preconceptions as to the courses evolution might take under unimaginably alien conditions. Some relationship even more incomprehensible to him might be the case.

So he had been patient, watching jealously as the lifeforms surveyed part of his domain in a flying artifact, but doing nothing. Then they had attempted, but failed, to capture some native organisms. Wanting to see what would take place, *Dominus* had delivered a few to them.

When he saw the mutated lifeform emerge from the construct on its escape bid, he knew it was as he had anticipated. The aliens must have made a genetic analysis of all their specimens. The massy construct was sealed against *Dominus*'s mutation-damping genes, and within that isolation they had carried out an experiment, subjecting one of the specimens to a challenge situation and prompting it to reproduce.

Dominus could forbear no longer. He issued the slipper with a stern command to stay fast. It was sufficiently its father's son to know what the consequences of disobeying him would be. Three alien lifeforms emerged in pursuit. To begin with, *Dominus* took one of the pair that were so nearly identical.

Alanie Lietner floated, deep within *Dominus*'s body, in a sort of protein jelly. Mercifully, she was quite dead. Thousands of nerve-thin tendrils entered her body to carry out a brief but adequate somatic exploration. At the same time billions upon billions of RNA operators migrated to her gonads (there were two of them) and sifted down to the genetic level where they analysed her chromosomes with perfect completeness.

"It killed her," Eliot was repeating in a stunned, muttering voice. "It killed her."

Abrak had persuaded him to return to the ship. They found

that Balbain had abandoned his vigil and was pacing the central chamber situated over the laboratory. His bird-eyes glittered at them with unusual fervour.

"We can delay no further," he boomed. "*Dominus*'s qualities cannot be gainsaid. The sense of him is overpowering. Therefore my quest is at an end. I shall return home."

"No!" crooned Abrak suddenly, in a hard tone Eliot had not heard him use before. "This planet also holds the promise of answering *our* requirements."

"You take second place. *I* originated this expedition, and therefore you are pre-empted."

"We shall see who will pre-empt whom," Abrak barked.

While the import of the exchange was lost on Eliot, he was bewildered at seeing these two, whom he had thought of as dispassionate men (beings, anyway) of science, quarrelling and snarling like wild dogs. So palpable was the ferocity that he was startled out of his numbness and waved his arms placatingly as though to separate them.

"Gentlemen! Is this any way for a scientific expedition to conduct itself?"

The aliens glanced at him. Balbain's mask had become wet — perhaps with the exudations of some emotion — and partly transparent. Through it Eliot saw the gaping square mouth that never closed.

"Let us laugh," Balbain said, addressing Abrak.

They both gave vent to regular chugging expulsions of air; it was a creaking monotone devoid of mirth, a weird simulation of human laughter. Neither species, to Eliot's knowledge, was endowed with a sense of humour at all; once or twice before he had heard them use this travesty to indicate, in human speech, where they believed laughter would be appropriate.

He felt chilled. A feeling of *alienness* wafted towards him from the two beings, whom previously he had regarded as companions.

Balbain made a vague gesture. "We know that you judge us by your own standards," he said, "but it is not so. Like you, we each came on this expedition to satisfy cravings inherent in our species. But those cravings are different from yours and from each other. . . ."

His voice softened and became almost caressing. Bending his

head slightly, he indicated the wall of the ship, as though to direct Eliot's attention outside.

"Try to imagine what evolution means here on Five. It takes not æons or millions of years to produce a biological invention, but only a few months. The Basic Polarity is not here to soften life's blows; competition is so intense that Five is the toughest testing ground in the universe. The result of all this should be obvious. What we have here is the most capable, potentially the most powerful source of life that could possibly exist. And *Dominus* is the fulfilment of that process. The most intolerant, the most *domineering* —" he put special emphasis on the word — "entity that the universe can produce!"

"Domineering?" echoed Eliot, frowning.

"But of course! Think for a moment: what special quality must a creature develop on Five in order to make itself safe? The ability to dominate everything around it! *Dominus* has that quality to the ultimate degree. He is the Lord, in submission to whom my species can at last find peace of mind."

Balbain spoke with such passion and in such a strange manner that Eliot could only stand and stare. Abrak spoke softly, turning his fox's snout towards him.

"It is hard for Balbain to convey what he is feeling," he crooned. "Perhaps I can explain it to your intellect, at least. First, the romantic picture you harbour concerning the fellowship of sentient minds is, I am afraid, quite incorrect. Mentalities are even more diverse in character than are physical forms. What goads us into action is not what goads you."

"Then we cannot understand one another?" Eliot said.

"Only indirectly. In almost every advanced species there is a central drive that comes from its evolutionary history and overrides all other emotions — in its best specimens. This overriding urge gives the race as a whole its existential meaning. To other races it might look futile or even ridiculous — as, indeed, yours does to us — but to the species concerned it is a universal imperative, self-evident and inescapable."

He paused to allow Eliot to absorb what he was saying.

While Balbain looked on, seeming scarcely any less agitated, he continued calmly: "For reasons too complex to describe, life on Balbain's world developed a submission-orientation. The physical conditions there, much harsher than those you are accustomed to, caused living beings to enter into an elaborate network of relationships in which each sought, not to dominate, but to *be* dominated by some other power, the stronger the better. This craving is thus the compass needle that guides Balbain's species. To them it is self-fulfilment, the inner meaning of the universe itself."

Eliot glanced at Balbain. The revelation made him feel uncomfortable.

"But how *can* it be?"

"Every species sees its own fixation as expressing the hidden nature of the universe. Do not you?"

Eliot brushed aside the question, which he did not understand. "But what's all this about *Dominus*?"

"Why, he represents the other half of this craving. His is a mentality of compulsive domination. He rules this planet, and would rule any planet with which he came in contact. Balbain knows this. With *Dominus* to command them, his people will feel something of completeness."

A small flash of insight came to Eliot. "That is *his* reason for this expedition?"

"Correct. On his own world Balbain is a sort of knight, or saint, who has set out in search of this . . . Holy Grail."

"We shall offer ourselves as *Dominus*'s slaves," Balbain boomed hollowly. "It is his nature to assume the position of master."

Eliot tried to fight off his feeling of revulsion, but failed. "You're . . . insane . . ." he whispered.

Once again Abrak's fake laughter chugged out. "But Balbain's assessment of *Dominus* is perfectly correct. Five *is* the source of potentially the greatest, and in many ways the strangest, power that existence is capable of producing, and *Dominus*, at this moment in time, is the highest expression of that power. There can be others — and that is why it is of interest to my people! We also have an existential craving!"

His snout turned menacingly towards Balbain. Eliot thought suddenly of his frightening ability to generate infra-sound.

"You will have no opportunity to satisfy it. Nothing will prevent us from becoming the property of *Dominus*." Balbain's words throbbed with passion. He was like an animal in heat.

The two began to circle one another warily. Eliot backed towards the door, afraid of infra-sound. He saw Abrak's snout open behind his mask.

Shuddering waves of vibration passed through his body. But, incredibly, in the same second Abrak died. His body was converting, from head down, into sand-coloured dust which streamed across the chamber in a rustling spray. Balbain's claw-like hand held the presumed source of this phenomenon: a device consisting of a cluster of tubes. When nothing remained of Abrak he put it away in a fold of his garment.

"Fear not," he said to Eliot in a conciliatory tone. "*You* have no reason to obstruct me. After I take home the glad tidings, you can return to Solsystem."

Eliot did not answer, but merely stood as if paralysed. Balbain gave a brief, apologetic burst of his simulated laughter, seeming to guess what was on Eliot's mind.

"As for Abrak, reserve your judgment on my action. I have given him what he desired — though to tell the truth he would have preferred the fate of your female, Alanie."

"Alanie," Eliot repeated. "How can we be sure she's dead? It may be keeping her alive. I don't know why you murdered Abrak, Balbain, but if you want me to help you, then help me to get Alanie back. Then I'll do anything you ask me."

"Defy *Dominus*?" Balbain looked at him pityingly. "Pointless, hopeless, perverted dreams. . . ."

Suddenly he rushed past Eliot and through the door. Eliot heard his feet clattering on the downward ramp.

The Earthman sat down and buried his face in his hands.

A minute or two later he felt impelled to turn on the external view screen to get another look at *Dominus*. A bizarre sight met his eyes. Balbain, about halfway between *Dominus* and the ship, had prostrated himself before the great beast and was making small gestures whose meanings were known only to himself. Eliot switched off the screen. A few minutes later, not having heard Balbain return, he looked again. There was no sign of the alien.

He was not sure how long he then sat there, trying to decide what best next to do, before a noise made him look up. The interstellar expedition's only other surviving member was entering the chamber.

Zeed was the least humanoid of all the team. He walked on limbs that could be said to constitute a pair of legs, except that they could also reconstitute themselves into tentacles, or a bunch of sticks, or a number of other devices to accommodate him to locomotion over a variety of different surfaces. Above these limbs a short dumpy body of indeterminate shape was hidden by a thick cloak which also hid his arms. Above this, a head of sorts: speckled golden eyes that did not at first look like eyes, other organs buried within fluted, bony grooves arranged in a symmetrical pattern.

The voice in which he spoke to Eliot, however, could have passed as human, although no mouth appeared to move.

"Explanations are superfluous," he said, moving into the chamber and looking down on Eliot. "I have consulted the ship's log."

Eliot nodded. The log, of course, automatically recorded everything that took place within the ship.

"It appears that Balbain could not constrain himself and has forfeited his life," Zeed continued. "It is not surprising. However, it determines our end, also, since only Abrak and Balbain knew how to pilot the ship."

This was news to Eliot, but in his present state the prospect of death caused him little alarm.

"Did *you* know Balbain's secret reason for this mission?" he asked.

"Of course. But it was no secret. Your people, being ignorant of alien races, made a presumption concerning its nature." Gliding smoothly on his versatile legs, Zeed moved to the view screen and made a full circle scan of their surroundings. Then he turned back to Eliot. "Perhaps it is a disappointment to you."

"Why did Balbain want any of us along at all?" Eliot said wearily. "Just to make use of us?"

"In a way. But we were all making use of one another. The universe is vast and quite mysterious, Eliot. It is an unfathomable darkness in which creatures arise having no common ground with each other. Hence, if they meet they may not be able to comprehend one another. Here in this ship we act as antennae for one another. We are not so alien to one another that we cannot communicate, yet sufficiently unalike so that each may understand some phenomena we encounter that the others cannot."

"So that's what we are," Eliot said resentfully. "A star-travelling menagerie."

"An ark, in which each has a separate quest. Yours is the obsession with acquiring knowledge. We do not share it, but the data you are collecting is your reward for the services you may, at some time, have been able to render one of us. You were enjoying yourselves too much for us to disillusion you concerning ourselves."

"But how can you *not* share it?" Eliot exclaimed. "Scientific inquiry is fundamental to intelligence, surely? How else can one ever understand the universe?"

"But others do not want to understand it, Eliot. That is only your own relationship to it; your chief ethological feature, whether you recognise it or not. You would still have joined this expedition, for instance, if it had meant giving up sex for the rest of your life."

"And yet you have a scientific culture and travel in spaceships."

"A matter of mere practicality. Pure, abstract science exists only for *homo sapiens* — I have not encountered it elsewhere. Other races carry out investigations only for the material benefits they bring. As an extreme example, think of *Dominus*: he, and probably countless of the animals here, possess vastly more of the knowledge you admire than do either of us, yet they have no interest in it and continue to live in a wild condition."

Eliot's thoughts were returning to Alanie and the disinterest all the aliens had shown in her horrifying death. He remembered Balbain's enigmatic remark. "Abrak," he said bleakly, "what was *he* seeking?"

"His species craves *abnormal death*. The cause of it is thuswise: life, however long, must end. Life, then, is conditioned by death. Hence death is larger than life. Abrak's people are conscious that everything, ultimately, is abnegated by death, and they look for fulfilment only in the manner of their dying. An individual of his species seeks to die in some unusual or noteworthy manner. Suicides receive praise, provided the method is extraordinary. Murderers, likewise, are folk heroes, if their killings show imagination. Ultimately, the whole species strives to be exterminated in some style so extraordinary as to make its existence seem meaningful. Five seemed to offer that promise — not in its present state, it is true, but after suitable evolutionary development, perhaps due to an invasion by Abrak's people."

"And *you*," Eliot demanded. "What do *you* seek?"

"We," answered Zeed with an icy lack of hesitation, "seek NULLITY. Not merely to die, like Abrak's species, but to wipe out the past, *never to have been.*"

Eliot shook his head, aghast. "How can *any* living creature have an ambition like that?"

"You must understand that on your planet conditions have been remarkably gentle and favourable for the arising of life. Such is not the general rule. Elsewhere there is hardship and struggle, often of a severity you could not imagine. The universe rarely smiles on the formation of life. On my planet . . ." Zeed seemed to hesitate, "we regard it as an act of compassion to kill our offspring at birth. The unlucky ones are spared to answer nature's call to perpetuate the species. If you knew my planet, you would not think that life could evolve there at all. We believe that ever since the first nervous system developed, the subconscious feeling has been present that it has all been a mistake. To you, of course, this looks weird and perverted."

"Yes . . . it does indeed," Eliot said slowly. "In any case, isn't it impossible? I presume you are travelling the galaxy in search of some race that has time travel, so that you can wipe out your own past. But look at it this way: even if you succeeded in that, there would still have to be a 'different past' — the old past, a ghost past — in which you still existed."

"Once again you display your mental agility," Zeed said. "Your reasoning is sound: it may be that our craving can be satisfied only if the universe in its entirety is nullified."

Springing to his feet, Eliot went to the viewscreen and peered out on to turbulent, lightning-struck Five. He thought of Alanie and himself slaving in the laboratory, and felt tricked and insignificant. Zeed seemed to think of their work as no more than the collecting instinct of a jackdaw or an octopus.

"Everything you've told me passes for psychosis back in Solsystem," he said finally. "I don't know . . . maybe this is really a travelling lunatic asylum. You could all be insane, even by the standards of your own people. Balbain had this kinky desire to be a slave. Abrak wanted to be killed bizarrely, and you want never to have been born at all. What kind of a set-up is that? If you ask me, the normal, healthy, human mentality is a lot closer to reality than all that."

"Every creature says that of itself. It is hard for you to accept that your outlook is not a norm, that it is an aberration, an exception. Let me tell you how it arose. Because of the incredibly luxurious conditions on the planet Earth there was able to develop a quite unique biological class: the *mammalia*. The specific ethological feature of the mammalia is *protectiveness*, which began within the family, then extended to the tribe, and finally, with your own species, has become so over-developed as to embrace the whole of the mammalian class. Every mammal is protected, by your various organisations, whether human or not. Now, the point is that within this shield of protectiveness qualities are able to evolve which actually are quite redundant, since they bear no relation to the hard facts of survival. One of these, becoming intense among monkeys, apes and hominids, is playful curiosity, or meddlesome inquisitiveness. This developed into the love of knowledge which became the overriding factor in the history of your own species."

"That doesn't sound at all bad to me," Eliot said defensively. "We've done all right so far."

"But not for long, I fear. Your species is in more trouble than you think. There is no future in this mammalian over-protectiveness. The dinosaurs thought themselves safe by reason of their excessive size, did they not? And yet that giantism was exactly what doomed them. Already you ran into serious trouble when your compulsive care for the unfit led to a deterioration of the genetic stock. You saved yourselves that time because you learned to eliminate defective genes artificially. But perhaps other consequences of this nature of yours will arise which you cannot deal with. I do not anticipate that your species will last long."

"While you — death-lovers — will still be here, I suppose?"

Zeed's golden eyes seemed to dim and tarnish. "We all inhabit a vast dark," he repeated, "in which there is neither rhyme nor reason."

"Perhaps so." Eliot's fists were clenched now. "Here's another 'ethological feature', as you call it — revenge! Do you understand that, Zeed? I'm going to take my revenge for the death of my mate! I'm going out there to destroy the animal that killed Alanie!"

Zeed did not answer but continued to stare at him and, so it seemed to Eliot's crazed imagination, lost any semblance to a living creature at all. Eliot ran to the lower galleries of the ship and armed himself with one of the few weapons the vessel carried: a high-powered energy beamer. As he stepped down from the ship and on to the booming, crashing surface of Five some of Zeed's words came back to him. An image came to his mind of the endlessness of space in which galaxies seemed to be descending and tumbling, and the words: *an unfathomable darkness without any common ground.* Then he pressed forward to challenge *Dominus*.

Dominus believed he had at last solved a perplexing riddle.

Following his initial seizure of one of the organisms, two others had emerged at short intervals so he had taken those also. A little later, he had moved in on the construct itself and taken a fourth organism from it. Of the fifth, there was no trace.

His analyses came up with the same result every time. The specimens were incomplete organisms: they were sterile. More accurately, they could only reproduce identical copies of themselves, like a plant. Together with this, their tissues suffered from an inbuilt deficiency which caused them to decay with age.

Plainly these facts were not consistent with their being motile, autonomous entities. *Dominus* now believed that the specimens he had were only expendable doll-organisms, created by some genuine entity as one might make a machine to carry out certain tasks, and dispatched here, in the metal construct, for a purpose.

And that entity, the owner of the construct and of the doll-organisms, having intruded on his domain once, would be back again.

With that realisation an urge beyond all power to resist came upon *Dominus*: the compulsion to *evolve*. He meditated in the depths of his being, and the entity to which he ultimately gave birth, amid great explosions, agonies and devastations, was as far above him in ability as he had been above his immediate inferior.

The new *Dominus* immediately set about the defence of his planet. The whole of the single continent became a spring-board for this defence, and was criss-crossed with artifacts which meshed integrally with the space-borne artifacts he sent ranging several light-years beyond the atmosphere. To crew this extensive system *Dominus* copied the methods of the invader and created armies of slave doll-organisms modelled on the enemy's own doll-organisms. And *Dominus* waited for the enemy to arrive. And waited. And waited. And waited.

The Problem of Morley's Emission

MEMO
To: Director, Orbit University.
From: Dean, Sociohistoric Faculty.
Date: 19 July A.D. 3065.

Dear Mansim: As you are aware, a month ago the Officiating World Steering Committee asked us to submit a bystander's report on the events surrounding the activities of the well-known philosopher Isaac Morley, giving our interpretation of their possible significance. Frankly, some of us are alarmed at the direction in which our conclusions are taking us. Below is a precis of the report which tentatively is shaping up and which *should* go to the Committee in a few days' time (most of it is rather elementary, as politicians, naturally, are ignorant of the subject of social energy fields). Are you happy to see it go through as it stands? Arthur.

CONFIDENTIAL

SPECIFICS: the building of the Antarctic Structure; the passage of the Extra-Solar Object; the economic deformations noted to have occurred in the period from March to December A.D. 3064.
1. The facts surrounding the edifice named the Antarctic Structure are simple, if not altogether explicable. The Structure is an immense pyramid, or ziggurat, five miles on the side, its faces worked into an intricate, baroque labyrinth. Five thousand people laboured on its construction for a year and a half, without payment and without any clear idea as to its purpose, having been inspired to assemble by the leadership of its architect the self-styled philosopher Isaac Morley, who had created a philosophical cult solely in order to complete his project.

Only later did it emerge that the Structure is actually a powerful, if somewhat over-elaborate, UHF transmitter, able to transmit a tight beam in a fixed direction spacewards at an angle of

5 degrees from the direction of the south polar axis, at longitude 93 degrees west. Its function as an ideological monument is probably secondary.

2. There seems no way in which Morley and his followers could have known beforehand of the passage of the mysterious object known simply as the Extra-Solar Object. Despite that, the beam from the Structure, after its one and only discharge on 1 April 3064, intercepted the Object exactly, at the point where it passed beneath the south pole, half a light year below the plane of the ecliptic.

The Object has an estimated rest-mass of a billion tons, and an estimated average diameter of three hundred and forty miles. It remained within detectable range for only one month. Apart from its high velocity, there is nothing to suggest that it is not of natural origin.

3. *Economic deformations*: all economic networks report an upsurge in new and unaccustomed directions from March to December of last year. Intermittent surges and subsidences in economic activity are by no means unusual, but several features of this one are perplexing. The networks unanimously claim that their new production initiatives were in response to demand arising from innovations in fashion; but it has proved impossible to trace any originating source for this demand. Even more puzzling, the new fashions seem suddenly to have dissipated before the production period was properly completed, and the networks are now left with vast stocks of useless articles.

One or two of the new commodities, such as the models of the Antarctic Structure which emit random buzzing noises, are clearly related to the influence of the Morleyites; but others, such as the holovid set able to screen nothing except the process of its own production, fulfil no obvious purpose.

4. To the layman it might seem that the above events, while concurrent in time, could not have very much bearing on one another. To explain how they possibly could, it will be necessary briefly to review the theory of *social energy fields*.

Early social science was separated, broadly speaking, into two camps. One view held that the individual human being is the only social reality, and that society itself has no substantive existence, but is only an arrangement, or "contract", between autonomous, self-conscious individuals. The opposing camp, however, denied that consciousness is an attribute of the individual mind at all. According to this doctrine, consciousness is an aggregate social function; the "self" has no independent existence and is a product, or reflection, of social forces. During the 20th and 21st centuries a series of wars was fought over this divergence in ideologies, as contending parties attempted either to destroy all forms of collective (or "state") control, or else to establish a world of collective harmony in which only group aims were admitted.

As with many diametrically opposed concepts, both were right and both were wrong. The individualist concept was erroneous because the social conditioning of individual consciousness is an observable fact, and in most cases is practically absolute. The collective concept is untenable on more theoretical grounds. If it were true, the collective cultural pool would be its own single source of influences and ideas, there being nowhere else from which to replenish them. Like any system denied an energy input, it would suffer a continuous downgrading of vitality. Since growth and novelty are more characteristic of cultures than is decline this doctrine also fails to answer the facts, and the regular injections into the common pool of fresh initiatives can only be attributed to individual qualities.

Gradually it came to be realised that society, with its properties of gregariousness and organisation, can be adequately expressed only as a *polar structure* in which the individual comprises one pole and the collective or "aggregate" entity the other pole, the two taken together having the properties of opposition, complementarity and inseparability.

It could be argued that the social polarity is a fictional concept since the "aggregate" pole is scattered over the surface of the Earth. However, the dimensions selected are not those of physical space but of "social space". Mathematically the "cultural polarity", as it is sometimes called, belongs to the same class of structures as does a magnetic field, with which it shares many characteristics.

The Psychological Aspect: Not only does the social polarity extend worldwide, it is also present in every individual brain. Human consciousness is clearly acted on by forces coming from two opposite directions: a man is both himself, and he is society. This ambiguity, an existential double-take, is absolutely ineradicable; neither pole can be omitted. The individual has innate qualities, urges and desires, but these cannot develop without appropriate stimuli; if bereft of society — if raised by animals, perhaps — he could not develop into a human person. Likewise, without individuals there could obviously be no society. Neither can persist without the other, and indeed until they coalesce within the brain no human being exists.

The Organisational Aspect: The substance of the psychological polarity is the substance out of which all forms of social organisation are constructed.

The polar binding force stretches from individual to total aggregate through a wide range of intermediate forms. The first manifestation of the binding force is known technically as *coherence*, in analogy to laser light which is of uniform wavelength and whose waves all move in step. Coherence refers to the principle of *conformity* in human affairs: the force of fashion, of national and cultural identity, of religious belief, and so on. Coherence involves no conscious organisation. The masses of individuals keep in step apparently of their own volition, but in reality because of the mimicking nature of this force.

Like magnetic fields, the SEF (social energy field) is fairly static in its ground state. A magnetic field can, however, be made to give rise to an electric current which flows at right angles to the field; the social polarity has a similar property in that it may give rise to a flow of *organised directiveness*, this being a general term implying the *intentionality* of a system, and covering anything having the nature of a project. Invariably it involves a movement from a past condition to a future altered condition; usually (but not necessarily) it involves the deployment of material forces.

Organised directiveness could therefore be said to be an SEF potential. When the flow actually occurs, however, it adds an extra dimension to the field, transforming it into a *quadropolar energy structure* requiring, for a complete description, not two, but four terms: individual and aggregate poles, positive and negative flow terminals.

Cohesiveness is the term used to describe the condition of an SEF which is giving rise to a flow of organised directiveness. The *economic system* is its most obvious manifestation.

The Principle of Conformation: The chemical term *conformation* describes the ability of some molecules to adopt various configurations, a different energy state being associated with each. The SEF is similarly capable of a range of conformations, in which the individual and aggregate poles are variously emphasised.

The most extreme aggregate-favoured conformation is the mass crowd, or mob, probably the closest the aggregate pole ever gets to leading an independent existence. The characteristics of a crowd, both physically and psychologically, differ so radically from those of a healthy individual that it has been held to constitute a separate form of life, or rather, to constitute an entity intermediate between animate creatures and inanimate forces. An invariable feature of crowds is that the faculty of self-determination, which to some degree is present in every individual, is totally lacking in them. A crowd exhibits the characteristics of raw energy or a body of water. It does not respond to instructions or appeals but only to physical barriers and conduits, provided they are strong enough. Any individual trapped in a crowd is, therefore, robbed of any control over his own movements, and should crowd control measures fail then internal pressures within the crowd can very quickly reach lethal proportions.

The crowd's power to submerge the individual is no less psychological than physical. Individuals who least expect it of themselves may find their judgment abdicated to crowd emotion, their feelings funnelled in a single direction like a torrent at full flood — a syndrome which has been a source of elation to those leaders who have learned to arouse it.

Crowds of gigantic magnitude have mostly been associated with religious occasions. The earliest historical mention of a giant crowd is for the year 1966, when five million people assembled for the Hindu festival of Kumbh-Mela. A Kumbh-Mela crowd of over twenty million is recorded for eighty years later. The largest recorded crowd ever was of an estimated two hundred and ten million people who assembled for the event of the Joyous Declaration of the World God Uhuru movement on the Central African

Plain in A.D. 2381, this number being compressed into a remarkably small area thanks to the ingenious open-plan multi-storey stadia erected for the occasion. When control measures failed fifty million people died as a result of internal crowd pressure. At several loci within the crowd the aggregated pressure rose to such a degree that several millions at a time were fused into a single bloody mass in which no individual bodies or parts of bodies were distinguishable. Gigantic crowds continued to be a feature of World God Uhuru despite attempts by civil authorities to have the gatherings banned.

A more disciplined crowd-like conformation yields mass regimentation ("the human dragon", as it has been called), the simplest and crudest means of accomplishing large-scale enterprises. This conformation was the basis of all the great engineering works of the ancient world, there being at the time no other form of economic organisation equal to the tasks involved. History furnishes many impressive examples of its use — for instance, the digging of a canal during the Chinese Sui dynasty to join the Yangtze and Yellow rivers, by order of the emperor Yang Ti (of whom it is recorded: "He ruled without benevolence"). Five and a half million workers were assembled and worked under guard by 50,000 police. In some areas all commoners between the ages of fifteen and fifty were drafted; every fifth family was required to contribute one person to help to supply and prepare food. Over two million workers were listed as "lost".

The history of civilisation is largely the story of the developing range of cohesive conformations.

Resolution Levels: The main success of the theory of social energy fields is that it at last brings human activity within the realm of purely physical phenomena, attributing to it properties as definitive as those of charge and mass. At first the energy field was looked on as only an analogy; but then T. R. Millikan pointed out that it is only in *scale* that the SEF is any different from, say, electromagnetism. Electrons are very small in relation to us; therefore it is easy to accept that they are acting on one another through the medium of an electric field. Were we able to study people reduced to the same resolution level as electrons, we would similarly infer that they were acting on one another through the medium of a field of energy.

From there it was but a short step to the idea that the SEF *actually exists* as a measurable field of force to which human beings respond. This field might, it was thought, consist of some subtle and undetected form of magnetism. It would go a long way towards explaining such phenomena as mass hypnotism, mass delusion, and the improbable feats of healing that are known sometimes to occur, since the human perception of reality must necessarily be tied to this field, and therefore would be malleable.

Attempts have been made to detect and measure the field, as well as to influence it by means of artificial field generators. In order to obtain a convenient resolution level Earth civilisation has been studied from satellite laboratories, from Luna, and from Triton. The effects of the "field generators" placed in some large cities, usually sending out low-powered magnetic and electrical oscillations, were initially quite promising, apparently producing either manic enthusiasm among the urban population, or else an unnatural lassitude. But due to the difficulty of isolating these results from other possible causes, none of them could be taken as conclusive.

The Theory of the Social Black Hole: If continued additions are made to force fields they become so powerful as to create weird and abnormal states of matter, such as the neutron star and the black hole. Social scientists have speculated on the results of endlessly adding to human populations, since the SEF also contains a gravitating principle: population tends towards centres, producing the well-known "skyscraper effect".

If large human communities were to exist in cosmic space the centripetal effect would tend towards the centre of a sphere. The "skyscraper effect" would then produce only increasing concentration and density, there being no extra dimension to ease the load as the dimension of height does on the ground. There being no theoretical limit to the size a population may ultimately assume, it has already been proposed to build a vast artificial sphere several hundred million miles in diameter (a development of the once-projected Dyson sphere) to trap all solar energy so as to power and accommodate a truly titanic civilisation. Leaving aside considerations of physical mass and gravity, the question that arises is what would happen to the SEF inside such a sphere (centred on the sun or built in interstellar space if provided with alternative sources of energy) if it were to fill up entirely with human population. It is believed that a condition of "psycho-social collapse" would occur towards the centre of the sphere. Individual and collective mentalities would assume unimaginable relationships; the two poles would perhaps disappear into one another, much as electrons and protons are forced to merge by the intense pressure inside a neutron star. Perception of reality, which is based on the polar relationship, would bear no resemblance to our perception of it. The whole of mankind within the sphere would ultimately be drawn into a "social black hole", and would be totally unable to perceive or conceive of an external physical universe.

The theory of the social black hole, while it might seem to verge on the limit of possibility, does indicate that a social energy field could become subject to wholly strange effects.

5. *Conclusions*: The quadropolar social energy field, with its properties of coherence and cohesion, can be looked on as a *cosmic instrument of action*: Its evolution has taken several hundred million years; it is now capable of a large range of accomplishments, many of them, no doubt, not even imagined as yet.

A disquieting feature of the SEF is that it is a self-conserving type of system beyond the scope of any of its parts to control. The reason for this is that any impulse arising within it is, after a period of time, answered by a re-equilibrating impulse from the opposite polarity. *Systems of this type are open to external control, however.* It is not idle to speculate that the universe may contain entities to whom Earth civilisation appears as a convenient ready-made tool or "machine" and who might be able to locate or devise external controls for such a machine — entities, perhaps, whose mentalities do not have a polar structure and whose perception of reality is therefore at variance with our own.

Isaac Morley, an acknowledged genius, had by his own account invented a new methodology of thought which included original concepts in ontology. He claims it was a coded statement of this system that was emitted by the Antarctic Structure. When asked why the project was undertaken, Morley said: "It seemed fitting that the information should be transmitted into the cosmos." When further asked why the transmission tapes were subsequently wiped clean, he merely replied that they had fulfilled their purpose; the concepts had been created and would travel through space for all eternity. Morley now claims not to be able to remember the salient features of his breakthrough in philosophical thought, their subtlety having proved too elusive for his memory.

Morley insists that the beam's interception of the Extra-Solar Object must have been coincidence. He laughs at any suggestion that, to put it crudely, he had been "manipulated" from interstellar space. How, he asks, could he have been "manipulated" into formulating entirely original concepts?

Morley, however, misses the point. External controls, if they existed, would not act on the individual, nor on the collectivity as such, but in some way on combinations of the two. Ideas, thoughts and schemes are all part of the social structure and might be treated by a controlling agency as interesting or valuable outputs.

The erecting of the Antarctic Structure, too, shows one of the classic combinations of individual (Morley) and collective (cult) action. Investigation of the subsequent economic deformations (during which transit of the Extra-Solar Object took place) has shown that the deformations travelled through the economic system in the form of ripples, much as if a stone had been dropped into a pond. Following this finding, the abandoned SEF detecting instruments on Luna and on two Earth satellites were broken into. It was discovered that they had recorded strong low-frequency oscillations of an unusual nature during this period. The magnetic pulses appeared, moreover, not to be restricted to the surface of the Earth but to be isotropic.

6. *Recommendations*:

(1) *It is imperative to ascertain whether entities capable of exercising external control exist.*

(2) While no human individual or institution can take charge of the SEF, the possibility perhaps remains that an artificial nonpolar intelligence could be constructed whose function would be,

not to control the SEF itself, but to act as a block on any other external agency that tried to effect control.

It must be said that the problems associated with the above two projects are not merely prodigious; we can offer no guidance as to where they should even begin.

CONFIDENTIAL MEMO

To: Dean, Sociohistoric Faculty.
From: Director, Orbit University.
Date: 20 July A.D. 3065.

Dear Arthur: This report alarms me, too. If this thing gets about it will provoke a whole new crop of crank religions. The government is finding lunatics like Morley and his followers exasperating enough as it is.

Two thoughts occur to me. (1) If an exterior intelligence *were* to control the SEF, could we be aware of it? Such an intelligence would surely take care not to intrude new sources of energy into the system, for fear of causing internal damage. (2) this being the case, what guarantee have we that the growth of the SEF was not controlled from the start? I'm reminded of the story of the man who woke up suddenly in the middle of the night, wondering why he had always presumed he was alive for his own convenience, and not for some other purpose entirely unknown to him.

For once I am inclined to think that ignorance is the better part of discretion. Do *not* send this report to the World Steering Committee — they're too democratic a body, some of them are bound to blab. Replace it with something more prosaic. It shouldn't be too difficult to suggest a reason why Morley *could* have known of the approach of the Extra-Solar Object in advance — he could then be arraigned for making a secret of scientific information.

Just between the two of us, I've already had a word with the WSC Chairman, and that's the kind of outcome he wants. He's been looking for a chance to nail Morley, anyway. Mansim.

The Cabinet of Oliver Naylor

Nayland's world was a world of falling rain, rain that danced on streaming tarmac, soaked the grey and buff masonry of the dignified buildings lining the streets of the town, drummed on the roofs of big black cars splashing the kerbs. Behind faded gold lettering on office windows constantly awash, tense laconic conversations took place to the murmur of water pouring from the gutterings, to the continuous, pattering sound of rain.

Beneath the pressing grey sky, all was humid. Frank Nayland, his feet up on his desk, looked down through his office window to where the slow-moving traffic drove through the deluge. *Nayland Investigations Inc.*, read the bowed gold lettering on the window. The rain fell, too, in the black-and-white picture on the TV set flickering away in the corner of the office. It fell steadily, unremittingly, permanently, while Humphrey Bogart and Barbara Stanwyck fled together in a big black car, quarrelling tersely in their enclosed little world which smelled of seat leather and rain.

They stopped at a crossroads. Bogart gripped the steering wheel and scowled while the argument resumed in clipped, deadpan tones. The windscreen wipers were barely able to clear away the rain; on the outside camera shots the faces of the two were seen blurrily, intermittently, cut off from external contact as the wipers went through their sweep.

In the office the telephone rang. Nayland picked it up. He heard a voice that essentially was his own; yet the accent was British, rather than American.

"Is that Oliver Nayland, private detective?"

"*Frank* Nayland," Nayland corrected.

"*Frank* Nayland."

The voice paused, as if for reflection. "I would like to call on your services, Mr Nayland. I want someone to investigate your world for me. Follow the couple in the black car. Where are they fleeing to? What are they fleeing *from*? Does it ever stop raining?"

Nayland replied in a professionally neutral tone. "My charge is two hundred dollars a week, plus expenses," he said. "For investigating physical world phenomena, however — gravitation, rain, formation of the elements — I charge double my usual fee."

While speaking he moved to the TV and twiddled the tuning knob. The black car idling at the crossroads vanished, was replaced by a man's face talking into a telephone. Essentially the face was Nayland's own; younger, perhaps, less knowing, not world-weary. There was no pencil-line moustache; and the client sported a boyish haircut Nayland wouldn't have been seen dead with.

The client looked straight at him out of the screen. "I think I can afford it. Please begin your investigations."

The picture faded, giving way to Gene Kelly dancing in *Singing in the Rain*. Nayland returned to the window. From his desk he picked up a pair of binoculars and trained them on a black car that momentarily was stopped at the traffic lights. Through the car's side window he glimpsed the profile of Barbara Stanwyck. She was sitting stiffly in the front passenger seat, speaking rapidly, her proud face vibrant with passion, angry but restrained. By her side Bogart tapped on the steering wheel and snarled back curt replies.

The lights changed, the car swept on, splashing rainwater over the kerb. Nayland put down his binoculars and became thoughtful.

For a few minutes longer Oliver Naylor watched the private dick's activities on his thespitron screen. Nayland held tense, laconic interviews in seedy city offices, swept through wet streets in a black car, talked in gloomy bars while rain pattered against the windows, visited the mansion of Mrs Van der Loon, had a brief shoot-out with a local mobster.

Eventually Naylor faded out the scene, holding down the "retain in store" key. At the same time he keyed the "credible sequence" button back in. The thespitron started up again, beginning, with a restrained fanfare, to unfold an elaborate tale of sea schooners on a watery world.

Naylor ignored it, turning down the sound so that the saga

would not distract him. He rose from his chair and paced the living room of his mobile habitat. How interesting, he thought, that the drama machine, the thespitron as he called it, should invent a character so close to himself both in name and in appearance. True, their personalities were different, as were their backgrounds — *Frank Nayland*, a twentieth-century American, was perfectly adapted to his world of the private eye, *circa* 1950, whereas he, *Oliver Naylor*, was a twenty-second-century Englishman and a different type altogether. But physically the resemblance was uncanny.

So close a likeness could not be coincidence, Naylor thought. The thespitron's repertoire was unlimited and in principle one could expect a random dramatic output from it, but in practice it showed a predilection for Elizabethan tragedy in one direction —devising dramas worthy, in Naylor's view, of the immortal Bill himself — and in the other for Hollywood thrillers of the 1930s-50s period. Both of these were firm favourites of Naylor, the thespitron's creator. Clearly he had unintentionally built some bias into it; sometime he would apply himself to locating its source.

The existence of Frank Nayland probably had a similar explanation, he concluded. It was probably due to an optional extra he had built into the machine, namely a facility by which the viewer could talk to the characters portrayed on the thespitron screen. In this respect the thespitron exhibited an admirable degree of adaptability — it was perfectly delightful, for instance, to see how it had automatically translated his stick-mike into a large, unwieldy 1950s telephone. Similarly, it must have absorbed his identity from earlier intrusions, fashioning it into the world of Frank Nayland.

Just the same, it was eerie to be able to talk to oneself, albeit in this fictional guise. A soupçon, perhaps, of "identity crisis".

He strolled to the living room window and gazed out. Millions of galaxies were speeding past in the endless depths, presenting the appearance of a sidewise fall of tiny snowflakes. The habitat was speeding through the universe at a velocity of c^{186}, heading into infinity.

At length Naylor turned from the window with a sigh. Crossing the room, he settled himself in a comfortable armchair and switched on the vodor lecturer which, before leaving Cambridge, he had stocked with all material relevant to the subject in hand. Selecting the talk he wanted, he rested his head against the leather upholstery and listened, letting the lecture sink into his mind much as one might enjoy a piece of music.

The vodor began to speak.

"IDENTITY. The logical law of identity is expressed by the formula $A=A$, or A is A. This law is a necessary law of self-conscious thought, and without it thinking would be impossible. It is in fact merely the positive expression of the law of contradiction, which states that the same attribute cannot at the same time be affirmed and denied of the same subject.

"Philosophically, the exact meaning of the term 'identity', and the ways in which it can be predicated, remain undecided. Some hold that identity excludes difference; others that it actually implies it, connoting 'differential likeness'. See B. Bosanquet, *Essays and Addresses*, 1889. The question is one of whether identity can be posited only of an object's attributes, or whether it refers uniquely to an object regardless of its attributes. . . ."

Naylor looked up as Watson-Smythe, his passenger, emerged from an adjoining bedroom where had been sleeping. The young man stretched and yawned.

"*Haw*! Sleep knits up the ravelled sleeve, and all that. Hello there, old chap. Still plugging away, I see?"

Naylor switched off the vodor. "Not getting very far, I'm afraid," he admitted shyly. "In fact, I haven't made any real progress for weeks."

"Never mind. Early days, I expect." Watson-Smythe yawned less vigorously, tapping his mouth with his hand. "Fancy a cup of char? I'll brew up."

"Yes, that would be excellent."

Watson-Smythe had affable blue eyes. He was fair-skinned and athletic-looking. Although only just out of bed he had taken the trouble to comb his hair before entering the habitat's main room, arranging his shining blond curls on either side of a neat parting.

Naylor had no real idea of who he was. He had met him at one of the temporary habitat villages that sprang up all over space. He was, it seemed, one of those rash if adventurous people who chose to travel without their own velocitator habitat, hitching lifts here and there, bumming their way around infinity. Apparently he was trying to find some little-known artist called Corngold (the name was faintly familiar to Naylor). Having discovered his whereabouts at the village, he had asked Naylor to take him there and Naylor, who had nowhere in particular to go, had thought it impolite to refuse.

Watson-Smythe moved to the utility cupboard and set some water to boil, idly whistling a tune by Haydn. While waiting, he glanced through the window at the speeding galaxies, then crossed to the velocitator control board and peered at the speedometer, tapping at the glass-covered dial.

"Will we get there soon, do you think? Is 186 your top speed?"

"We could do nearly 300, if pushed," Naylor said. "But any faster than 186 and we'd probably go past the target area without noticing it."

"Ah, that wouldn't do at all, would it?"

The kettle whistled. Watson-Smythe rushed to it and busied himself with warming the teapot, brewing the tea and pouring it, after a proper interval, into bone-china cups.

Naylor accepted a cup, but declined a share of the toast and marmalade which Watson-Smythe prepared for himself.

"This fellow Corngold," he asked hesitantly while his guest ate, "is he much of an artist?"

Watson-Smythe looked doubtful. "Couldn't say, really. Don't know much about it myself. Don't know Corngold personally either, as a matter of fact."

"Oh." Naylor's curiosity was transient, and he didn't like to pry.

Watson-Smythe waggled a finger at the thespitron, which was still playing out its black-and-white shadow show (Naylor had deliberately eschewed colour; monochrome seemed to impart a more bare-boned sense of drama). "Got the old telly going again, I see — the automated telly. You ought to put that into production, old chap. It would be a boon to habitat travellers. Much better than carrying a whole library of play-back tapes."

"Yes, I dare say it would."

"Not in the same class as this other project of yours, if it comes off, of course. That will be something."

Naylor smiled in embarrassment. He almost regretted having told his companion about the scheme he was working on. It was, possibly, much too ambitious.

After his breakfast Watson-Smythe disappeared back into his bedroom to practise callisthenics — though Naylor couldn't imagine what anyone so obsessed with keeping trim was doing space travelling. Habitat life, by its enclosed nature, was not conducive to good health.

His passenger's presence could be what had been blocking his progress, Naylor thought. After all, he had come out here for solitude, originally.

He switched on the vodor again and settled down to try to put his thoughts back on the problem once more.

"The modern dilemma (continued the vodor) is perhaps admirably expressed in an ancient Buddhist tale. An enlightened master one day announced to his disciples that he wished to enter into contemplation. Reposing himself, he closed his eyes and withdrew his consciousness.

"For thirty years he remained thus, while his disciples took care of his body and kept it clean.

"At the end of thirty years he opened his eyes and looked about him. The disciples gathered around. 'Can the noble master tell us,' they asked, 'what has engaged his attention all this time?' The master told them: 'I have been considering whether, in all the deserts of the world, there could conceivably be two grains of sand identical in every particular.'

"The disciples were puzzled. 'Surely,' they said, 'that is a small matter to monopolise the attention of a mind such as yours?'

" 'Small it may be, but it was too great for me,' the master replied. 'I still do not know the answer.'

"In the twentieth century a striking *scientific* use of the concept of identity seemed for a while to cut across many logical and philosophical definitions and to answer the Buddhist master's question. In order to handle paradoxical findings resulting from experiments in electron diffraction, equations were devised which, in mathematical terms, removed from electrons their individual identities. It was pointed out that electrons are all so alike as to be, for all intents and purposes, identical. The equations therefore described electrons as exchanging identities with one another in a rhythmic oscillation, without any transfer of energy or position. . . ."

Naylor's first love had been logic machines. As a boy he had begun by reconstructing the early devices of the eighteenth and nineteenth centuries: the deceptively simple Stanhope Demonstrator invented by an English earl, which with its calibrated window and two cursors was probably the very first genuine logic machine (though working out the identities was a tedious business); the Jevons Logic Machine (the first to solve complicated problems faster than the unaided logician) which in common with Venn diagrams made use of the logic algebra of George Boole. He had quickly progressed to the type of machine developed in the twentieth century and known generically as the "computer", although only later had it developed into an instrument of pure logic for its own sake. By the time he was twenty he had become fully conversant with proper "thinking machines" able to handle multi-valued logic, and had begun to design models of his own. His crowning achievement, a couple of years ago, had been the construction of what he had reason to believe was the finest logic machine ever, a superb instrument embracing the entire universe of discourse.

It was then that he had conceived the idea of the thespitron, a device which if marketed would without doubt put all writers of dramatic fiction out of business for once and all. Its basic hardware consisted of the above-mentioned logic machine, plus a comprehensive store and various ancillaries. After his past efforts, he had found the arrangement surprisingly easy to accomplish. In appearance the machine resembled an over-large, old-fashioned television set, with perhaps rather too many controls; but whereas an ordinary television receiver picked up its programmes from some faraway transmitter, the thespitron generated them internally. Essentially it was a super-plotting device; it began with bare logical identities, and combined and recombined them into ever more complex structures, until by this process it was able to plot an endless variety of stories and characters, displaying them complete with dialogue, settings and incidental music.

Naylor had watched the plays and films generated by the thespitron for several months now, and he could pronounce himself well pleased with the result of his labours. The thespitron was perpetual motion: because the logical categories could be permutated endlessly, its dramatic inventiveness was inexhaustible. Left to its own devices, it would eventually run through all possible dramatic situations.

Naylor had once heard a theological speculation that, laying aside his own philosophical training, he thought was lent added piquancy by the existence of the thespitron. The speculation was that God had created the universe for its theatrical content alone, simply in order to be able to view the innumerable dramatic histories it generated. According to this notion all ethical parameters, all poignancies, triumphs, tragedies and meaningless sufferings were, so to speak, literary devices.

The thespitron, Naylor reasoned, repeated this situation exactly. For was it not a private cosmic theatre? The cosmos in miniature, complete in itself, self-acting, consistent with its own logical laws just as the greater cosmos was? The idea that the thespitron had some sort of cosmic significance was made even more alluring by its present location here in intergalactic space, googols of light years from Earth. Here, too, was the miniature cosmos's creator and the observer of its presentations — Naylor himself, who was thus pleasingly elevated to the status of a god.

The perverse amusement he derived from this thought did not affect him seriously. Theological notions were all crude and simplistic to a man of education. But even with the redundant God-concept left out of account the Spectatorist Myth was interesting enough, leading to the idea of the universe interpreted as a logic of theatre — which was, after all, what he had achieved in the thespitron. Mulling over this idea brought a fascinating, compelling vision to the recesses of Naylor's mind. He imagined, at the source of existence, a transcendental logic machine — preternatural archetype of his own — which ground out the categories of logical identity in pure form; he saw the categories passing down a dark, immensely long corridor, combining and recombining as they went, until eventually they permutated into concrete substance — or in other words, into the physical universe and all its contents.

But even as he entertained this image Naylor smiled, shaking his head, reminding himself how corrupting to philosophy were all such idealist fancies. He was well aware of how fallacious it was to imagine that logic was antecedent to matter.

Philosophically Naylor held fast to the tradition of British empiricism (while not descending, of course, to American pragmatism) and saw himself very much as a child of the nineteenth century, harbouring a nostalgic fondness for the flavour of thought of that period — though the outlook of J. S. Mill had been much updated, naturally, by the thoroughgoing materialist empiricists of Naylor's own time. He eschewed the manic systems-building of the continentals and was suspicious of any lapse into idealist formulations (such as "rationalism") all of which ended up sooner or later in some version of the hysterical "world-soul" doctrine.

In his attachment to nineteenth-century values Naylor was typical of his time. Most of his fellow Englishmen were equally proud to think of themselves as products of the great Victorian age, for in recent decades there had been a genuine and far-reaching renaissance in the qualities that had given that period its vigour. The Victorians, with their prolific inventiveness, their love of "projects", their advocacy of "progress" combined with an innate and rigid conservatism, embodied, it was commonly believed, all that was best in civilisation. And indeed it was hard to imagine any period more closely resembling the age of England's Great Queen than the present one.

As often happens, economic forces were in some measure responsible for the change. During the twenty-first century it had gradually become apparent that the advantages of global trade were finally being outweighed by the disadvantages. The international division of labour was taking on the aspect, not of a constant mutual amelioration of life, but of a destructive natural force which could impoverish entire peoples. The notion of economic progress came to take on another meaning: to signify, not the ability to dominate world markets, but the means by which a small nation might become wealthy without any foreign trade whatsoever. Britain, always a pioneer, was the first to discover this new direction. With the help of novel technologies she reversed what had been axiomatic since the days of Adam Smith, and for a time was once again the wealthiest power on Earth, aloof from the world trade storm, reaping through refusal to trade all the benefits she had once gained through trade.

It was a time of innovation, of surprising, often fantastic invention, of which the Harkham Velocitator, a unit of which was now powering Naylor's habitat through infinity, was perhaps the outstanding example. The boffin had come into his own again, outwitting the expensively equipped teams of professional research scientists. Yet in some respects it was a cautious period, alert to the dangers of too precipitous a use of every new-fangled gadget, and keeping alive the spirit of the red flag that once had been required to precede every horseless carriage. For that reason advantage was not always taken of every advance in productive methods.

Two devisements in particular were forbidden. The first was the hylic potentiator, an all-purpose domestic provider commonly known as the matter-bank. This worked by holding in store a mass of amorphous, non-particulate matter, or hyle, to use the classical term. Hylic matter from this store could be instantly converted into any object, artifact or substance for which the machine was programmed, and returned to store if the utility was no longer needed or had not been consumed. Because the hylic store consisted essentially of a single gigantic shaped neutron, very high energies were involved, which had led to the device being deemed too dangerous for use on Earth. Models were still to be found here and there in space, however.

The second banned production method was a process whereby artifacts were able to reproduce themselves after the manner of viruses if brought into contact with simple materials. The creation of self-replicating artifacts had become subject to world prohibition after the islands of Japan became buried beneath ever-growing mounds of still-multiplying TV sets, audvid recorders, cameras, autos, motor-bikes, refrigerators, helicopters, pocket computers, transistor radios, portphones, light airplanes, speedboats, furniture, sex aids, hearing aids, artificial limbs and organs, massage machines, golf clubs, zip fasteners, toys, typewriters, graphic reproduction machines, electron microscopes, house plumbing and electrical systems, machine tools, industrial robots, earthmovers, drilling rigs, prefabricated dwellings, ships, submersibles, fast-access transit vehicles, rocket launchers, lifting bodies, extraterrestrial exploration vehicles, X-ray machines, radio, video, microwave, X-ray and laser transmitters, modems, reading machines, and innumerable other conveniences.

Of all innovations, however, the invention to have most impact on the modern British mind was undoubtedly the Harkham velocitator, which had abolished the impediment of distance and opened up infinity to the interested traveller. Theoretically the velocitator principle could give access to any velocity, however high, except one: it was not possible to travel a measured distance in zero time, or an infinite distance in any measured time. But in practice, a velocitator unit's top speed depended on the size of its armature. After a while designing bigger and bigger armatures had become almost a redundant exercise. Infinity was infinity was infinity.

Velocitator speeds were expressed in powers of the velocity of light. Thus 186, Naylor's present pace, indicated the speed of light multiplied by itself 186 times. Infinity was now littered, if littered was a word that could be predicated of such a concept, with velocitator explorers, most of them British, finding in worlds without end their darkest Africas, their South American jungles, their Tibets and Outer Mongolias.

In point of fact the greater number of them did precious little exploring. Infinity, as it turned out, was not as definable as Africa. Early on the discovery had been made that until one actually *arrived* at some galaxy or planet, infinite space had a soothing, prosaic uniformity (provided one successfully avoided the matterless lakes), a bland sameness of fleeting mushy glints. It was a perfect setting for peace and solitude. This, perhaps, as much as the outward urge, had drawn Englishmen into the anonymous universe. The velocitator habitat offered a perfect opportunity to "get away from it all", to find a spot of quiet, possibly, to work on one's book or thesis, or to avoid some troublesome social or emotional problem.

This was roughly Naylor's position. The success of the thespitron had emboldened him to consider taking up the life of an inventor. He had ventured into the macrocosm to mull over, in its peace and silence, a certain stubborn technical problem which velocitator travel itself entailed.

The problem had been advertised many times, but so far it had defeated all attempts at a solution. It was, quite simply, the problem of how to get home again. Every Harkham traveller faced the risk of becoming totally, irrevocably lost, it being impossible to maintain a sense of direction over the vast distances involved. The scale was simply too large. Space bent and twisted, presenting, in terms of spatial curvature, mountains and mazes, hills and serpentine tunnels. A gyroscope naturally followed this bending and twisting; all gyroscopic compasses were therefore useless. Neither, on such a vast and featureless scale, was there any posibility of making a map.

(Indeed a simple theorem showed that large-scale sidereal mapping was inherently an untenable proposition. *Mapping consists of recording relationships between locations or objects.* In a three-dimensional continuum this is only really practicable by means of data storage. However, the number of possible relationships between a set of objects rises exponentially with the number of objects. The number of possible connections between the 10,000 million neurons of the human brain actually exceeds the number of particles within Olbers' Sphere [which, before the invention of the velocitator, was thought of as the universe]. Obviously no machine, however compact, could contain the information necessary to map the relationships between objects whose number was without limit, even when those objects were entire galaxies.)

Every velocitator habitat carried a type of inertial navigation recording system, which enabled the traveller to retrace his steps and, hopefully, arrive back at the place he had started from. This, to date, was the only homing method available; but the device was delicate and occasionally given to error — only a small displacement in the inertial record was enough to turn the Milky Way Galaxy into an unfindable grain of sand in an endless desert. Furthermore, Harkham travellers were apt, sometimes unwittingly, to pass through powerful magnetic fields which distorted and compromised the information on their recorders, or even wiped the tapes clean.

Naylor's approach to the problem was, as far as he knew, original. He had adopted a concept that both philosophy and science had at various times picked up, argued over, even used, then dropped again only to resume the argument later: the concept of *identity*.

If every entity, object and being had its own unique identity which differentiated it from the rest of existence, then Naylor reasoned that it ought to be uniquely findable in some fictive framework that was independent of space, time and number. Ironically the theoretical tools he was using were less typical of empiricist thought than of its traditional enemy, rationalism, the school that saw existence as arising, not from material occasions, but from abstract categories and identities; but he was sufficiently undogmatic not to be troubled by that. He was aware that empirical materialists had striven many times to argue away the concept of identity altogether, but they had never, quite, succeeded.

Naylor imagined each individual object resulting from a combining, or focusing together, of universal logic classes (or universal identities), much as the colour components of a picture are focused onto one another to form a perfect image. It was necessary to suppose that each act of focusing was unique, that is to say, that each particle of matter was created only once. It would mean, for instance, that each planet had a unique identity: that a sample of iron from the Earth was subtly different from a sample of iron taken from the Moon, and it was this difference that Naylor's projected direction-finder would be able to locate.

But was it a warrantable assumption, he wondered?

"Ah, the famous question of identity," he said aloud.

The vodor lecture, heard many times before, became a drone. He turned it off and opened his notebook to scan one section of his notes.

"IDENTITY AND NUMBER: The natural numbers, 1, 2, 3, 4, 5 . . ., are pure abstractions, lacking identity in the philosophical meaning of the word. That is to say, there is no such entity as 'five'. Identity in a set of five objects appertains only to each object taken singly . . . 'Fiveness' is a process, accomplished by matching each member of a set against members of another set (e.g. the fingers of a hand) until the set being counted is exhausted. Only material objects have identity. . . ."

In his fevered imagination it had seemed to Naylor that he need but make one more conceptual leap and he would be there, with a sketch model of the device that would find the Milky Way Galaxy from no matter where in infinity. He believed, in fact, that he already had the primitive beginnings of the device in the thespitron. For although no *physical* mapping of the universe was possible, the thespitron *had* achieved a *dramatic* mapping of it, demonstrating that the cosmos was not entirely proof against definition.

But the vital leap, from a calculus of theatre to a calculus of identities, had not come, and Naylor was left wondering if he should be chiding himself for his lapse into dubious rationalist tenets.

Dammit, he thought wryly, if an enlightened master had no luck, how the devil can I?

Gloomily he wrote a footnote: "It may be that the question of identity is too basic to be subject to experiment, or to be susceptible to instrumentation."

His thoughts were interrupted by the ringing of the alarm bell. The control panel flashed, signalling that the habitat was slowing down in response to danger ahead. In seconds it had reduced speed until it was cruising at only a few tens of powers of the velocity of light.

At the same time an announcement gong sounded, informing them that they had arrived within beacon range of someone else's habitat — presumably Corngold's.

Naylor crossed to the panel to switch off the alarm. As he did so Watson-Smythe appeared from the bedroom. He had put on a gleaming white suit which set off his good looks to perfection.

"What a racket!" he exclaimed genially. "Everything going off at once!"

Naylor was examining the dials. "We are approaching a matterless lake."

"Are we, by God?"

"And your friend Corngold is evidently living on the shores of it. Can you think of any reason why he would do that?"

Watson-Smythe chuckled, with a hint of rancour. "Just the place where the swine would choose to set himself up. Discourages visitors, you see."

"You can say that again. Do I take it we are likely to be unwelcome? What you would call a recluse, is he?"

The younger man tugged at his lower lip. "Look here, old chap, if you feel uneasy about this you can just drop me off at Corngold's and shoot off again. I don't want to impose on you or anything."

But by now Naylor was intrigued. "Oh, that's all right. I don't mind hanging about for a bit."

Watson-Smythe peered out of the window. They were close to a large spiral galaxy which blazed across the field of vision and swung majestically past their line of sight.

"We'll get a better view on this," Naylor said. He pressed a small lever and at the front end of the living-room a six-foot screen unfolded, conveniently placed in relation to the control panel. He traversed the view to get an all-round picture of their surroundings. The spiral galaxy had already receded to become the average smudged point of light; in all directions the aspect was the usual one of darkness relieved by faintly luminous sleet — except, that was, for directly ahead. There, the screen of galaxies was thin. Behind that screen stretched an utter blackness: it was a specimen of that awesome phenomenon, the matterless lake.

For the distribution of matter in the universe was not, quite, uniform. It thinned and condensed a bit here and there. The non-uniformity of matter mainly manifested, however, in great holes, gaps — lakes, as they were called — where no matter was to be found at all. Although of no great size where the distances that went to make up infinity were concerned, in mundane terms the dimensions of these lakes were enormous, amounting to several trillion times the span of an Olbers' sphere (the criterion of cosmic size in pre-Harkham times, and still used as a rough measure of magnitude).

Any Harkham traveller knew that it was fatal to penetrate

any further than the outermost fringes of such a lake. Should anyone be so foolhardy as to pass out of sight of its shore (and in times past many had been) he would find it just about impossible to get out again; for the simple fact was that when not conditioned by the presence of matter, space lacked many of the properties normally associated with it. Even such elementary characteristics as direction, distance and dimension were lent to space, physicists now knew, by the signposts of matter. The depths of the lakes were out of range of these signposts, and thus it would do the velocitator rider no good merely to fix a direction and travel it in the belief that he must sooner or later strike the lake's limit; he would be unlikely ever to do so. He was lost in an inconceivable nowhere, in space that was structureless and uninformed.

As the habitat neared the shore the lake spread and expanded before them, like a solid black wall sealing off the universe. "Will Corngold be in the open, do you think, or in a galaxy somewhere?" Naylor asked.

"I'd guess he's snuggled away in some spiral; harder to find that way, eh?" Watson-Smythe pointed to a cluster of galaxies ahead and to their right. "There's a likely-looking bunch over there. Right on the edge of the lake, too. What do the indicators say?"

"Looks hopeful." Naylor turned the habitat towards the cluster, speeding up a little. The galaxies brightened until their internal structures became visible. The beacon signal came through more strongly; soon they were close enough to get a definite fix.

Watson-Smythe's guess had been right. They eventually found Corngold's habitat floating just inside the outermost spiral turn of the largest member of the cluster. The habitat looked like two or three eskimo igloos squashed together, humped and rounded. Behind it the local galaxy glittered in countless colours like a giant Christmas tree.

Watson-Smythe clapped his hands in delight. "Got him!"

Naylor nudged close to the structure at walking pace. The legally standardised coupling rings clinked together as he matched up the outer doors.

"Jolly good. Time to pay a visit," his passenger said.

"Shouldn't we raise him on the communicator first?"

"Rather not." Watson-Smythe made for the door, then paused, turning to him. "If you'd prefer to wait until. . . . Well, just as you please."

He first opened the inner door, then both outer doors which were conjoined now and moved as one, and then the inner door of the other habitat. Naylor wondered why he didn't even bother to knock. Personally he would never have had the gall just to walk into someone else's living-room.

With tentative steps he followed Watson-Smythe through the short tunnel. Bright light shone through from the other habitat. He heard a man's voice, raised in a berating, bullying tone.

The door swung wide open.

The inside of Corngold's dwelling reminded Naylor of an egg-shaped cave, painted bright yellow. Walls and ceiling consisted of the same ovoid curve, and lacked windows. The yellow was streaked and spattered with oil colours and unidentifiable dirt; the lower parts of the walls were piled with canvases, paintings, boxes, shelves and assorted junk. The furniture was sparse: a bare board table, a mattress, three rickety straight-backed chairs and a mouldy couch. An artist's easel stood in the middle of the room. Against the opposite wall was the source of Corngold's provender and probably everything else he used: a matter-bank, shiny in its moulded plastic casing.

Corngold was a fat man, a little below medium height. He was wearing baggy flannel trousers and a green silk chemise which was square-cut about the neck and shoulders and was decorated with orange tassels. He had remarkably vivid green eyes; his hair had been cropped short, but now had grown so that it bristled like a crown of thorns.

He reminded Naylor of early Hollywood versions of Nero or Caligula. He did not, it seemed, live alone. He was in the act of browbeating a girl, aged perhaps thirty, who for her dowdiness was as prominent as Corngold was for his brilliant green shirt. Corngold had her arm twisted behind her back, forcing her partly over. Her face wore the blank sullenness that comes from long bullying; it was totally submissive, wholly drab, the left eye slightly puffy and discoloured from a recent bruise. She did not even react to the entry of visitors.

Corngold, however, eased his grip slightly, turning indignantly as Watson-Smythe entered. "What the bloody hell do you mean barging in here?" he bellowed. "Bugger off!" His accent sounded northern to Naylor's ears; Yorkshire, perhaps.

To Naylor's faint surprise Watson-Smythe's answering tone was cold and professional. "Walter Corngold? Late of 43 Denison Square?"

"You heard me! Bugger off! This is private property!"

Watson-Smythe produced a slim Hasking stun beamer from inside his jacket. With his other hand he took a document from his pocket. "Watson-Smythe, M.I.19," he announced. "I have here a warrant for your arrest, Corngold. I'm taking you back to Earth."

So that was it! Naylor wondered why he hadn't guessed it before. Now that he thought of it, Watson-Smythe was almost a caricature of the type of young man one expected to find in the "infinity police", as it was jocularly called — M.I.19, the branch of security entrusted with law enforcement among habitat travellers.

He felt amused. "What are the charges?" he asked mildly.

"Two charges," Watson-Smythe replied, turning his head slightly but still keeping the Hasking carefully trained on Corngold. "Theft, and more serious, the abduction of Lady Cadogan's maid, who unless I am very much mistaken is the young lady you are now mistreating, Corngold. Take your hands off her at once."

Corngold released the girl and shoved her roughly towards the couch. She plomped herself down on it and sat staring at the floor.

"Ridiculous," he snorted, then added, in a voice heavy with irony: "Betty's here of her own sweet will, aren't you, dearest?"

She glanced up like a frightened mouse, darting what might have been a look of hope at Watson-Smythe. Then she retreated into herself again, nodding meekly.

Corngold sighed with satisfaction. "Well, that's that, then. Sod off, the two of you, and leave us in peace." He strolled to the easel, picked up a brush and started to daub the canvas on it, as though he had banished them from existence.

Watson-Smythe laughed, showing clean white teeth. "They

told me you were a bit of a character, Corngold. But you're due for a court appearance in London just the same."

He turned politely to Naylor. "Thanks for your assistance, Naylor old boy. You can cast off now if you're so inclined, and I'll take Corngold's habitat back to Earth."

"Can't," Corngold said, giving them a sideways glance. "My inertial navigator's bust. I was stuck here, in fact, until you two turned up. Not that it bothers me at all."

Watson-Smythe frowned. "Well. . . ."

"Is it a malfunction?" Naylor queried. "Or just a faulty record?"

Corngold shrugged. "It's buggered, I tell you."

"I might be able to do something with it," Naylor said to the M.I.19 agent. "I'll have look at it, anyway. If it's only the record we can simply take a copy of our own one."

Corngold flung down his brush. "In that case you might as well stay to dinner. And put that gun away, for Chrissake. What do you think this is, a shooting gallery?"

"After all, he can't go anywhere," Naylor observed when Watson-Smythe wavered. "Without us he'll *never* get home."

"All right." He returned his gun to its shoulder holster. "But don't think you're going to wriggle out of this, Corngold. Kidnapping's a pretty serious offence."

Corngold's eyes twinkled. He pointed to a clock hung askew on the wall. "Dinner's at nine. Don't be late."

Wearily Naylor slumped in his armchair in his own living-room. He had spent an hour on Corngold's inertial navigator, enough to tell him that the gyros were precessing and the whole system would need to be re-tuned. It would be a day's work at least and he had decided to make a fresh start tomorrow. If he couldn't put the device in order they would all have to travel back to Earth in Naylor's habitat — as an M.I.19 officer Watson-Smythe had the power to require his cooperation over that. At the moment the agent was in his bedroom, bringing his duty log up to date.

The business with the navigator had brought home anew to Naylor the desirability of inventing some different type of homing mechanism. He was becoming irritated that the problem was so intractable, and felt a fresh, if frustrating, urge to get to grips with it.

Remembering that he had left the vodor lecture unfinished, he switched on the machine again, listening closely to the evenly-intoned words, even though he knew them almost by heart.

"The question of *personal* identity was raised by Locke, and later occupied the attentions of Hume and Butler. Latterly the so-called 'theorem of universal identity' has gained some prominence. In this theorem, personal identity (or *self*-identity) is defined as *having knowledge* of one's identity, a statement which also serves to define consciousness. Conscious beings are said to differ from inanimate objects only in that they have knowledge of their identity, while inanimate objects, though possessing their own identity, have no knowledge of it.

"To be conscious, however, means to be able to perceive. But in order to perceive there must be an 'identification' between the subject (self-identity, or consciousness) and the perceived object. Therefore there is a paradoxical 'sharing' of identity between subject and object, similar, perhaps, to the exchange of identity once posited between electrons. This reasoning leads to the concept of a 'universal identity' according to which all identity, both of conscious beings and of inanimate objects, belongs to the same universal transcendental identity, or 'self'. This conclusion is a recurring one in the history of human thought, known at various times as 'the infinite self', 'the transcendental self' and 'the universal self' of Vedantic teachings. 'I am you,' the mystic will proclaim, however impudently, meaning that the same basic identity is shared by everyone.

"Such conceptions are not admitted by the empirical materialist philosophers, who subject them to the most withering criticism. To the empiricist, every occasion is unique; therefore its identity is unique. Hume declared that he could not even discover self-identity in himself; introspection yielded only a stream of objects in the form of percepts; a 'person' is therefore a 'bundle' of percepts. Neither can the fact that two entities may share a *logical* identity in any way compromise their basic separateness, since logic itself is not admitted as having any *a priori* foundation.

"The modern British school rejects the concept of identity

altogether as a mere verbalism, without objective application. Even the notion of electron identity exchange is now accepted to be a mathematical fiction, having been largely superseded by the concept of 'unique velocity' which is incorporated in the Harkham velocitator. It is still applied, however, to a few quantum mechanical problems for which no other mathematical tools exist."

Naylor rose and went to the window, gazing out at the blazing spiral galaxy which was visible over the humped shape of Corngold's habitat. "Ah, the famous question of identity," he murmured.

He knew why the question continued to perplex him. It was because of the thespitron. The thespitron, with its unexpected tricks and properties, had blurred his feeling of self-identity, just as the identity of electrons had been blurred by the twentieth-century quantum equations. And at the same time, the thoughts occurring to him attacked materialist empiricism at its weakest point: the very same question of identity.

There came to him again the image of the categories of identity, proceeding and permutating down a dark, immensely long corridor. He felt dizzy, elated. Here, in his habitat living room, his domain was small but complete; he and the thespitron reproduced between them, on a minute scale, the ancient mystical image of created universe and observing source, of phenomenon and noumenon; even without him here to watch it, the thespitron was the transcendental machine concretised, a microcosm to reflect the macrocosm, a private universe of discourse, a mirror of infinity in a veneered cabinet.

Could the characters and worlds within the thespitron, shadows though they were, be said to possess *reality*? The properties of matter itself could be reduced to purely logical definitions, heretical though the operation was from the point of view of empiricism. The entities generated by the machine, obeying those same logical definitions, could never know that they lacked concrete substance.

Was there identity in the universe? Was that *all* there was?

Now he understood what had made him include a communication facility in the thespitron; why he had further felt impelled to talk to Frank Nayland, his near-double. He had identified himself with Nayland; he had tried to enlighten him as to the nature of his fictional world, prompted by some irrational notion that, by confronting him, he could somehow prod Nayland into having a consciousness of his own.

Who am I? Naylor wondered. Does my identity, my consciousness, belong to myself, or does it belong to this — he made a gesture taking in all that lay beyond the walls of the habitat — to infinity?

Sitting down again, he switched on the thespitron.

Naylor's sense of having duplicated the logical development of the universe was further heightened by the inclusion of the "credible sequence" button. This optional control engaged circuits which performed, in fact, no more than the last stage of the plotting process, arranging that the machine's presentations, in terms of construction, settings and event-structure, were consonant, if not quite with the real world, at least with a dramatist's imitation of it.

With the button disengaged, however, the criterion of mundane credibility vanished. The thespitron proceeded to construct odd, abbreviated worlds, sometimes from only a small number of dramatic elements. Worlds in which processes, once begun, were apt to continue forever, without interruption or exhaustion; in which actions, once embarked upon, became a binding force upon the actor, requiring permanent reiteration.

The world of Frank Nayland, private investigator, was one of these: a world put together from the bare components of the Hollywood thriller *genre*, bereft of any wider background, moving according to an obsessive, abstract logic. A compact world with only a small repertoire of events; the terse fictional world of the private dick, a world in which rain was unceasing.

Summoning up Nayland from store, Naylor watched him pursue his investigations, his gabardine raincoat permanently damp, rain dripping from the brim of his slouch hat. So absorbed did he become in the dick's adventures that he failed to notice the entry of Watson-Smythe until the M.I.19 officer tapped him on the shoulder.

"It's nine o'clock," Watson-Smythe said. "Time we were calling on Corngold."

"Oh, yes." Naylor rose, rubbing his eyes. He left the thespitron running as they went through the connecting tunnel, tapping on Corngold's door before going in.

A measure of camaraderie had grown up during the hour they had spent with the artist earlier. Naylor had come to look on him more as an eccentric rascal than a real villain, and even Watson-Smythe had mollified his hostility a little. He had still tried to persuade Betty Cooper, the maid allegedly abducted from the home of Lady Cadogan (from whom Corngold had also stolen a valuable antique bracelet), to move in with them pending the journey back to Earth, but so great was Corngold's hold over her (the hold of a sadist, Watson-Smythe said) that she would obey only him.

There was no sign of the promised dinner party. Corngold stood before his easel, legs astraddle, while Betty posed in the nude, sitting demurely on a chair. Though still a sullen frump, Naylor thought that when naked she had some redeeming features; her body tended to flop, and was pale and too fleshy, but it was pleasantly substantial, in a trollopy sort of way.

Corngold turned his head. "Well?" he glared.

Watson-Smythe coughed. "You invited us to dinner, I seem to remember."

"Did I? Oh." Corngold himself didn't seem to remember. He continued plying the paint onto the canvas, a square palette of mingled colour in his other hand. Naylor was fascinated. The man was an artist after all. His concentration, his raptness, were there, divided between the canvas and the living girl.

Naylor moved a few paces so he could get a glimpse of the portrait. But he did not see what he had expected. Instead of a nude, Corngold had painted an automobile.

Corngold looked at him, his eyes twinkling with mirth. "Well, it's how I see her, you see."

Naylor was baffled. He could not see how in any way the picture could represent Betty, not even as a metaphor. The auto was sleek and flashy, covered with glittering trim; quite the opposite of Betty's qualities, in fact.

He strolled to the other end of the egg-shaped room, glancing at the stacked canvases. Corngold had a bit of a following, he believed, among some of the avant-garde. Naylor took no interest in art, but even he could see the fellow was talented. The paintings were individualistic, many of them in bright but cleverly toned colours.

Corngold laid down his brush and moved aside the easel, gesturing to Betty to rise and dress. "Dinner, then," he said, in the tone of one whose hospitality may be presumed upon. "Frankly I'd hoped you two would have got tired of hanging around by now and cleared off."

"That would have left you in a bit of a spot," Naylor said. "You have no way of finding your way home."

"So what? Who the hell wants to go to Earth anyway. I've got everything I need here — eh?" Corngold winked at him obscenely, and, to the extreme embarrassment of both Naylor and Watson-Smythe, stuck his finger in Betty's vulva, wiggling it vigorously. Betty became the picture of humiliation, looking distressfully this way and that. But she made no move to draw back.

Naylor bristled. "I *say!*" he protested heatedly. "You *are* British, aren't you?"

Corngold's manner became suddenly aggressive. He withdrew his finger, whereupon Betty turned and snatched for her clothes. "And why shouldn't I be?" he challenged.

"Well, dammit, no proper Englishman would treat a woman this way!"

There was a pause. Corngold gave a peculiar open-mouthed grin which grew broader and broader as he looked first at Betty and then back and forth between Naylor and Watson-Smythe.

"Fuck me, I must be a Welshman!"

"Perhaps the best thing *would* be to leave you here, Corngold," Watson-Smythe commented, his tone one of coldest disapproval. "It might be the punishment you deserve."

"Do it, then! You'd never have got to me at all, you bastards, if I'd found a way to turn off the fucking beacon."

"It can't be done," Naylor informed him. It would be typical of such a character, he thought, not to know that. The beacon signal was imprinted on every velocitator manufactured, as a legal requirement. Otherwise habitats would never be able to vector in on one another.

Corngold grunted, and dragged the board table to the centre of the room. Around it he arranged the three chairs his dwelling boasted, and with a casual gesture invited his guests to sit down.

"What's all this 'Corngold', anyway?" he demanded as they took their places. "Have I agreed that I am Corngold? Establish the identity of the culprit— that's the first thing in law!"

"I am satisfied that you are Walter Corngold," Watson-Smythe said smoothly.

Corngold banged on the tabletop, shouting. "Supposition, supposition! Establish the identity!"

He laughed, then turned to Betty, who was clothed now and stood by in the attitude of a waitress. "Well, let's eat. Indian curry suit you? How do you like it? Mine's good and hot."

While Corngold discussed the details of the meal Betty went to the matter-bank and returned with a large flagon of bright red wine and four glasses. Corngold sloshed out the wine, indicating to her that she should knock hers straight back. As soon as she had done so he emptied his own glass, instantly refilling it.

"One good hot vindaloo, one lamb biriani and a lamb korma," he instructed curtly.

Betty moved back to the matter-bank and twisted dials. Spicy aromas filled the room as she transferred bowls of food from the delivery transom to a tray. Naylor turned to Corngold.

"You can't seriously contemplate spending the rest of your life in this habitat? Cut off from humanity?"

"Humanity can go jump in a lake." Corngold jerked his thumb towards the great nothingness that lay beyond the local galaxy. "Anyway, who says I'm habitat-bound? You forget there are other races, other worlds. As a matter of fact I have a pretty good set-up here. I've discovered a simply fascinating civilisation on a planet of a nearby star. Here, let me show you."

Rising, he pushed aside a pile of cardboard cartons to reveal the habitat's control board. A small golden ring of stars appeared, glowing like a bracelet, as he switched on an opal-surfaced viewscreen.

Corngold pointed out the largest of the stars. "This is the place. A really inventive lifeform, not hard to get to know, really, and with the most extraordinary technology. I commute there regularly."

"And yet you always bring your habitat back out here again?" Naylor remarked. "You must love solitude."

"I do love it indeed, but you misunderstand me. The habitat stays here. I commute to Zordem by means of a clever little gadget the natives gave me."

Heavily he sat down at the table, licking his lips. His visitors tried to ask him more about these revelations, their curiosity intensely aroused; but when the food was served he became deaf to all their questions.

Taking up a whole spoonful of the pungent-smelling curry Betty served him, and without even tempering it with rice, he rolled it thoughtfully round his mouth. Then suddenly he spluttered and spat it all out.

"This isn't vindaloo, you shitty-arsed cow! It's fucking Madras!"

With a roar Corngold picked up the bowl and flung it at Betty, missing her and hitting the wall. The brown muck made a dribbling trail down the yellow.

"You must excuse my common-law wife," he said to Naylor, his expression turning from fury to politeness. "Unfortunately she is a completely useless pig."

"But I don't dare dial vindaloo," Betty protested in a whining, tearful voice. "The bank's been going funny again. On vindaloo—"

"Get me my dinner!" Corngold's bellow cut off her explanations. Submissively she returned to the machine, operating it again. As she turned the knobs an acrid blue smoke rose from the matter-bank, coming not from the transom but from the seams of the casing.

Naylor, with a glance at Watson-Smythe, started to his feet with the intention of beating a retreat to his own habitat and casting off with all haste. But Corngold sprang up with a cry of exasperation, marched over to the ailing bank and gave it a hefty kick, at which the smoke stopped.

"It's always giving trouble," he exclaimed gruffly as he rejoined them. "That's what comes of buying second-hand junk."

"You do realise, don't you," Watson-Smythe said, in a tone Naylor found admirably calm and even, "that that thing can go off like a nuclear bomb?"

"So can my arse after one of these curries. Ah, here it comes. Better be right this time."

Corngold's vindaloo was *very* hot. The sweat started out on his forehead as he ate it, grunting and groaning, deep in concentration. He was a man of lusty nature, Naylor decided, carrying his enjoyment of life to the limit. Afterwards he sat panting like a dog, calling for more wine and swallowing it in grateful gulps.

Then, the meal over, Corngold became expansive. With a wealth of boastful detail he began to describe his contacts with the inhabitants of the planet Zordem.

"Their whole science is based on the idea of a certain kind of ray," he explained. "They call them *zom* rays. They have some quite remarkable effects. Let me show you, for instance —"

He opened one of the egg-shaped room's four doors, disclosing a cupboard whose shelves contained several unfamiliar objects. Corngold picked one up. It was smooth, rounded in shape with a flat underside, easily held in one hand, and about three times as long as it was broad. He carried it to the viewscreen and slapped it against the side of the casing, where it stuck as if by suckers.

On the screen, the ring of stars vanished. In its place was intergalactic space, and in the foreground a long, fully equipped spaceship of impressive size, the ring-like protuberance about her middle indicating the massiveness of her velocitator armature. They all recognised her as a Royal Navy cruiser, one of several on permanent patrol.

"Rule Britannia!" crowed Corngold. "It's the *Prince Andrew*, ostensibly seeing that we habitat travellers don't mistreat the natives. But really, of course, having a go at a second British Empire. I should ko-ko!"

"It's no joking matter," Watson-Smythe said sternly. "There have been quite a few incidents. I dare say your relations with Zordem will come under scrutiny in good time, Corngold."

"Is she close?" Naylor asked.

"No, she's quite a way off," Corngold said, taking a look at a meter. "Roughly a googol olbers."

"Your gadget can see *that* far? But good God — how do you find a single object at that distance?"

"The Zordems put a trace on her the day I arrived. To make me feel at home, I suppose. Don't ask me how. They did it with zom rays!"

Naylor was stunned. "Then *these* are the people who are masters of infinity!" he breathed.

Corngold sighed, strolled back to the table and sat down, placing his bare, fat arms among the empty dishes. He wiped up a trace of curry sauce with his finger and licked it. Then he looked up at Naylor.

"You really are a clown," he said. "Masters of infinity! That's a lot of crap newspaper talk. The Zordems are nowhere into infinity, any more than we are. If you're going to talk about *infinity*, well then, the whole spread anyone's gone from Earth, or anywhere else for that matter, is no more than a dot. Okay, build a velocitator armature a light year across and ride it for a billion years. You've still only gone the length of a dot on the face of infinity. That's what infinity means, isn't it? That however far you go it's still endless? For Chrissake," he ended scathingly, "you ought to know that."

"Just the same, you've misled us with this talk of being stranded," Watson-Smythe accused him. "With equipment like this you can obviously find your way to anywhere."

"Afraid not. This gadget gives the range but not the direction. And even the range is limited to about fifty googol olbers. The Zordems have hit on a lot of angles we've missed, but they're not that much in advance of us overall."

"Still, it must be based on a completely new principle," Naylor said intensely. "Don't you see, Corngold? This might give us what everybody's been looking for — a reliable homing device! It might even," he added shyly, "mean a reduction in sentence for you."

He stopped, blushing at the emerald malevolence that brimmed for a moment from Corngold's eyes. If he were honest, he was beginning to find the man frightening. There was something dangerous, something solid and immovable about him. His knowledge of an alien technology, and his obvious intelligence which came through despite his outrageous behaviour, had dispelled the earlier impression of him as an amusing crank. All Watson-Smythe's trained smoothness had failed to make the slightest dent in his self-confidence; Betty remained his slave, and Naylor privately doubted whether the charge of abduction could be made to stick. There was something ritualistic in Corngold's treatment of her, and in her corresponding misery. It looked to Naylor as though they were matched souls.

"I thought I had dropped plenty of hints," Corngold emphasised, "that I don't really want to come back to Earth. Betty and I want nothing more than to remain here, thank you."

Watson-Smythe smiled. "I'm afraid the law isn't subject to your whims, Corngold."

"No?" Corngold's expression was bland. He raised his eyebrows. "I thought I might be able to bribe you. How would you both like to screw Betty here? She's all right in her way — just lies there like a piece of putty and lets you do which and whatever to her."

Watson-Smythe snorted.

"What is it you want, then?" Corngold asked in sudden annoyance. "The fucking bracelet? Here — take it!" He went to the mattress on the floor, lifted it and took a gold ornament from underneath, flinging it at Watson-Smythe. "It's a piece of sodding crap anyway — I only took it because Betty had a fancy for it."

Watson-Smythe picked up the bracelet, examined it briefly, then wrapped it in a handkerchief and tucked it away in an inside pocket. "Thanks for the evidence."

Corngold sighed again, resignedly. He reached for the flagon of wine and drained the dregs, finishing with a belch.

"Well, it's not the end of the world. I expect Betty will be glad to see London again. But before you retire for the night, gentlemen, let me answer your earlier question — how I make the transition between here and Zordem. It's quite simple, really — done by zom rays again, but a different brand this time."

He went to the cupboard and brought out something looking like a large hologram plate camera, equipped with a hooded shutter about a foot on the side. "This is really a most astonishing gadget," he said. "It accomplishes long-distance travel without the use of a vehicle. I believe essentially the forces it employs may not be dissimilar to those of the velocitator — but instead of moving the generator, they move whatever the zom rays are trained on. All you do is line it up with wherever you want to go and step into the beam — provided you have a device at the other end to de-translate your velocity, that is. Neat, isn't it? The speed is fast enough to push you right through walls as though they weren't there."

"Why, it's a matter transmitter!" Naylor exclaimed.

"As good as."

Already Watson-Smythe had guessed his danger and was reaching for his gun. But Corngold was too quick for him. He trained the camera-like device on the agent and pressed a lever. The black frontal plate flickered, exactly as if a shutter had operated — as indeed one probably had. Watson-Smythe vanished.

Naylor staggered back aghast. "*Christ*! You've murdered him!"

"Yes! For trying to disturb our domestic harmony!"

Naylor stuttered: "You've gone too far this time, Corngold. You won't get away with this . . . too far."

Scared and flustered, he scrambled for the exit. He scampered through the tunnel, slammed shut the outer doors and disengaged the clutches so that the two habitats drifted apart. Then, slamming shut the inner door, he rushed to the control board.

In the egg-shaped room, Corngold had quickly set up the Zordem projector on a tripod. He aligned the instrument carefully, focusing it through the wall, onto the intruding habitat a few yards away. He opened the shutter for an instant: Naylor and his habitat were away, projected out into the matterless lake.

A faint voice came from the communicator on the nearly-buried control board. "I'm falling, Corngold. Help me!"

"I'll help you," Corngold crowed, grinning his peculiar open-mouthed grin. "I'll help you fall some more!"

He opened the shutter again, uttering as he did so a wild, delighted cry: "*FUCK OFF!* . . . ." Naylor was accelerated by some further trillions of light years per second, carried by the irresistible force of zom rays.

Corngold turned to Betty. "Well, that's him out of the way," he exclaimed with satisfaction. "Bring on the booze!"

Pale and obedient, Betty withdrew a flagon of cerise fluid and two glasses from the matter-bank. She poured a full measure for

Corngold, a smaller one for herself, and sat crouching on the couch, sipping it.

"We'll move on from here pretty soon," Corngold murmured. "If they could find us, others can."

He tuned the opal-glowing viewscreen into the lake and surveyed the unrelieved emptiness, drinking his wine with gusto.

Corngold's mocking "Fuck off" was the last message Naylor's habitat received from the world of materiality, whether by way of artificial communication, electromagnetic energy, gravitational attraction or indeed any other emanation. These signposts, normally informing space of direction, distance and dimension, were now left far behind.

There had been no time to engage the velocitator and now it was too late. Corngold had had the jump on them from the start. At the first discharge of the Zordem projector Naylor's speedometer had registered c^{413} and his velocitator unit did not have the capacity to cancel such a velocity even though the lake's shore, in the first few moments, had still been accessible. At the second discharge the meter registered c^{826} and unencumbered, total space had swallowed him up. He was now surrounded by nothing but complete and utter darkness.

Within the walls of the habitat, however, his domain was small but complete. He had, in the thespitron, an entire universe of discourse; a universe which, though nearly lacking in objective mass, conformed to the familiar laws of drama and logic, and on the display screen of which, at this moment, Frank Nayland was pursuing his endless life. Naylor's mind became filled yet again with his vision of the long dark corridor down which the logical identities eternally passed, permutating themselves into concretisation. Who was to say that out here, removed from the constraints of external matter, the laws of identity might not find a freedom that otherwise was impossible? Might, indeed, produce reality out of thought?

"The famous question of identity," he muttered feverishly, and sat down before the flickering thespitron, wondering how it might be made to guide him, if not to his own world, at least to some world.

As the big black car swept to a stop at the intersection Frank Nayland emerged from the darkness and leaped for the rear door, wrenching it open and hustling himself inside. His gat was in his hand. He let them see it, leaning forward with his forearm propped over the top of the front seat.

Rainwater dripped from him onto the leather upholstery. Ahead, the red traffic lights shone blurrily through the falling rain, through the streaming sweep of the windscreen wipers.

Bogart peered round at Nayland, his face slack with fear.

"Let's take a walk," Nayland said. "I know a nice little place where we can talk things over."

Bogart's hands gripped the steering wheel convulsively. "You know we can't leave here."

"No . . . that's right," Nayland said thoughtfully after a pause. "You have to keep going. You have to keep running, driving —"

The engine of the car was ticking over. The lights had changed and Bogart started coughing asthmatically, jerking to and fro.

Stanwyck put her hand on his arm, a rare show of pity. "Oh, why don't you let him go?" she said passionately to Nayland. "He's done nothing to you."

Nayland clambered out of the car and slammed the door after him. He stood on the kerb while the gears ground and the vehicle shot off into the night. He walked through the rain to where his own car was hidden in a culvert, and drove for a while until he spotted a phone booth.

Rain beat at the windows of the booth. Water dripped from his low-brimmed hat as Nayland dialled a number. While the tone rang he dug into his raincoat pocket, came up with a book of matches, flicked one alight and lit a cigarette with a cupped hand.

"Mr Naylor? Nayland here. This is my final report."

A pause, while the client on the other end spoke anxiously. Finally Nayland resumed. "You wanted to know about the couple in the car. Bogart is wanted for the snatch of the Heskin tiara from the mansion of Mrs Van der Loon. It was the Stanwyck woman — Mrs Van der Loon's paid companion — who got him into it, of course. The usual sad caper. But here's the rub: there's a fake set of the Heskin rocks — or was. Mrs Van der Loon had a legal exchange of identity carried out between the real jewels and the paste set. A real cute switcheroo. It's the paste set that's genuine now, and Bogart is stuck with a pocketful of worthless rocks and a broad who's nothing but trouble."

"Can that be done?" Naylor asked wonderingly.

"Sure. Identities are legally exchangeable."

Staring at the thespitron screen, the stick-mike in his hand, Naylor was thinking frantically. He watched a plume of smoke drift up the side of Nayland's face, causing the dick to screw up one eye.

Something seemed to be happening to the thespitron. The image was becoming scratchy, the sound indistinct.

"Why does it never stop raining?" he demanded.

"No reason for it to stop."

"But are you *real*?" Naylor insisted. "Do you *exist*?"

Nayland looked straight at him out of the screen. The awareness in his eyes was unmistakable. "This is *our* world, Mr Naylor. You can't come in. It's all a question of identity."

"But it will work — you just said so," Naylor said desperately. "The switcheroo — the fake me and the real me —"

"Goodbye, Mr Naylor," Nayland said heavily. He put down the phone.

Without Naylor as much as touching the controls, the thespitron ground to a halt. The picture dwindled and the screen went blank.

"Ah, the famous question of identity!" boomed the thespitron, and was silent.

Naylor fingered the restart button, but the set was dead. He fell back in his chair, realising his mistake. He realised how foolish had been his abandonment of the solid wisdom of materialist empiricism, how erroneous his sudden hysterical belief, based on fear, that logic and identity could be antecedent to matter, when in truth they were suppositions merely, derived from material relations. Deprived of the massy presence of numerous galaxies, signposts of reality, the thespitron had ceased to function.

The closing circles were getting smaller. Now there was only the shell of the habitat, analogue of a skull, and within it his own skull, that lonely fortress of identity. Naylor sat staring at a blank screen, wondering how long it would take for the light of self-knowledge to go out.

Printed in the United States
148192LV00003B/108/A